LAKE EFFECT SNOW

by

C.P. Rowlands

2008

LAKE EFFECT SNOW

ISBN 13: 978-1-60282-068-5

THIS AEROS EBOOK IS PUBLISHED BY
BOLD STROKES BOOKS, INC.
P.O. BOX 249
VALLEY FALLS, NY 12185

ORIGINAL BOLD STROKES BOOKS EBOOK EDITION: SEPTEMBER 2008

CREDITS
PRODUCTION DESIGN: STACIA SEAMAN
COVER DESIGN BY BOLD STROKES BOOKS GRAPHICS

Acknowledgments

I would like to thank Len Barot for coming back, finding me, and believing in this book. What an amazing experience you are, Rad. Thanks to the entire BSB support group and authors who help each other out every day in more ways than publicity and promotion. I am proud to be associated with this group of people. I drop to my knees in front of my first-ever editor, Cindy Cresap. I was literally struck mute when I saw what beautiful things she had done with my prose, and she did it with patience, humor, and many, many kind words of instruction.

Thanks to my loyal and protective first readers, beginning with my best childhood friend, Jan Frazier, and a virtual friend, Lee Coates. My outstanding book club in Milwaukee: in particular, Jan Berman, Lynn Drumm, and Cathy Pollack, who read this book every time I asked. My family was tremendous. Thanks to Josh, Tammy, Lisa, and the other Tammy for your help with computer issues and for being the best kids on this planet. My partner, Gloria, read every draft I wrote with love, support, and patience. She is the most extraordinary woman I have ever known.

Dedication

This book is dedicated to every American who has ever
defended our country in whatever form they could:
with words or goodwill, or as a military person. And to each
of us here in America, for every single time we are respectful
and kind to each other. If we don't take care of one another,
no one else will.

CHAPTER ONE

Reporter Annie Booker and her driver drove slowly away from the military morgue into Baghdad's quiet, black night. Her exhausted body gave a slight jerk as she stared numbly at the passing landscape. She felt as dark as the air around her. They had killed Jack Kcegan. He had stood beside her, white shirt gleaming under his body armor beneath the lone streetlight, when suddenly, a hole blossomed in his forehead. The crack of a gunshot reached her ears a second later. Instinctively, she had reached for him, and they fell to the ground together as gunfire crackled like lightning around them. She felt the stubble on his face as she ran her hands over him frantically looking for signs of life.

"Jack," she said and felt as if she had shouted, but then realized she had actually whispered. He had been dead weight, unmoving, until the Marines lifted him off her. She and her driver had followed them to the hospital at breakneck speeds, but Annie had not even hoped. She had held him, and her clothes were soaked with his blood.

The car stopped at her hotel, and she pounded up the stairs in the dark to change clothes and wash Jack's blood off. She would be on the air in a little under two hours, and no one cared about the condition of her heart or mind.

They still had thirty minutes until airtime when her driver made his usual stop for cigarettes at his uncle's food market. Annie stepped out into the gritty dawn and stretched. Three trees leaned against the building, catching her eye, and she reached back into the car for her sketchbook. She wanted to focus her mind on something else, on anything but Jack Keegan. Sitting on the sandbags with her back against a cement wall, she zipped her jacket up and closed her eyes. God, she was tired. She crossed her legs, letting the sketchbook lay in her lap. It was the rainy, cool season, and she was glad for the coat she was wearing. The air was the usual combination of dust and gas fumes as traffic began to pick up behind her. She looked at the market again and studied two older ladies sitting on a bench, one holding a small handful of flowers.

She flipped the pages of her sketchbook, found a blank sheet of white paper, and quickly laid the building onto the paper, then the three trees that tipped tiredly against the shop. Leaning over to blow dirt off the paper, Annie pushed her mind again away from Jack. She had to get through this report without crying. She had called her New York producer from the morgue. This would be big news in the United States, but she had cried for a friend. Then she had called his wife and cried again.

Looking down again, she forced herself to draw steadily until children's voices broke her concentration. Two women, dressed in the traditional black abayas of Iraqi women, were leading a group of youngsters who were eight or nine years old. This was no place for a child to be, even under the protection of the teachers. One of the women caught Annie's eye, and a sudden look passed between the them, one Iraqi woman and one American. Annie wondered what the woman was thinking and smiled just as a bomb exploded. The world went silent, turned red with her own blood, and then black as Annie was blown into the street, unconscious.

❖

The descent into New York City was bumpy, and the plane jolted Annie awake. She stared at the ceiling until the echoes of the nightmare faded. Finally, she pushed into an upright position and rolled her head slowly back and forth, easing the kinks in her neck.

Looking out the window, she saw snow, the first in a long time, and she wondered how much surrounded her Wisconsin home by now. She absently adjusted the sling on her left arm and straightened further, motioning to the flight attendant with her good arm. Annie tucked her headphones into her backpack and checked her watch. She'd slept over ten hours and had been on this airplane over fourteen.

She swallowed some aspirin and looked down at her boots. They were coated with Iraqi dust, and her last clean pair of pants weren't in much better shape. Or maybe it was dust from the Jordan airport where they'd sat over twenty hours, unsure if they'd ever get out of there. The worst three months of her life was over. She was home.

Forty minutes later she was jammed between other passengers, trying to get to her baggage. This noise would put a rock concert to shame, Annie thought, but was too tired to care. She stood, wondering how to get her luggage with one arm in a sling. A child screamed, and Annie swung around, heart pounding, back in Baghdad in a moment. A firm hand gripped her elbow, startling her, and she jerked away.

"Annie Booker?" a friendly male voice asked. She frowned at the young man smiling at her. "Welcome home," he continued, pulling an ID from his suit pocket. "I'm Special Agent Josh Palmer, FBI, and if you don't mind, I'll give you a ride to the network offices."

"Really?" Annie was surprised. What would the FBI want with her? "What's wrong?" she asked, reaching for a bag, but he beat her to it, not answering.

"Just point out your luggage, and I'll get it," he said, stacking the cart. "I'll talk to you in the car."

"That's all," Annie said, pointing to the last piece of luggage. He took the handle, maneuvering it through the crowd. She had no choice but to follow.

They drove through the crowded New York City streets, and Annie watched the snow, falling like lace from the gray sky. Almost two weeks ago, she had dreamed of snow in Baghdad while lying on the bed, mind drifting with painkillers for her arm.

Annie looked at the streets, enjoying being in her own country. New York City traffic was hectic, but she relished it, leaning back into the comfortable sedan. Even the car smelled American, smelled like freedom. Josh swore as a taxi cut in front of him and then he apologized.

She grinned at him. "Stop it. You make me feel like your mother. I'm only thirty-eight years old."

"You're not old, but sorry. I just know you're beat. How's your arm?"

"Fine," she answered firmly. "Just hit with some concrete."

"A car bomb is something."

Annie turned away, looking out the window, and her stomach knotted again. "I'm fine," she repeated softly, thinking of Jack Keegan. Jack's death, that was "something."

"What's it like over there? I've never been out of the country."

"Dirty, usually hot, dangerous. In the last three years I've watched a city almost disappear." As the houses, roads, and businesses disappeared, so had society. Annie forced her thoughts back to the here and now, wondering again why an FBI agent was talking to her. "The car bomb, is that why you want to talk with me? Or is it Jack Keegan?"

They pulled into the parking ramp and he said, "Actually, I'd rather show you. That way your producer can talk with you at the same time."

They got off the elevator, and as Annie brushed by a group of women who were probably on their way to lunch, she wished for a shower. She settled for a quick scrub of her hands and face in the washroom, enjoying the hot water and clean bathroom. Running her hands over the immaculate counter, Annie glanced at herself in the mirror. Her tanned skin looked out of place in the New York winter.

Bill Simpson, producer and friend, was waiting, leaning against the wall when she came out. Good, now she'd get answers. She smiled at his wrinkled shirt and undone tie.

"Time for a treadmill?" She tapped his tummy, teasing.

"Smart-ass," he muttered, steering her into a conference room close to his office. "Welcome home, girl. This one had me worried."

"Why? I escaped. And don't get too close. I haven't bathed in a while." Annie grinned at him as they walked into the room. "Do you have anything to eat? I'm starving."

Bill ducked out and was back in a moment with bagels. Annie grabbed one and was busy with the cream cheese, listening to her stomach grumble. She looked at both men. "I don't suppose I'm here for good news, so let's have it."

Josh pushed the monitor in front of her.

"This just came up," Bill began. "Josh, why don't you show her what you folks found and then we'll talk? Thought maybe we could get this done this afternoon, but we really need to look at more of your reports, so you're not going to get out of here until tomorrow."

Annie sipped her coffee and then reached for another bagel,

watching the screen as Josh flipped to a Web site she had seen before. She caught her breath, stunned, as she read her name.

"My God, is this for real? Jaish al-Basca scares me to death. That group beheads people." She was quiet for a moment, then she turned and looked again. "This is a mistake. I'm not important enough to be on this list." They were all quiet, reading the religious rhetoric and radical political goals on the site, militant Muslims urging action to oust the invaders. It was the main post for the Islamic Jihad.

"I knew you'd say that." Bill looked at her. "That's why I wanted you to see it with Josh. When they brought this to us, especially after the car bombing, I thought we'd better bring you in for a talk."

Annie started to say something, but his tired face stopped her. She looked out the office window instead and watched a pigeon make its way along the window ledge in the snow. She thought back to a time in Kosovo. She and Bill had been huddled together near part of a wall in the snow, trying to stay warm, and Bill had been shot. After he recovered, he'd taken himself out of the field, saying he just didn't have the heart for it anymore. His eyes were asking her the same thing—was she ready to stay home? And she knew he was thinking of Jack, just as she was. Annie sighed. She just might be ready.

"Does this have anything to do with the bomb?" she asked.

Josh walked around the table and sat, facing her. "I'd like to say we know exactly what's going on here, but honestly, we're right at the beginning. Usually they target our politicians, businesspeople, or the military, but now, here you are. You're not the first woman, but you are the first American reporter to appear on their enemy list."

"Let's hope that bomb wasn't theirs. I'd hate to think those children died because of me." Annie pushed her chair back a bit. "The only thing I can think of is that piece on honor killings that I did last month. I heard from a number of people about that, but nothing as extreme as this."

She watched the young agent, wondering if he'd ever been in danger, breathing hard, frightened beyond words. His face certainly didn't show it if he had been. Annie looked him in the eye. What did she see? Youth, innocence. Did he really know what he was doing, or was he just a desk jockey?

Josh dropped his eyes first. "Truthfully, we don't know why

you're on this list. Please look at the rest of the women's names. Have you worked with them? Is there anything that would connect you?"

Annie leaned forward and looked. *No need to be rude just because the boy is young. I was young. Once.* She felt his lack of experience and remembered the feeling. Both men looked expectantly at her, but she just shook her head. "I know all seven of them, but I can't see what we have in common other than we're all correspondents, in the same place at the same time. I've worked beside most of them for quite a while." She stood. "Honestly, I'm tired, hungry, and I need a bath. God, do I need a bath. Can we pick this up tomorrow?"

Bill nodded. "Josh, do you think this warrants someone being assigned to her for a while?"

"Yes, we do. At least until we understand why these women are being targeted."

"No." Annie raised her voice. "I'm the only American, right? I don't like seeing my name, or my fellow reporters, listed as an *enemy.* It's scary. But wouldn't they have done something over there, not here? Why wait until I left the country to make a move? I don't think we need the FBI."

"Annie—" Bill started to say, but she interrupted him.

"No. Bill, I don't need someone with me. Yes, this is a well-organized group of zealots, and I'm afraid of them. Still, I know what I'm talking about. They won't pursue me here."

"That's true, but I have to think about three years ago, Annie. We're still not sure about the car bomb, and then Jack Keegan was standing next to you. Maybe they did try to do something over there, as you said."

Annie stared at him. "Surely you don't think Jack was killed because he was standing next to me?"

"We just don't know. That's the problem."

She turned away, swallowing tears. "Okay, we'll do it your way. Let me know what you want me to do and I'll do it, but I'd like to go to the hotel now." She took one more look at the young FBI agent. *If they assigned someone like Josh Palmer, who was too untried to know what the hell he's doing, I'd be better off alone,* she thought as she opened the door.

Later that night, lying in bed after a bath and dinner plus more than several drinks, Annie ran the meeting through her mind. Was this really serious? If she had known about it in Iraq, she would have just ignored it because everything was dangerous there, and now that they had started targeting journalists, who knows? The car bomb was probably random anyway. And Jack? She refused to let her mind consider that possibility. *Actually*, Annie corrected herself, *I'd probably have contacted several of the other women on the list, and we would have ignored it together.* She had seen Kerry's name on the list, her English friend, and she worried that Kerry might not know about this. Kerry would be there for at least another month. Annie made a mental note to e-mail her in the morning. She could hear Josh in the living room of the suite, talking on the phone, and she hoped he'd get some sleep.

The restaurant had felt good tonight, jazz playing in the background, candlelight on the table, good food and better drinks, all in her own language. Annie had watched Bill across the table, noting the extra lines on his face and the additional gray hair. They'd talked about what was going on in the political world in the United States, their families, the mess in Iraq, and, after more drinks, the things they wished they'd never seen. Finally, they'd talked about Jack, the man who had broken them into this business, their mentor, and someone they loved. Annie told Bill the things no one else would ever hear, and she wanted to tell it just once, then never again. She needed to talk to Nancy, Jack's wife, one more time and would call her tomorrow. The mention of Jack's wife had stopped their conversation, and they knew it was time for the night to be over. They'd meet again tomorrow, go over the film, and perhaps find a clue in there, but she doubted it.

Still, she was home. She'd left two messages on her home phone, but Mary hadn't called her back. She turned over, trying to put her aching arm in a more comfortable position, thinking about tomorrow instead. *Nothing like watching several hours of yourself.* Annie groaned. She turned the light off, curled into a ball, and was asleep instantly.

CHAPTER TWO

F BI agent Sarah Moore came through the doors of Milwaukee's
airport, muttering, "Damned cold," as she stomped snow off
her boots. The airport was almost deserted at this time of night, and she
moved quickly toward the passenger areas. The New York redeye was
due any minute, and she checked the monitors. *Just landing.* She held
her ID at security, opened her coat so they could view the gun, and then
began the long walk to the gate where the reporter would be coming
in.

She slouched tiredly against a wall in the shadows, closing her
eyes for a moment. Her phone had gone off in the middle of a dream
of a warm body against hers, hands in just the right places, and she had
groaned as the noise from the phone swept body and hands away but
left the desire. Annie Booker wasn't supposed to be in until tomorrow,
but here she was. Sarah shifted her legs, leaning against the wall as
the dream still worked on her. She scanned the area as she tried to
remember what Josh had called her new assignment. *Golden?*

She had started the day checking out Jack Keegan, the murdered
network news producer. Then she had looked over the three-part award-
winning series done by Keegan and Annie Booker two years ago that
had created a furor in the United States. Sarah had sent this on to her
group in Virginia that specialized in domestic terrorism. They would go
over each and every response the network and the reporter had received.
Her team had finished the day watching news reports filed by Annie
from Baghdad. Annie was a true celebrity, and Sarah wondered if she
would be one of those pushy, demanding people. She'd dealt with them
before. The network had described her as "savvy" and "a risk taker," but

the "down to earth" was hopeful. Another statement had irritated Sarah: "She looks so good we have to have her in front of the cameras." *Sure, like a target,* Sarah thought, *and attractive women collect viewers.* The final filmed report had quieted everyone in the room as the reporter had leaned against a burned-out vehicle, talking to a soldier. They had come under fire, and she had glanced unflinchingly at the camera, mint green eyes catching sunlight before she went down. Definitely a risk taker, as they had said, but she had been standing beside Keegan when he was killed, and then, less than twelve hours later, she had been injured in an explosion. Sarah knew her head had to be spinning.

Sarah spotted Annie behind a noisy group of people obviously traveling together. "Lord," she murmured and forgot to move. Finally, she pushed off the wall and matched Annie's pace, watching her struggle with the sling on her arm and her backpack. With that tanned face and sun-bleached hair, Sarah understood why Josh had said "golden." The other passengers looked at Annie in the quiet, curious way truly attractive people gathered attention.

"Ms. Booker?" Sarah approached her.

"Pardon me?" Annie stopped and turned to look at her.

"I'm Sarah Moore, the agent Josh Palmer asked you to meet." She held up her ID.

"Oh." Annie shifted, studying her. They were about the same height. "Okay, guilty, I forgot about you. Is there something I'm supposed to do?"

"Let's get you to my car. I know you're tired, and so am I. Here, let me carry that backpack for you."

"Thanks, I'm fine. I can carry it." Annie gave her a polite smile but kept the bag, moving toward the baggage area. Sarah put a light hand on her shoulder. "The other two agents will get your luggage. Let's just go to my car, okay?" Annie stopped again.

"Where's my car?" Annie was frowning, and Sarah braced herself.

"It's already at your house. We checked it this morning and took it home for you. I have a car here."

"My coat, I always leave it in the car when I'm coming home in cold weather."

"I have it in my car," Sarah said and watched Annie's frown smooth into the professional expression she had seen on film today.

Annie finally nodded. "All right, let's go," she said, but Sarah heard her mutter something as they walked away.

A few minutes later they were in the ramp and the bitter cold slammed into them. Sarah opened the back door and grabbed Annie's coat, holding it for her. "Crap," Annie said, trying to get it on around the sling on her arm in the bitterly cold wind.

"Hop in while I warm the car up," Sarah said as two men came toward them with Annie's luggage and put it into the backseat of the car next to them.

Annie looked across the seat at Sarah. "This is a first for me. I've never been involved with the FBI. I mean, I've known several of you, but I've never dealt with something like this."

Sarah smiled, remembering Annie's voice from the films. It certainly made you turn your head and look at the TV. She pulled a thermos from a cup holder. "I've got some coffee. Want some?" She poured the steaming liquid into the thermos lid and offered it to Annie. "Here, it'll help. Have you tried driving with one hand? I wasn't sure and thought this would work since I'll be staying with you." She watched Annie's reaction to the information that she would be staying at the house. Josh had said she had pitched a fit when they had discussed this in New York.

"Is it really necessary?" Annie gave her that cool television look again.

"Yes, it is. You are my assignment as long as you're in town, and that means I stay at your house. This is serious, Ms. Booker, and I or one of the agents on my team will be with you until we get this resolved." Sarah put her gloves on, waiting, but Annie was quiet and finally just sighed. "Ready?" Sarah asked and backed the car out, driving into the cold Wisconsin night. Snow blew in front of the headlights as the two cars drove down the ramp.

Less then an hour later they pulled into Annie's driveway. They'd talked a bit about Annie's injury and her flight home, and Sarah had complained about Milwaukee winters. Sarah had grown up in the Arizona desert and made Annie smile with stories about learning to drive in Wisconsin snow. Annie said how nice it was to drive on a freeway that didn't have enormous holes in the cement, even if there was snow. Sarah talked about a case that she'd just finished, a federal judge that had been threatened. Annie had read about it in the paper that morning, and they were still talking about it when they pulled into her driveway.

❖

Inside the house, Annie automatically walked to the indoor/ outdoor thermometer on the wall. "Twelve above out there. It's been a while since I've seen weather this cold."

"I hate it, the cold I mean," Sarah said. "Please stay here while we check the house." The three agents disappeared down the hallway, turning on lights as they went. Sarah had tossed her coat over the back of a chair, and Annie absently hung it beside her own at the back door. Annie stood, enjoying the feeling of her home, looking at the baggage piled on her kitchen table. She moved some of it, sorting out her backpack and laptop, and then started toward her office.

"Wait," Sarah said, coming back into the room. "Where are you going?"

"My office."

"Let me go ahead. Want these bags in there?" she asked, and Annie nodded, following Sarah into the dark room. She flipped the lights on. "Stay here while we do the rest of the rooms."

Annie put her laptop on the desk, tossed the backpack on the daybed, and looked around. She took a deep breath, touching her desk. She'd been gone over three months, but it seemed like three years right now.

Sarah popped back into the room. "Looking good. Oh, do you have a basement? Of course you do. This is Wisconsin."

"That way, in the laundry room." Annie pointed across the hall-way. "Only door in there. Would you like me to make some coffee?"

"Thanks, but no. I don't know about you, but I'm whipped." She turned toward the laundry room. Annie looked at her athletic body and well-tailored suit as she left the room. Those brown eyes were calm, and she seemed efficient, experienced. That was good. The basement took a bit of time before Sarah returned. "Okay, you're secure. Beautiful home, Ms. Booker."

"It's Annie, and thank you."

"All right, Annie it is, but only if you'll call me Sarah. Just show me where to dump my stuff and I'll give you some privacy and let these guys go on home. Oh, one of your windows was unlocked. Is that usual?"

"What? That messes with my alarm system. Mary should have—" Annie looked up. *Where is Mary?*

"By the way, when is your roommate returning?"

"I didn't know she was gone."

Sarah looked at her for a moment and then said, "Her employer said she was on vacation."

Annie shook her head. "I imagine she left me a note or some information somewhere. I'll let you know."

"Please do." Sarah gestured to her bag. "So, where do you want me to bunk?"

Annie felt utterly exhausted. Mary was on vacation? Annie mulled that over in her mind as she walked down the hallway to the first guest room. Mary had been using the one farther on down the hall.

"My bedroom's directly across from this one," Annie said. "There's a full bath for you." She pointed at a door. "Feel free to use the dressers or whatever you need."

Sarah tossed her bags on the bed and looked around. "Thanks, and by the way, if I leave before you get up in the morning, there'll be another agent here, probably a man. Just a warning." Annie gave a brief nod and turned to leave the room, but Sarah stopped her. "I'm sorry. We'll pretty much be in your space. I know you're going to want to get yourself together after being gone so long, but it can't be helped."

Annie nodded tiredly. "I still think this is wrong. If they had wanted to do something, they would have, over there, not here at home." She walked back to her office, grabbing several bags and taking them to the laundry room. She swore softly at Mary. Why hadn't she told her she'd be gone?

She retreated into her bedroom and took her favorite old robe off a hook behind the bathroom door. She let her clothes drop in a heap then snuggled into the robe and stood for a moment, feeling it against her skin. Finally, she moved to the big bed. The clean sheets felt like the robe, like home. She listened to the wind howl and was glad it wasn't desert sand hitting the windows. "I made it," she said and snuggled deeper into the warm blankets and sleep.

❖

Sarah took her shoes off and stretched out on the bed, listening to Annie moving around. She set her clock and smiled, remembering the airport. *You won't let me carry your bag? Okay, but I caught you smiling at my stories about snow. Stubborn but thoughtful,* she decided, remembering the offer of coffee. *Also, injured and exhausted, but I certainly didn't expect her to look like she did. Everyone looks good on film, but she's better looking in person, and her voice is incredible, like a calm, blue-skied autumn day.* After the lights had gone out, Sarah got up and made one last silent walk around the house. Finally, she took her clothes off and got into bed, sleep taking her immediately.

CHAPTER THREE

Sarah Moore sat in her office, bent over a county plat map. Surrounded by photos and other papers, she had been looking over the property, thinking about protection around the house for more than in-house surveillance. Most of it seemed to be wooded. She looked up when a new agent rapped his knuckles on her open door.

"Time for a second cup?" Scott Fraizer asked, holding a tray with two coffee cups She nodded and looked back at the large book spread out on her desk.

"What have you got for me on the family?" she asked, pushing her hair from her face as she reached for the coffee. Looking at the cup in her hand, Sarah smiled. "Thanks, Scott, I appreciate this." He was coming along nicely for a newbie, including trying to get into her good graces with her favorite coffee.

"How was it last night?" Scott asked, putting his large frame onto one of the small chairs she kept in front of her desk. Sarah didn't want anyone to get too comfortable in her office. It was her space, and she protected it, even if it meant having narrow chairs that no one in their right mind could sit on comfortably for more than ten minutes.

"She's very nice, thankfully." Sarah looked across the desk and caught him watching her. "And?"

"Well, how does she look?" He grinned at her. "I mean, she's thirty-eight."

Sarah leaned back in her chair. "Look? Well, she's tall, slender, and attractive, but a very tired lady right now." Sarah paused, watching him. "Her hair is, I'm not sure, brown essentially, but sunburned almost white on top and streaked with blond."

He frowned, and Sarah wondered what else he was asking. "No one ever looks as good in person as they do on television," he finally said.

Sarah started to laugh. "Wrong, and I was surprised. She's every bit as good as television, probably better because you get a wider range of expressions to go with that voice. Here, set these on the table." Sarah handed him the books and network photos of Annie. "Now, what did you find out on the family?"

Taking papers out of his briefcase on the chair beside him, Scott said, "Shall I just read it to you?" Sarah nodded and he began, "Dad, James Booker, has owned a nursery business for over thirty-five years and just expanded with a second location. Mother, that is, Dr. Hannah Booker, began the Milwaukee Women's Clinic when she returned from Vietnam. She started an organization called Charlene's Angels. It's sort of a good old girl network, women-helping-women organization."

"Scott, follow up a bit further on the family, including any siblings. We need to be sure of everything. Oh, and take a further look at what I've outlined here with security for her house. You might have some additional suggestions that I'd be willing to consider, including temporary motion sensors around the house. As a matter of fact, call Jim at the house for me, will you? We'll do that and include a walk-around." She stood and smiled down at him. "What about Ms. Booker?"

"I thought we'd covered her yesterday?"

"We had network information, that's true, but what about the local take on her? That's really what I want from you, Scott. Local stuff. Maybe I was unclear?"

He finally stood, and she could see the relief on his face. No one liked her chairs. "I'm sorry. I just assumed you wanted the rest of the family."

"No harm, no foul. Don't get too personal. Just anything you feel is pertinent to what we need." She hadn't heard a word about Annie's lifestyle, but they needed to know everything, legally, they possibly could to provide even adequate protection.

"Do the usual, Scott. We know about her job and her family, but what about her friends? Has she ever been investigated for anything illegal? I know she's a national personality, but they have problems too. What about gambling or even drugs? As I said, just run her through the usual background checks."

He looked apprehensive and so she smiled. "Thanks for the coffee. I appreciate it. When you feel comfortable with what you have, see me. If I'm not here, I'll be with Ms. Booker. Just give my phone a ring."

After he had left she walked to the window and looked at the busy street below her fourth floor office. She hoped she and Annie could have a conversation tonight. There had to be something that connected her and the others on that list, but what? They didn't know enough about that bunch of crazies in Iraq to put in a teaspoon, but she would by tonight. And then there was that damned bomb and the network executive who'd been standing right next to her when he was shot. Annie had been living very close to the edge. Sarah frowned, going back to her desk, and looked at the old Rolodex on her desk, flipping it to a card. One of her college roommates worked for the CIA. She'd talk to her before she went one step further.

CHAPTER FOUR

Annie lay in the gray space of dreams, the nightmare shadowing her once again. Her mind knew she would wake soon, and with a final nudge of energy, she opened her eyes, her body trembling. She dreamed of the same dark figures: Jack, rising out of the sand, the woman's eyes that had looked into hers before the explosion, and the screaming voices of children. She closed her eyes, trying to calm herself, ears straining for the noise of the Baghdad hotel. She sat up, moving to the edge of the bed. The gray space held her mind a moment longer and then dissolved. "I'm home," she mumbled and lay back, snuggling into the warm covers of her own bed.

Thin winter sun caught the crystal snowflake that hung on the French doors to the deck, tossing colors around the large bedroom. Annie tracked the colors. She and Mary had picked the bed out together when they were just beginning. Staring at the colors on the ceiling, she thought about beginnings, a time when you just did and followed your heart. Mary was finishing her first year at the clinic, and Annie had just begun at the network when they moved in here.

Annie grabbed her pillow, holding it close, and looked over at the other side of the bed. The covers lay still, untouched, like a grave. She couldn't even remember what it felt like to wake up with someone on the other side of the bed, any bed. Mary had been sleeping in their guest bedroom for almost three years.

As she stretched her sore muscles, a sudden memory walked across Annie's mind. Mary, in a restaurant, sunlight raining down on her pale, golden hair. Annie had come in with her team after a summer softball game, and the bright hair had caught her eye. The team had settled down at a long table with the usual noise, shoving and laughing, but Annie had kept her attention on the nice-looking blonde wrapped in the shaft of light. She was alone, engrossed in the papers spread out on the table, ignoring the noisy group. Annie had taken a drink of her beer, told her friends she was in for a pizza, and then headed for Mary's table.

"Excuse me?" Annie had stood before her.

An impatient "yes" floated out into the air. Mary had not even looked up.

"Excuse me, as in I know I'm interrupting," Annie had persisted, "but I think I met you at the hospital." And she had, helping her best friend Rebecca with her little boy who had fallen into a table. He'd been a handful, but Mary had been patient, calming him down. Annie had stared until Rebecca began to tease her.

"Could be, but that was the end of my med school emergency med rotation. Now I'm a doctor." Mary finally looked up. She had been filling out forms for Annie's mother's clinic, but Annie had said nothing. That had been the beginning and now, over eleven years and millions of words later, the house was strewn with tears and arguments.

Now I can think about endings, Annie thought as she got out of bed and checked herself out in the mirror. "And I need a haircut," Annie muttered. She pulled on warm socks and jeans, then searched for a sweatshirt in the chest of drawers. All of Mary's things were gone, and she opened more drawers, finding the same. "What the heck?" She went to Mary's room. The result was the same, empty drawers and cabinets in the bathroom. Annie sank down on the bed and looked at the empty room. She realized this was the last place they had talked, face-to-face, over three months ago. The night that Mary had told her about Meg. Too exhausted to even think straight, Annie had simply stared. They had agreed to settle it while Annie was home, but that moment had never happened. Jack Keegan had called from New York and Annie was soon back in Baghdad. She'd been home less than five days.

She headed to the bathroom where she brushed her teeth and tried to tame her hair, which was now several inches longer than she was used to wearing it. Something on the counter glinted as she moved the toothbrush around in her mouth, and she stared at the mirror. She closed her hand over the shiny metal object without looking. She turned it in her hand, knew what it was, and jammed it into her pocket. Someone coughed, a man, and she paused, listening, then remembered Sarah telling her that a male agent might be here today. Annie walked out of her bedroom but didn't see anyone. Sighing, she walked down the hallway to the large kitchen and looked into the living room.

"Morning," she said, startling the man bent over a laptop.

"Good afternoon." He stood. "I'm Mike Easton, FBI, working with Agent Moore." He held out his hand, and she thought about Sarah last night. Apparently, all FBI agents were tall. "Please, just do whatever it is you need to do," he continued. "I walk the house about every twenty minutes, inside and out. A crew will be here soon to install temporary motion sensors outside, but it shouldn't take them long. Just a heads up, all right?"

Annie nodded, thinking of all the time and money being wasted on her. She was home and safe. She started the coffee and walked around the house. No doubt about it, Mary's personal belongings were gone. *Does that mean I get the furniture*, Annie wondered as she checked her desk. If Mary had wanted to leave her any information, it would be here, but there was nothing. Well, what was there left to say anyway? Mary had just quit asking, quit talking, quit arguing, and found Meg. And left.

Annie tried calling her mother, but got her voicemail and left a message. She walked back into the kitchen and poured a cup of coffee, looking out over Lake Michigan. Steam rose off the frozen lake as the sun warmed it, something she loved to watch. The white snow against green pines and coppery oak trees was soothing. Any color but sand, she thought. The clock showed one o'clock, and she turned to the laundry room. First load of clothes in and boots cleaned and put away, she went into her office. Annie soon had some of her parents' old rock playing, and then she booted up her laptop. The music warmed her some, cutting into the curl of loneliness creeping into her mind. She heard the doors to the deck close and remembered there was someone else in the house. Perhaps it wouldn't be so bad after all, having people around.

Annie reread a page of notes from her final piece in Baghdad but finally gave up. She couldn't concentrate, and switched to e-mail. There was nothing from Kerry in Baghdad, and that bothered her. The network had her in Iraq almost ten months out of last year, and she hadn't been home in over three months. There was a missed holiday season in there somewhere, not to mention Mary. Annie slid her hand into her pocket, feeling the ring, turning it with her fingers. "I wouldn't want to live with me," she muttered. She stared at the laptop again. The U.S. involvement in Iraq was confusing and dangerous. It had never been about weapons of mass destruction or democracy. It was about money and politics, maybe oil. Worse, she had a sliding suspicion that revenge had also played a big part in the beginning, and that feeling grew each time she went back. *I love my work*, Annie thought, *but it's changing, evolving slowly into something I'm not happy with*. The Jaish al-Basca list was a new wrinkle in her life, but she couldn't believe they'd bother with her, not here, in the U.S.

The doors opened in the kitchen, and she heard the agent come back into the house. The phone rang just as the music ended.

Her mother's voice sparkled on the telephone. "Welcome home, honey. Want to have dinner with us tonight?"

"I've died and gone to heaven," Annie said, amazed that there were still moments when her mother's voice would bring tears to her eyes.

Her mother laughed and asked how she was.

"Homesick, Mom. I'm just glad to be home." Annie checked out the refrigerator while talking to her mother. "Do you want me to bring anything?"

"No, just be there by six. Love you, honey, have to go." As they hung up Annie spotted the carton of eggs.

"Cool, eggs. Beats crackers and dried fruit." She pulled them out. A white object on the table caught her eye, and she reached for Sarah's business card. Annie called and left Sarah a message, following her instructions to notify her if Annie needed to leave the house. Annie walked into the living room, clearing her throat first so she didn't startle the man working at the big coffee table. He looked up with a smile, and she told him that she would be going to her parents' for dinner and she had left a message for Agent Moore. He frowned at her.

"If Sarah's not back by then, I'll have to go with you," he said. Annie nodded, then walked back into the kitchen. She saw her mail, neatly stacked and weighed down by a statue of a crow. Annie picked up the statue, rubbing the carved heavy hardwood with her thumb. Black with green undertones, the statue was a beautiful piece of work.

Rebecca had given it to her when they had shared a house during their final year of college. Annie picked up the phone one more time and left Rebecca a message too. "What is it with me and voicemail today?"

She looked through the mail and pulled out a newsletter from Charlene's Angels. She was pleased to see that some of her own e-mailed comments from Iraq had been included. Iraqi women were struggling. Annie remembered the last woman she had interviewed. A teacher before Saddam's government began to decline in the eighties, she was now washing linens at the hospital. Her English had been excellent, and Annie had gone to her house later and met her husband and her children. The notes were on her computer, and her mind swung back. The family was stuck in what remained of their house with very little food and infrequent electricity. What little water they had was unfit for drinking. They had given their children Valium until the supplies had run out. Annie had shared some of her own bottled water with this family when possible, and she wasn't the only journalist or military person doing this. Looking around her kitchen, Annie felt her heart sag. Watching those people struggle just to make it from day to day had saddened her. She had hoped the American presence would enrich and help them, but it wasn't happening. Her worst fear was that it never would. The last Iraqi official she had interviewed said it would take his country at least twenty-five years to recover from the Americans.

Annie frowned down at her cooling eggs. It always took her several days to adjust to being home, something Mary had never understood. She straightened and tried to redirect her mind. She wasn't on call here. She had brought home gifts for each of her nephews and nieces, as well as Rebecca's two kids, and she wondered how tall they would be when she saw them next. Once again, the unfamiliar sensation of loneliness threaded through her. *Alone is not the same as lonely*, she thought and then realized this was the first time she had come home and Mary had been gone, out of town. *I wonder if this was how she felt*, she thought as she cleaned up her dishes.

Annie struggled again trying to get her coat on over the sling and finally got the zipper to engage. She stepped out into the snow on the deck and took a deep breath of the cold air. The sunlight was shallow but felt good. Leaning on the railing, she looked down the bluffs to Lake Michigan. Annie loved the lake, its restlessness and the fact that she couldn't see across it. It seemed to go on forever. This land was once fully covered with trees, mostly oak, maple, and pine. Her family had owned the land for over one hundred and fifty years, and each family member that had lived here had taken care of the trees, saving as many as possible.

Annie walked through the snow to the back of the deck, checking out the roof and the loft above it. Her mother's uncle had come home from war in the forties and torn down the existing house, building this spacious log cabin with a loft for a stained glass studio. Long and graceful, glassed in on three sides, the loft was modeled after the widow's walk common to the Great Lakes and the East Coast. He had salvaged pieces of beautifully colored glass that had been part of the family business and used them to line the bottom of the studio windows. When Annie and Mary had bought the house she had remodeled it as her painting studio but kept the stained glass, installing shutters to cover them when she painted to use true light. When she wasn't painting, she would open the shutters to a storm of color.

She stretched to see the boathouse but could only see the dock. They'd had so many parties on this lawn. Her mother's uncle had loved to entertain. In the winter this had been the "official" sliding hill for their sleds, toboggans, or whatever the family could find to make the trip down the long hill. She and Mary had planted a row of blue spruce, and she checked them out. Surprised at their height, she smiled. *Guess I get the trees too.*

The old plum tree at the side of the deck looked as if it was wintering well, and she envied its simple, safe quiet in the snow. *I wonder if I could run away, just disappear*, she thought, kicking snow off the edge of the deck. *It'd be easy, just pack a couple of small bags, pick up my car keys and walk out the door, stay in motels. I could see my country again, forget the FBI and my job.* Annie moved to the right and kicked more snow, running the possibility through her mind. She'd let her parents and Rebecca know where she was, but no one else.

A crow screamed above her, startling her, and she watched the large bird glide down toward the lake. This was beginning to feel a lot like three years ago, that black hole in the earth, and she held her injured arm with her right hand, rocking slightly. The last time she had stood here, the leaves had turned and she didn't want to leave. Annie's artist mind re-created the scene in her memory. *God, I love this land,* she thought, and was surprised to feel tears on her cheeks. "Dammit," she said softly. "Stop." But she couldn't and then frowned as the FBI agent stepped out on the deck.

"I'm sorry, Ms. Booker, but you shouldn't be out here alone."

"Not even on my own deck?"

"Not alone," he said. "Just let me know where you're going and I'll tag along."

She turned her back. This was impossible. Time to pack a bag. Annie wiped her eyes and checked the tree line up to the house. She looked again at the loft and squinted against the sun rocketing off the large panes of glass. Something looked different. All the shutters were closed. Mary might have done it if the winds had been strong off the lake. Had one of the FBI agents been up there last night? She had been so tired she couldn't remember.

Annie studied the snow, watching a spot melting into a tiny puddle on the wood. It would be ice before the sun went down.

❖

Hamel stood in the woods, watching the house and the two people on the deck at the back. He had been there quite a while, taking the measure of the property, and he would stay longer. He was dressed in white camouflage, the anorak blending into the snow. He barely moved, quieting his breath. The closest house was over a half mile away, the distance between them filled with woods. The reporter and the man had looked right at him but had not seen him against the snow. He smiled inwardly at his unexpected good luck. He had just found out she was back in town, and he had come out here to check it out for himself.

CHAPTER FIVE

Agent Easton drove to them to Annie's parents' home and parked behind her father's company pickup.

"Do you go inside with me?" Annie asked, tightening her jaw. It irritated her even though she knew he was just doing his job. He looked at her and dialed Sarah.

"She's on her way," he said, and they waited in silence.

When Sarah drove up, Mike said a few words to her and drove away.

"How was your day?" Sarah asked, studying Annie's expression.

"Glad to be home," she answered. "Sarah, my parents know nothing about this, about you, so bear with me, please."

Sarah nodded, following her to the family entrance on the enclosed back porch. Sarah stopped to look at an old red bicycle with a crow painted on the front fender. "What's this?"

Annie stopped and ran her hands over the handlebars. "Remind me later tonight, when we go home, and I'll tell you about this. It's special. Mom and Dad keep it around for the grandkids."

A mouthwatering aroma greeted them as they reached the door. "Yum," Annie said, "Dad's fried chicken."

"Hi, sweetie," her father said, bending down for a kiss. "Missed you." His thick gray hair shone in the light.

"Daddy, this is Agent Sarah Moore from the FBI." Annie did the introductions while her father took their coats. When he came back he looked pointedly at Annie's arm, raising his eyebrows in a question.

"I'm fine," Annie said. "I'll start with wine. How about you, Sarah?"

Sarah declined, and Annie petted Maggie, their four-year-old golden retriever. "How's business, Dad?"

"Fine, but you know the nursery business in Milwaukee in the winter. Slow and ramping up for spring, but the new location is growing, so I can't complain."

Annie looked out at the greenhouse in the backyard. "Spending time out there?"

"As much as possible. Your mother's on her way, so we'll eat soon." Annie watched him look at Sarah and could see that he had decided to wait until her mom came home to ask about her.

"Great, I'm starved," Annie replied.

The garage door hummed, and Maggie barked at the back door as Annie's mother bustled into the room. "James, that smells delicious. Hello, youngest daughter. Give me a hug." She held out her arms and gave Annie a careful hug around the sling on her arm, pushing her hair off her forehead a bit. "Need a haircut, huh?" She smiled at her and then frowned. "But you've lost way too much weight."

She stepped back, taking one last look and then noticed Sarah. "And who's this?"

Annie went through the introductions again and her mother reached out her hand, smiling. "Let me get my things into the office and we'll eat." She gave Maggie some attention, then exited through a doorway.

Annie's dad raised his eyebrows, remarking dryly, "So laid back, isn't she?" Annie and her dad laughed.

"Actually, she's perfect and so are you," Annie replied just as her mother entered the room.

"You look good, Mom. How is the clinic going?" Annie asked, watching her mother's expression, knowing she was trying to decide how she could tactfully ask about the FBI agent. Annie grinned. This was fun.

Her mother shot her a look and answered Annie's question. "Good, very good. Hired three new doctors and another psychiatrist to help me out. Thank God. I was having trouble keeping up."

"Never thought I'd hear those words out of your mouth, Mom." Annie took another look at her mother. *More gray hair than the last time I checked*, she thought.

"Just a good front, my dear. How hungry are we? Do we have a little time?"

Years around her mother had taught Annie what to say. "Let's talk. And have more wine."

"Not that I'm impatient." Her mother laughed. "Don't you wonder how I never manage to send my patients off the closest bridge?" She turned to Sarah. "Are you here officially, or as Annie's guest?"

Annie spoke before Sarah could open her mouth. "Officially, and I don't think it's anything other than just odd. There's an extremist group in Iraq called Jaish al-Basca, a group that I've known about for a few years. When I flew into New York City, the FBI met me at the airport and we went to Bill Simpson's office. It seems my name is on their latest Web site. Mine and seven others. All women and all reporters."

"Web site?" her dad said, looking startled.

"Actually," Sarah answered, "let me take this one, if that's all right with you, Annie."

Annie nodded, got up, and began setting the table for another person as Sarah began. She wanted to hear what they said, officially.

"Your daughter's name, along with the other female reporters, appeared several weeks ago on this particular Web site. We regularly monitor domestic Web sites, but in this case, our intelligence in Iraq first alerted us and we began to watch it. Sometimes our citizens' names will appear once and then just disappear. This time, Annie's name was initially one of three, and then it grew to eight names. Her network is concerned, and we're not going to take a chance."

"Annie," her dad began, "this sounds serious."

"I think the FBI sounds like a good idea," her mother finished his thought.

Annie sat down and took a drink of wine, looking at her dad over the rim of her glass. *He looks older too, just like Mom*, she thought.

"I'm sorry, you two. The FBI is new to me too. Mom, I should have said something on the phone to you earlier. I don't want to worry either of you."

Sarah spoke up. "We don't like to be in a citizen's private space, but the alternative is not nice. Would it be all right if we have dinner first?"

Annie's mother broke into a smile. "Wonderful idea. Are you all as hungry as I am? Here, James, let me help." They got up, putting food on the table, and she asked about Annie's arm.

"The doctor said to tell you that little pieces of concrete got into the muscle, but it's healing. Wait, I've got some information." She reached in her pocket for the paper the Army doctor in Baghdad had given her. "Here, Mom, this was for you. The stitches haven't been looked at for two days, actually longer. Maybe before I leave tonight?"

Her mom nodded. "Yes, I've been wanting to see it anyway." She leaned toward Annie. "Jack Keegan, what a loss, honey."

Annie stopped. Her throat constricted, and she hoped she wouldn't cry. Her parents had been close to Jack and his family. Annie cleared her throat. "Did you get to the funeral?" she asked.

"Yes, we flew in for two nights. Nancy said to thank you personally for calling her."

Annie had felt it was her responsibility since she had been with him. "I called her again when I got back the other day." She stopped, unable to say another word.

Her dad told a humorous story about a fishing experience last summer with Jack, and her mom changed the subject, launching into stories about the grandchildren. Annie got her mind together and led Sarah into a conversation about growing up in Scottsdale, Arizona, and she complained again about the Midwest climate.

"And I miss the hot food," Sarah confessed.

"You mean hot as in spicy, right?" her dad asked with a grin.

"No one has the right salsa here. Mom sends me some now and then, but it's not the same when I go out."

Annie's dad went into the kitchen pantry, returning with a glass jar filled with something green and held it out to Sarah. "I'd like you to try this stuff. A friend of mine in New Mexico loves my concoction, and I'd be grateful if you tried it too. Be honest."

Sarah looked around. "Do you folks eat this?" They all laughed as she took a taste, and Annie held her breath. Her dad's salsa made her eyes water.

Sarah laid some on her plate and dipped a piece of chicken into it. "Oh, this is so good, truly excellent, Mr. Booker."

"Then it's yours," he said, obviously pleased. "Would you like the recipe?"

"Me? I can't cook. Don't tell anyone, but I struggle boiling water. My mother would kill me for admitting this, Lord knows she tried."

Amid the ensuing laughter Annie watched Sarah's dark eyes sparkle and liked her for being careful and warm with her parents. Her dad's salsa didn't make her eyes water, and she was cute. No, she was downright attractive.

They moved to the den for coffee before her dad asked Sarah again about Jaish al-Basca. Sarah looked at Annie, who had settled on the floor, her back resting on the sofa next to her mom.

Annie said, "It's weird for me to be here, in the United States, worrying about something in Iraq. If I were still in Baghdad and knew this, we would have noticed, paid attention, but gone on doing our jobs anyway."

Sarah took a deep breath. "I don't know, Annie. From where I sit, they are everywhere. I've been assigned to you simply because they are here." She looked at Annie who looked away.

"Here? You mean the U.S., or Milwaukee?"

"Both. Milwaukee and the entire United States." Sarah set her cup on the table. "We're coordinating with the other countries on your case, and I have to admit that we're all wondering why we have eight women from different countries on their Web site with such dire threats. You have to have something in common other than just being correspondents. I know you were all living within a two-mile radius of each other in Baghdad and you've all been there the longest of any women reporters, but there has to be something else."

Annie was struck by a quick memory of the children on the ground, dead, and she took a quick breath. "I can't think of a single thing. I swear. I mean, we saw each other, but never in a planned or structured setting. It's all so unstable over there."

Sarah nodded. "We're just not prepared for terrorism in our everyday lives here in America. It's easy to forget that we're at war, and it's not because we don't care. It seems remote to most people in this country. Just to be very clear, there is a terrorism cell active here, in Milwaukee, a branch of the main group in Chicago. The money comes primarily from Chicago, but they funnel illegal Iraqis through this city, figuring, of course, it'll be less apparent. We need something that ties these women together, and then we'll have more information.

The other women are equally puzzled. Two of them are still in Iraq, for that matter."

Annie nodded, thinking of Kerry.

Sarah continued. "You're a lot safer in the United States, that is true, but we have discussed moving you to a safe area until we know more about the quality of the threat."

"The quality?" Annie asked in disbelief.

"A safe place?" her mom asked. "A different house, or state?"

"Probably in-state, up north," Sarah said. "This is typical terrorism. Thriving on the unknown. As I said, we have good intelligence and knowledge of the locals, but I don't know if this Web site is connected to these people. I'm just trying to prepare you. If it looks as if it's becoming more dangerous, we'll get Annie out of here. And, Annie, to answer your question about quality, I mean intent. As I said, our locals are traditionally information gathering centers, disseminating people to other areas."

Her dad spoke up. "Do you mean they wouldn't organize an attack?"

"Oh no, Mr. Booker. They very well might, and, in fact, we believe they will. We just don't know where or when, and believe me when I say they're patient. They certainly have the resources and are capable of carrying out an attack, possibly like the one we've already experienced. But at this point, they are just funneling Iraqis into the country. What we don't know is if they have any connection to the Web site Annie's name is on."

Sarah looked at her. "Annie, you are at risk. That's why we've installed the sensors around the house and why I'll be there with you, or someone else will, around the clock."

Annie shut her mind down. She was home. This wasn't Iraq. She thought about the two bags she had packed at home. She looked at Sarah's dark hair that curled down to the top of her collar and wondered what it would feel like to run her hands through it. Sarah was looking at her, so she asked, "Am I safe in my house?"

"You have an excellent alarm system," Sarah said. "I checked it out last night, when we got to your house. In fact, it's pretty sophisticated. Any special reason for that?"

Annie took a deep breath. "My ex-partner, Mary, was home alone most of the time." She looked at Sarah, trying to gauge her reaction. It was the first time she had ever used the word "ex" about Mary, and it felt strange in her mouth. She glanced at her parents. She hadn't said a word to them about Mary leaving. Sarah's eyes never left hers or changed, and Annie realized there was probably very little this woman didn't know about her. "Since I'm gone most of the time, I thought the least I could do was put in the best system available."

"Whatever, it's a good one. It doesn't bother you to be alone?"

Annie shook her head and then remembered this afternoon. Maybe it did bother her.

"By the way, where will you go next, on your job?" Sarah asked after a moment.

"As of now, the only thing they want is for me to get my arm taken care of."

"Okay. By the way, can I use your workout equipment? That's a great setup you have in the basement."

"Anytime. And I may be using it too, depending on what Mom and the doctors at the clinic have to say when they look at my arm."

"Let's do that before you go." Her mom stood. "I'll look at your arm and we'll have another cup of coffee in the kitchen."

Her mom poured more coffee for both of them and sat at the table. "Tell me about Mary, and to be truthful, she talked to me about Meg. She knew you were coming home and they took off on vacation."

"What did she say?"

"That she's leaving," her mom said gently.

"Sorry I haven't said anything to you or Dad. The network got me out of here so fast the last time we didn't get a chance to talk about much. Today I noticed her things are gone, clothes, pictures, even books, so I assume she's moving into Meg's. Maybe I get the furniture in the divorce." She reached into her pocket and pulled the ring out, setting it carefully on the table. The gold glowed softly in the kitchen lights. "This was lying on the counter in the bathroom."

Her mother looked at the ring. "Divorce? I have people in my office every day over divorce. It's a big deal. Then the injury, Jack's death, and now this Web site thing. It's a lot, sweetie, and it worries us. I'm glad the FBI is there." She looked at Annie with a little twinkle in her eyes. "I don't mean to pry, but I'm going to. Anyone…?"

Annie was surprised but teased her mom right back. "You want the gory details, huh? Let's see, just one-nighters or—"

"All right. I hear enough of that from my patients. I'm talking to my daughter now."

"There's no one, Mom." Annie sobered. "I am taking this seriously, but it's always so deadly there. You should see Baghdad, all burned, broken up. They didn't love Saddam, but they love Iraq, the ones that are left."

"Your dad and I caught your report on the exodus estimate."

Annie nodded. "The worst part is that the ones who left were the people who could have helped the most now—the leaders, the truly resourceful people who might have held the country together. The people who wouldn't have been afraid to be bold and imaginative."

"I wonder if that's who Sarah is talking about when she says illegal immigrants?"

"I don't know," Annie said, "but you can bet I'll ask."

Her mom sighed. "The arm. Did the doctor in Baghdad say you need to see a specialist? Any problems sleeping? Or nightmares?"

"The surgeon there said I'd probably need rehab. It's on that paper I gave to you. I know they put stitches in and thought my doctor at the clinic would look at it. And, yes, I'm having nightmares, but, Mom, I would have talked to you about them."

Her mom took the paper and then helped Annie take her arm from the sweatshirt. She looked at the wound and stitches, then back down at the paper, reading the military doctor's description of the injury.

"Let's see, tendon and tissue damage from the impact and the cement. Oh, a possible stress fracture? And ligament damage." Hannah read from the paper. "That was, what? Almost two weeks ago? This seems incomplete."

"You of all people know what field hospitals are like, and damn, it was the same place we had taken Jack. I was brought in with several other groups. It was a woman doctor, and she said the arm would have to be looked at again. She was so busy, Mom. There were so many injuries and bodies. It was crazy. They assumed I would just leave Baghdad right away, and I meant to, but I had to finish up. Really, compared to just about everyone else in there, my injury was minor."

What she had done was take two days to rest so she could stand up straight without falling over or move her arm without crying. Then she had gone to find the families of the women and children involved in the blast. She had found the families of the two women immediately and talked with them off camera. Annie had left their homes, sat in the car, and cried. The women were university students from established families, and the children had been their little brothers, sisters, and cousins. She had tried to film it, make it a story for the network, but every time she began the tears would start. Nothing worked, and so she had waited in Kerry's room, then in her own hotel, feeling broken and frightened until she thought she could go home in a human form.

"All right. Come to the clinic tomorrow. We'll have some tests run and check it out. Looks like the doctor was right. You'll probably need some rehabilitation. By the way, how are your ears? This doesn't say anything about a concussion."

"She talked about that and was surprised that I just had temporary hearing loss. My ears are fine. I was sitting on sandbags and leaning against a concrete wall. I think that saved me." They worked at getting her arm back in the sleeve. "The advantages of having a doctor in the family." Annie grinned. "I'm going to go home, put some music on, and call Rebecca. Have you heard from her?"

"She called the day after you left the last time. Wanted to talk with you, but you'd already gone."

"I was only here five days. I didn't even feel as if I'd been home," Annie said, picking the ring up and putting it in her pocket.

❖

Hamel had easily swung himself up to the top of the garage after everyone had left the reporter's home. He had watched from the woods as they installed the motion sensors. *If I were doing that, I would have hidden them better and installed more of them*, he thought, watching them through his binoculars. He powered up the binoculars and tried to read the numbers on the equipment, but he couldn't and decided to wait until after dark. The American sensors weren't as accurate as his, and he was familiar with almost all of them.

Getting into the loft was easy. He simply took a tool from his pack and ran it over the wood and metal until he heard the lock disengage inside. He took a small flashlight and carefully pushed things away from the wall, then slid inside. This was just to familiarize himself with the house. He stood for a while, thinking about the alarm system, wondering why it didn't extend up here, to this room. It was a good system, but electronics were simple. Finally, he took latex gloves from his pocket and moved forward, going down the steps and into the house.

He started at the back. He would want to draw this for his sister so she would be as familiar with it as he was. He was certain the reporter had the information Jack Keegan had gotten and he quickly looked through the office but found nothing. There was time. He would be back. He sat down at the laptop on the table in the front room. He laid his pack on the table and began to insert his program into the FBI computer. It was another piece of luck to find their computer here, unattended. When done, he repacked his bag, moving to the kitchen and then walking the perimeter of the room, pausing at the big French doors to the deck. They were the easiest locks he had found so far. Finally satisfied, he opened the kitchen door, reset the alarm, and left through the garage side door into the woods. He stripped the gloves off, stuffing them in his parka pocket, and walked to the car he had left there much earlier.

CHAPTER SIX

S arah pulled into a local convenience store on their way home. "The owner of this store, Sam, is a Pakistani and had just bought the place when Mary and I were moving into the house," Annie said as Sarah parked the car. "We've taught each other a lot of things, from language to culture, and he's one of my favorite people. I had Charlene's Angels, Mom's organization, come in and help him with his legal difficulties, and we've become close over the years. I usually manage to smuggle one of his favorite alcoholic beverages home, and we trade news, but I left in such a hurry I forgot it. Watch his face when I tell him I don't have it." Annie chuckled, getting out of the car. "If you see anything you want, just pick it up, all right?"

Sam came from behind the counter to greet Annie, but when he saw her arm he stopped, making a face. He wouldn't even let her pay as she apologized for not bringing a bottle home for him. They talked until a man came to the counter from the back of the store. Annie moved her items to the side to let him check out, glancing at him and then taking a longer look. He looked familiar. It happened to her often, traveling so frequently, but this felt different, urgent somehow. She noted his expensive boots and heavy coat that looked new. He was tall, and his short black hair curled about his head. Annie asked Sam about him after the man left, but he hadn't seen him before.

Annie was quiet when they got into the car and started for her house. As the garage door rolled up, she finally said, "I can't remember where I've seen that man, but I know him. It's more than just seeing him somewhere. I know that I know him. I've been around him for more than just a few minutes at some point." She shook her head and opened the kitchen door. "I give up. I just don't remember where." She pointed at a peg beside the door. "Just hang your coat here, Sarah. I'll put the groceries away."

Sarah put the bags on the kitchen counter, asking Annie to wait while she checked the house out. "Did Jim show you the house monitor, the system we installed this afternoon?" she said, walking back into the kitchen. Annie shook her head. "All right, after I get done with my workout, we'll go over it. I want you to be familiar with it too." She left for the basement.

After starting a fire, Annie moved the rocking chair closer to the big fireplace and turned the stereo on to a local jazz station. Her grandfather had built the rocker, and Annie ran her hands over the arms, thinking of their cabin on the lake. It had been sold after they were gone and she missed it. Now that Mary was leaving, maybe she could buy a cabin on a lake. *Not that I want to sell this place*, she grumbled as a log shifted in the fireplace. She glanced at her watch.

"Damn," she said, jumping up. She went and checked her phone for a message from Rebecca. She grinned, listening to her friend's voice, and then dialed her number.

"Larsen residence, Shelly speaking," her eight-year-old goddaughter answered.

"Shelly, it's Aunt Annie. How're you doing?"

Shelly screamed her name, and Annie held the phone away from her ear. "Annie, are you coming to our house?"

"Well, sweetie, I need to talk to your mother first, and we'll set up a time to get together."

"Don't come tonight. I have to go to bed soon, and I won't get to see you."

"Okay, honey, I promise. Is your mother there?"

Annie could hear Rebecca's voice telling Shelly to go upstairs and get ready for a bath. Rebecca was laughing when she answered the phone.

"Hey, deep throat, bedtime at the Larsen house. Can I call you back?"

"Sure, I'll be up."

"Missed you, glad you're home," Rebecca said.

Annie hung up and took the black and green crow statue with her as she eased back into the rocking chair. On the fireplace mantel she could see the photo that Mary had taken at a picnic four years ago—David holding Shelly, Rebecca, and Simon with Annie, arms entwined, laughing. That had been the last good year she could remember.

Annie rubbed the smooth wooden statue thinking about the camp where she had met Rebecca when they were five years old. The thirty-some years since had been theirs together. They had shared secrets, the mysteries of growing up, even clothes until Annie had grown two inches taller. The final year of college they had rented a house together, and a week before graduation, had gone out celebrating, ending up at Annie's favorite gay bar. Drunk and having the time of her life, she had made a flagrant pass at her, and Rebecca had left her standing in the middle of the dance floor, alone. Annie had chased her home, and they had argued in the kitchen until she made one too many rude suggestions. Rebecca had slapped her. Hard. And then called her boyfriend, David, and disappeared for the weekend. She had come home to Annie with the wooden statue of the crow, apologetic when she didn't have to be, and worse, pregnant. Annie looked back up at the photograph. They weren't punished with their oldest child, Simon; they were rewarded.

No one knew her like Rebecca, and she wondered if David knew his wife as well as she did. She had held her hand and cried with her as Simon had been born while David flew back from California. Annie sipped her beer, thinking of that moment. It still made her feel good. She had taught Rebecca golf and Rebecca had taught her sailing. *So many good times*, Annie thought, *but not lately. Damn. I haven't had time for the boat or golf or Rebecca.*

Annie stood, stretching carefully and feeling off center. It felt like the free fall she'd taken through her life three years ago. She walked to her office and rummaged around in her backpack. She found her sketchbook and flipped through pages as she went back to her chair in front of the fire. The drawing of the food market in Baghdad made her take a quick breath as she recalled the two old people sitting on the bench. Annie remembered the young woman she had traded glances with as the bomb exploded. She remembered the eyes that died seconds later. Annie had lain unconscious until an Army med-tech had put an ice pack on the back of her head and began working on her arm. Annie had seen the dead children around her, something she would never forget. The next coherent moment had been in the military hospital.

Kerry, the English photojournalist, and Tom, her field producer, were sitting beside the bed.

Annie bent over the book, examining the smudges and a suspicious brown spot on the paper. Was that blood? And how had she gotten the sketchbook back?

She tossed the book on the nearby coffee table, just as Sarah came into the room carrying a soda. She groaned and flopped down on the couch by the fireplace. "That shower felt good, and you have great equipment down there." She leaned back and closed her eyes. "Like that music you're playing?" Sarah asked, taking a drink and raising her eyebrows in a question.

Annie smiled at her. "We grew up on it. Mom and Dad always had music playing, and all four of us had to take piano lessons. If you don't like it, I'll turn it off, or I've got some great old rock I could put on instead."

"I'm fond of country." Sarah smiled back and then relaxed with a sigh. "Like that word, fond?" She stretched and rolled onto her back, one knee up, eyes closed. Annie tried to look away, but her eyes wouldn't leave Sarah's body. Her white shirt was pulled up, exposing a few inches of taut stomach muscles above the faded jeans and bare feet. Sarah reached down and put a hand around the bottle sitting on the floor, accentuating small, firm breasts. Annie held her breath.

"Annie!" Sarah's voice cut into her breathlessness.

"What?"

"What's your answer?" Sarah said.

"What's the question?" Annie answered, thoroughly confused. Sarah rolled on her stomach, staring at her.

"I asked about those trophies in the basement."

"Oh," Annie said, "what about them?"

"Whose are they?"

"Trophies, where did you see those?" Annie frowned.

Sarah sat up, looking at her. "They're on a shelf down there, behind the bar in the room with the pool table."

"Mary must have done it when she moved her things out of here." Annie took a sip of beer and looked back at Sarah. "She actually has my golf trophies on a shelf down there?" Sarah nodded. "That's odd. I've never unpacked them."

"Are you all right?" Sarah was staring at her now.

Annie shook her head. "Probably not. Oh hell, definitely not. Less than a week ago I was stranded in an airport in Jordan. About twelve of us, huddled on the floor, drinking and smoking anything we could find, afraid we wouldn't get out. When we finally did, fourteen hours later I was in New York City, talking to your people." She let out a long breath and was quiet for a moment. "My body may be here, but I'm not sure where my head is."

Annie was quiet again, then changed the subject. "You had asked about anything that I could think of that was out of the norm. I'm working on some notes for Dr. Majer at the university. He has taught Middle East religion here for about five years."

"What kind of information?"

"His sister and her family are still in Iraq, but just kind of hanging on. I always stop by, shoot a few photos of her family and friends, and talk with her. It's just family stuff."

"Who knows about this? How long have you been doing it?"

"I met him when I first started going to Iraq. That's at least three years ago. My friend Rebecca teaches history at the university, and he was at a party that we went to. I was trying to pick up as much background as I could. I've known his sister and the girls since I began reporting from Baghdad."

"Did he find you, or did Rebecca introduce him?"

"You know, I don't remember."

"Well, let's do a little background on him, shall we? I think we should cover anything you think of." She was quiet a moment. "What were his sister's friends like?"

"She was a professor, like Dr. Majer. Still teaches occasionally when she can and invites me to their dinners. I enjoy them and take photos for her. Pretty good source of information for me, as well." Annie got up to put another log on the fire.

"Individual shots?" Sarah asked. Annie was wrestling with the poker, one-handed. "Wait, let me do that." Sarah got up and helped, finally getting the log where Annie wanted it.

"Group shots and sometimes individual shots."

"And what do you do with the photos?"

"I give them to Dr. Majer. I just drop them off at his house when I'm in town. Nothing arranged." She felt unsure. "This isn't involved with the Web site, is it?"

"I don't think so," Sarah said. "It's just better to look at everything and anything we can. I swear, sometimes I'm just amazed at what's right in front of my eyes."

"It's about the only thing I bring home to Milwaukee. It doesn't feel risky. You know, over there, you just get into a zone, and it's not that you get used to it, but it becomes part of every moment."

"Annie," Sarah said softly, "you've been in many dangerous places. Didn't you start out in Kosovo over ten years ago? That was hazardous, and I know you've worked in Pakistan and Afghanistan. Your last few weeks in Iraq were pretty scary."

"It's always dangerous," Annie said. "The riskier it is, the more focused I become. I'm not this reckless reporter who loves the thrill, although I admit to moments. My real love is people. I want to know what happens to them. Jack Keegan hired me to go to Kosovo. We started going after the truth and the real story instead of just winging it with rumor." She shook her head. "No matter how often we report it, people have no idea how things are in Iraq right now. It's desperate, bad, and it breaks my heart."

"Annie, let's go look at that computer. I should have checked it when we came home." They moved to the living room where a small flashing pink light made the dark room look eerie.

"Damn." Sarah pulled her phone out and called the office. "Someone's been in here. Look at that." Annie stood behind her, watching the light as Sarah talked rapidly into the phone. "This is my fault. I should have checked it when we came home. What the hell? This usually means security's been breached. The techs are on their way."

"Wait, someone was in here, in my home? Why didn't the house alarm go off?"

Sarah walked to the kitchen and opened the panel on the alarm pad. "Maybe I did something when I checked it earlier. I'll have the techs look at it too." She shook her head and followed Annie into the den. "Is there anything else you're working on that we should check out?"

Annie went toward her office and Sarah walked over to look at the rows of books on the wall. "Like to read?" she asked when Annie came back into the room

Annie started to laugh. "They're my buddies and my companions."

"Are they both of yours?"

"Mary's books are gone. See those empty shelves over there?" Annie pointed across the room. "You don't see any medical books where you're standing, do you? That just gives me more room for my books."

They sat, side by side, on the brown leather sofa, and Annie took papers out of her backpack. Sarah reached for a dark green sheet of paper with a white insignia and white print.

"That's a flyer from the FFI in Iraq. I got that when they opened the country's first women's shelter in Baghdad. Did a report on it. Are you familiar with that?"

Sarah shook her head and looked over the notes and photos. "We don't have any of this. Our counterparts over there probably do, but we don't that I know of. What was that, FFI?"

"It's the FFI, Freedom First in Iraq, a women's organization." Annie glanced at Sarah and noticed the long dark eyelashes shading her eyes.

"What's your story? How did you get into the FBI?"

"Well, my dad's ex-FBI, so I grew up in it. Then a friend, actually more than a friend, steered me into it after college, and I liked what I saw. Ah, youth." She grinned at Annie. "Later, I found out that it was just a way to get me out of town. What a way to break up with someone."

Annie grinned back. "Yeah, that does suck. So, is there someone else?"

"Nope, that was the last one. I get out, bars, movies, what have you, but nothing serious."

"What's your job? I mean do you have a specialty or something?" Annie searched for the right words. "I think what I'm asking is, are you primarily behind a desk?"

Sarah looked serious. "If I told you, I'd have to kill you." They laughed at the old joke.

Annie relaxed. It'd been too long since she had just laughed like this.

"I work on special cases," Sarah said, "and also as a profiler now and then. Actually, that's my specialty, but this is a small office, so I usually do fieldwork. Lately, I've been working with a special agent in charge of this area's Joint Task Force on Terrorism, so here I am."

"Listen, it's not personal that I don't want anyone with me at the house or everywhere. I'm alone most of the time, but I can share my space if needed. Right now, with Mary leaving and some other things I'm dealing with, I'm not easy. I admit it." Annie thought of the packed bags in her bedroom. The idea of leaving still felt good to her. "A Web site just doesn't seem very threatening to me. I've been pinned down, under fire, and I'm sure you know about Jack Keegan. Then the dead children when I was injured. Can you understand why a list doesn't feel threatening?" She looked at Sarah. "However, if someone's been in here, my own home, that does upset me."

Sarah frowned and turned to Annie, putting her arm protectively on the back of the couch, close to Annie's shoulders. "Believe me, they're here. The group I mentioned tonight, the one I'm assisting on, is very organized. My fear is that whatever this is, no matter how small it looks to you, has attracted enough attention to fall into their sights. Please take this seriously."

Annie heard the plea and closed her eyes. "You're the expert," she said softly. "I'm shocked by all of this, and as many places as I've been, that's not easy to do, Sarah. I'm not afraid. I understand fear. I think I'm just kind of...stunned." Annie sat straighter, glancing into the calm brown eyes. She had never said that to anyone, and she looked again at the steady eyes next to her, wondering if she saw trust. No, trust was what she was feeling.

"How long are you usually gone?" Sarah said.

"Usually three to four months. It's about as much as I can take and still be civilized. Now, I get back here, and it looks like they've followed me home. Plus, the house is empty because my doctor has gone off with another doctor."

"Not that it's any of my business, but how are you with that?" Sarah took her arm away and straightened.

"With Mary? I was surprised when I found out about the other person, but truthfully, we've been in bad shape for a long time. The only thing that surprises me is that she didn't tell me that she was moving out now. You must have seen that when you asked me when she was coming back?"

Sarah nodded.

"Mary deserves a life. Someone to talk to and live with every day, not just two or three times a year. I was never honest with myself as to how lonely she was. Never thought how she might worry while I was out there, in the world's neighborhoods where they shoot people or blow them up. There are a gazillion other things working here. I mean, we've lived together over ten years, but I just keep thinking about being gone so much."

Sarah simply nodded again.

"I've been in places so seriously dangerous that I finally quit talking to Mary about them, but this—Jack Keegan and the explosion—got to me. God, eight children, Sarah." She brought her knees up under her chin and rested her head. "Surely you've been there too?"

"Not that extreme, but yes, danger. There is that to be said for both of us. Do you think there's hope?" Sarah quirked an eyebrow at Annie.

"I'm not sure what I believe anymore or even how I feel. You were right when you told Mom and Dad that we forget, here in the U.S., that we are actually in a war. Of course I know they're here. I hear crazy stories everyday over there, but home always feels safe to me. The world fascinates me, but I think I'd like to stay here for a while." She trailed off. "I'm whining. Sorry."

"Please do. That means I can whine too." Sarah gave her a grin and leaned over, picking up the open sketchbook. "What is this, by the way?"

Annie took the book. "I sketch while I'm on assignment. It relaxes me and helps me remember details." She thought of the morning after Jack. "It also helps me discipline my mind." She flipped a couple of pages. "This is my hotel room in Baghdad." She tipped the book so Sarah had a better look.

Sarah whistled softly. "You're good. You lived in this room?"

Annie laughed. "And glad to have it. Not the Ritz, huh? Kept the gin under the bed, along with the crackers and dried fruit I lived on." She turned the page to a drawing of a woman with a wistful expression. "This woman is a chemical engineer. At first, women, under Saddam, had quite a bit of freedom. Many are well educated and articulate, but now, with less education and freedom available, the young girls gravitate to the old patriarchal ways."

Annie was aware of the lavender scent of soap on Sarah, and moved closer, enjoying the fragrance. "I respect the religion of any country I'm in, but this one is a problem for me. It doesn't want to include women. It wants them home, obedient, and uneducated." She flipped a few more pages in the sketchbook, stopping at the drawing of a cleric coming out of a mosque. "I think fundamentalism thrives when a culture goes through a dramatic change. The more afraid a society becomes, the more it tolerates from its government or its leaders. Look at us after nine-eleven, we've had fundamentalists falling out of the woodwork, and I won't even speak of the government."

❖

The phone rang and Annie reached across Sarah, answering and immediately smiling, "Hey, Rebecca, what's happening?" She unfolded from the couch and took the phone out of the room.

The FBI team arrived a few minutes later, and Sarah sat with them in the living room. Someone definitely had been inside the house and messed with the computer. She put her coat and boots on and went outside with the others to look for footprints in the snow. They found tracks leading away from the side door of the garage. Sarah wanted the prints measured and the house gone over. Her breath blew white puffs into the air as she talked to the forensics team, and she stayed with them until her fingers began to go numb.

Annie was back in the den with her knees drawn up under her chin again, looking at the sketchbook. Sarah stood by the fireplace trying to warm up as she told Annie about the computer, the footprints, and what the team was hoping to find as they went through Annie's home. They would print, photograph, and videotape the scene. The two women walked slowly through the house to see if Annie could find anything missing or out of place, but found nothing. They talked with the team for a bit and then went back to the den. Annie was pale and quiet, so Sarah picked up the sketchbook, asking about the drawings again.

There were drawings of Annie's driver, Saddam's palaces before and after the American invasion, bombed-out cars, Iraqis of all ages. Annie stopped at the drawing of the marketplace, the one done just before the explosion. Annie had disappeared for two days after the injury, and Sarah wondered where she had been. And what if Annie had been the target when they shot the network producer or set off the car bomb? Annie held up the green paper again.

"The situation for women is declining. Sexual assaults and human trafficking are on the rise. That's what this flyer is about, the FFI." She laid the paper flat and pointed to a piece of its text. "See, shelter and protection for women, safety from the oppression of fundamentalism." Annie sighed. "Sometimes being in Iraq is like being on the moon, all sand, dirt, and dust. I miss the brightness, the oxygen of this place. Home. And the right to be able to say these things out loud."

Sarah loved listening to Annie talk but didn't like what she was hearing behind the words—the isolation and hurt. She changed the subject, hoping to change the mood.

"Oh, before I forget, what's the story of the red bicycle at your parents' house, the one with the crow painted on it?"

Annie finally laughed again, "When I was ten, my oldest brother, Noah, took me to the dump and we found that bike. He wanted to teach me mechanical things, so we took it home, put it in the basement, and took it apart. God, there were hundreds of pieces. Then, over the next few months, he helped me reassemble it and paint it. That bike is the first thing I ever built from scratch, and I named it the Red Crow. It was the fastest bike on the block." She grinned at Sarah.

The FBI techs were done and called out for Sarah. When she came back into the room, Annie looked up at her. "I just remembered, when you checked the house last night, did you go into the loft?"

Sarah stopped, surprised. "What?"

"The loft, the second story here?"

"Damn," she said, "I looked at it from the outside but missed it when we came in. Show me, please. Is it locked?" Annie shook her head and they moved to Annie's office. She pointed at what appeared to be a wall.

"What? That's a wall."

Annie touched a small indentation in the wall and it slid open, revealing clothing hanging in front of them, boxes of computer paper, and shoes on the floor. "It's a closet?" Sarah held her hands out.

"Not your fault. I was so tired last night," Annie said, hitting a light switch that illuminated steps to the right. "I can see how you missed this." She entered the closet, starting up the steps.

"Wait, me first. Wow, talk about hidden. Was it supposed to be?"

"What?" Annie asked, backing down and letting Sarah go by.

"Hidden," Sarah replied as she walked up the steps.

"Not at all, this was originally a stained glass studio. You should see it when the sun shines through the colored glass along the bottom of the big panes of glass. I had it remodeled as my studio when Mary and I moved in and had this and another sliding door put in. Noah, the brother who helped me with the bike, is an architect, and he designed both doors plus the remodeling of this studio."

"No, I meant the door is hidden. Where's the other door?" Sarah asked.

"In the master bathroom," Annie replied, laughing. "And I dare you to find that one."

"Oh, my God, how beautiful," Sarah said from the top of the stairs, staring at a large painting on an easel. "This is someone you know quite well, I presume." She turned and grinned down at Annie.

Annie came up behind her. "Presume away. That's Mary." They walked across the studio floor. Sarah stood quietly before the painting of a slender blond woman, sitting on the edge of a bathtub, draped only in a towel, bent over but smiling up at the artist.

"This is wonderful, Annie." Sarah stood motionless.

"I'll offer it to Mary, or hell, who knows? Maybe I should just burn the thing."

"Well, I don't think it should be burned. Look how it shines. It's radiant."

Annie looked at Sarah for a moment and then walked away. "It was painted over five years ago," she said, her voice flat. She walked to the shutters and knelt down, balancing herself on her good right hand. "This is what I wanted to show you. I never close these shutters like this, and Mary normally wouldn't have come up here. There are two tiers of these things. The shorter ones cover the stained glass. The big ones cover the clear windows, and I open them when I paint so I can use the true light."

"Is there anything out of place here? Look around for me," Sarah said.

Annie started at the south end of the large room and walked slowly around the benches, desks, and paintings until she was back where she started. "Nothing, Sarah. I just have the feeling that things have been moved around."

"Well, do this again tomorrow, just to be sure, especially with the business with the computer tonight. Maybe seeing it with fresh eyes in the daylight will help. By the way, is this tied into your alarm system?"

Annie shook her head. "I just didn't see the need." She looked momentarily lost. "I'm beginning to feel like my red bike, in a trillion pieces."

Sarah walked toward the steps. "Come on. Have one more beer, and you can tell me what you have against country music."

CHAPTER SEVEN

After her shower the next morning, Sarah went to Annie's office. She studied the wall, then the door for a few moments. It really was ingenious. She went up the stairs and opened the big shutters for the extreme light Annie had talked about. The sunlight crept into every corner, and she turned, feeling like she was outside in the air. She checked for skid marks, footprints, or anything she could find, and then she saw them. Slide marks scratched a thin layer of dust under the smaller shutters that were closest to the garage roof. A wooden crate holding pieces of framing had been moved.

"Not hardly small," Sarah said, taking a piece of framing and lifting the shutter. A pane of red glass swung out when she gently touched it with the wood. It had to be at least three feet wide and just as tall. She called the forensic team and asked them to come out again to dust for prints or anything else they could find. *The team is going to love me if I keep this up,* Sarah thought as she backed away, trying not to disturb anything anymore than she already had. She went to the painting that Annie had covered last night. She pulled the canvas flap up, admiring the painting once again, and thought about the two women. Her sources had said they were a striking couple. But it appeared they'd struck each other in a ten car pile-up. Relationships were a tricky ride.

She frowned as she went down the stairs. *I'm just like Annie. Gone all the time. Someone would be left home by herself, and then I'd be alone, just like she is.*

She looked around the office. The light gray walls with white trim set off the black-and-white photos on the wall. She stopped at a picture of a young Annie with a fishing pole, but minus some front teeth. There was a wedding photo of Hannah and James Booker, along with other family photos. She looked closely at a picture of Hannah with what Sarah assumed were all four of her children when they were much younger. Two of the kids resembled their mother and two looked like James Booker. There was a large shot of a U.S. military tank with Annie standing in front with a microphone, but she couldn't tell what country she was in. Sarah paused at the state-of-the-art computers. At least one monitor was set up for video conference. Shelves with more books, photos, and statues, finished the area around the desk. *Nifty*, Sarah thought, *I could work in here all day*.

Wandering out into the large open kitchen, she found the coffee maker and coffee. Sarah leaned on the cooking island and looked out the wide French doors that led to the deck, the same graceful doors that were in Annie's bedroom. Lake Michigan was bright this morning, a blue that could fool you into thinking it was warm. The house was flooded with sunlight, and she was struck by the brightness, the space and color. Green plants sat on the counter and window ledges. It was like a breath of summer.

This woman likes space and she likes to cook, Sarah decided, turning slowly. Even the floor tile looked Italian. There was a large round oak table with chairs and she wondered if it was handcrafted. She walked down to three comfortable-looking upholstered chairs around a low coffee table. There was a small fireplace beside the chairs and a tall, narrow window lined with stained glass chips. The glass looked old to Sarah, and she leaned forward to see if there were straw marks in it. Yes, the glass was wavy. She smiled. Annie valued old things too. The stained glass threw colors onto the chairs, and a bonsai tree stood proudly at one end with several books lying in front of it. Curious, she picked up Kawabata's *Snow Country* and sat in the closest chair, browsing through pages bathed in the silent colors.

"Sarah?" Annie's voice penetrated the quiet.

Startled, Sarah looked up at Annie standing in the sunlight. It almost hurt to look at her, and she pulled in a breath. She held the book up so Annie could see what she had been reading.

Annie gave her a smile. "Stay there. I'll get us some coffee and join you."

Sarah went back to the book and read until Annie put two cups on the table. Annie's sleepy face looked young as she smiled at Sarah. "Don't tell me you read him too?"

Sarah reached for the coffee. "No, not since college. First Japanese to win the Nobel Prize. Late sixties, I believe. Is that right?"

Annie leaned back in the chair and nodded. "I usually take at least one of his books when I travel. About three years ago I had a doctor who was a bit of a Zen person, and she loved his books. She got me into them."

Sarah laid the book on the table and looked out at the open kitchen area. "This is beautiful, Annie. Reminds me of a place in Italy where my family stayed when I was young. Dad was taking some special training."

"It's my favorite room. Wait until you see it in the summer. It's like another house." She nodded at Sarah's cup, "Try the coffee. See if you like it."

It was bitter and sweet at the same time, but definitely tasted like coffee. "It's strong but delicious. What is it?"

"I have it ground downtown. Mary hates it. Says it makes her teeth ache." Annie gave a soft laugh and pointed at the book. "Those guys are a bit too masculine and sentimental for my tastes, but I love the haiku, so I read their work. Actually, I went to Japan and spent time in the area where *Snow Country* was located."

Sarah looked over the rim of her cup, peeking at Annie's face. She could tell Annie was somewhere else, so she waited. Finally, Annie's eyes moved back to her.

"That was an incredible place and I loved it. Do you know much about Eastern religion or living?"

"Bits and pieces."

"Look on the chair next to you."

Sarah spotted a tape on top of more books about Japan.

"Sometime, when you have a moment, look at that video. I followed his book and shot film. My own private documentary." She stood, holding her cup. "I'm going to shower and get dressed. Thanks. It was nice waking up to the smell of coffee in the house."

Sarah nodded. "Did you go alone?"

"Well, I wasn't supposed to, but as it all fell out, yes, I did."

Later, after the forensic team had come back to the house, Sarah and Annie sat in the living room with coffee, looking at the FBI computer.

"Not that I'll ever be in the house without one of you, but do you think I should go over this, especially now that you know someone was in here?" Annie asked. They looked at the computer, sitting close, and Sarah showed her where the FBI had located the electronic bug.

"The device that was put in here destroyed our memory, so we can't say who was here. Only that someone definitely was inside the house." Sarah punched a few more keys. "Also, the house alarm was tweaked but reset, and whoever did this has an excellent knowledge of electronics. Very smart."

"This is crazy. My hotel room was routinely searched in Baghdad. I used to set little traps for them. Since there was nothing there that I cared about except the gin, it became a little game. But my home is not a game."

"I'm sorry," Sarah said. "I'm sure I don't need to tell you this, but these guys are excellent with electronics."

Annie tucked her hair behind her ear, and the morning sun caught a flash of gold. Sarah cleared her throat. It was a wonderful morning to be around Annie.

"Right." Annie's hair fell forward as she studied the coffee cup in her hand. "I have to go to the clinic for my arm this morning, and I'm having dinner with my friend Rebecca and her kids tonight. What's the drill here?"

Sarah looked at her watch. "My backup, Scott Frazier, is on his way, and he'll go with you to the clinic. The task force has a six o'clock meeting tonight. It usually runs two or more hours, so he'll go with you to your friend's house. Have you told her?"

Annie nodded. "She knows. Sarah, this is my oldest and best friend. Do we have to have an agent with us, inside the house?"

Sarah sighed. This was always the hard part. "In view of what happened yesterday, I have to say yes."

Annie tried to negotiate, saying she didn't want to alarm the children, but Sarah stood her ground.

"What are you talking about?" she teased. "Almost everyone in the office has children. Do you think we'll pull our guns and shoot up the place?"

"No." Annie managed to keep a straight face, but her mouth tipped up at the corners. "I just wanted a normal private visit."

"Actually, you shouldn't even be leaving the house, Annie, but for tonight, let's do it this way."

Annie studied her a moment. "It was worth a try, and of course, you're right."

❖

"Whoa," Annie yelled. "We missed the driveway." Snow blew through the dark winter night into the car's headlights as Agent Frazier steered the SUV into a U-turn and plowed through a sizeable snowdrift. He turned the car into the opening in the tall brick wall marking the driveway to Rebecca and David's home. The soft lights in the windows looked so inviting that Annie sat for a minute, relishing the scene and forgetting her driver entirely.

The front door opened, and Simon, Rebecca's oldest, came running out. "Annie!" he yelled, grinning.

"Simon, where's your coat?" Annie hugged him tightly, "Oh boy, have you grown!" He was almost as tall as she was. "You look like your mom," she said as he put his arm around her shoulder. "Bet you're fighting off the girls." She grinned at him.

"Oh no, Annie, I love 'em," he shot back, looking all of his sixteen years. *God*, Annie thought, *I'm talking girls with Simon.*

She heard footsteps running down the hall and turned just in time to catch her eight-year-old namesake. "Annie," Shelly yelled, blond hair flying and blue eyes sparkling. Annie held her tight and gave her a kiss on the top of her head.

"Behave, Shelly Anne," Rebecca said, hugging Annie too. "About time you got here. Put that child down before you hurt yourself worse than you already have." Rebecca pointed at Annie's arm.

"Just a scratch, Slider." Annie grinned, hugging her hard. "I've missed you."

Agent Frazier had waited patiently in the entryway, and Annie introduced him. Rebecca pointed up the stairs. "Go ahead. There's four bedrooms, a bath, and an office up there. Simon, why don't you show him where everything is?" Rebecca and Annie grinned at each other, knowing how this would fascinate any sixteen-year-old.

"Why do you call her Slider?" Shelly asked as they walked toward the dining room.

"Long story, and I'm not sure your mama wants me to tell it," Annie said raising her eyebrows at Rebecca.

"Uh, well." Rebecca and Annie smiled at each other. "How about over dinner? Are you up to my famous lasagna? Or you can eat a peanut butter sandwich."

"Oh no, the dread lasagna," Annie said as they started to laugh. Lasagna was the first meal Rebecca had learned to cook, and they had eaten it at least once a week for almost a year.

"I'm going to ask Agent Frazier to join us for dinner," Rebecca said, "and then put him in front of the TV in the den."

Scott and Simon came down the stairs and went through to the back porch. Simon was speaking seriously to the FBI agent. As they passed by, Scott turned and grinned at them, endearing himself to Annie. He was enjoying Simon as well. The minute they left the room, both women started to laugh.

"Where's David? Back in China?" she asked over dinner.

"Yep," Simon answered.

"How was the trip home, and what did the doctors say about your arm?" Rebecca asked.

"The trip home was long." Annie really didn't want to talk about it right now. "Doctors did the scan thing this morning, and it looks like I'll need minor therapy, but it's healing."

"When are you going to stop going over there?" Rebecca grumbled. "How long for the sling?"

Annie made a face at her. "Don't know yet. More to come tomorrow." She changed the subject by asking the kids about school.

Later, they sat the table while the kids cleared the dishes. Much to Annie's surprise, Scott had gotten up to help also. "Coffee?"

"Coffee. You've got the lasagna down to perfection, and yes, I know I've lost weight. Lack of edible food will do that to you."

Rebecca patted her stomach. "I, on the other hand, have to do thirty minutes on the treadmill from hell just to maintain weight." Turning, she yelled into the kitchen, "Kids, time for bath or homework. Tomorrow's a school day." Two groans floated back at her, and she turned to Annie with a truly evil grin. "Don't you like the way I managed to get out of the Slider story? I haven't lost my touch."

Annie laughed. "I'll get the coffee and you get Scott into the den. I know there's basketball on the TV."

Alone at the dining room table, Annie looked at Rebecca over her coffee cup. "Okay, what's up? I can see your mind practically doing cartwheels."

"There's a job opening at the university next year, and before you laugh at me, think about it. You've been playing around with this crap long enough. You're going to get yourself killed and leave me to fend my way though life without you. I don't think I can deal with that."

"You know, I actually have been thinking about a change. Surprised?"

"Good grief, yes, but at least if you were teaching, you wouldn't end up with an FBI escort. Annie, this is more than just not getting hurt, or worse. I thought the 'Big A' with Mary would have done it, but no, there you go, back to Iraq again. You're good. That's not what this is about. I'm proud of what you do and how well you do it, but I just wish you'd be safer."

"The big what?" Annie laughed. "What did you say about Mary?"

"A, as in absence."

"Guilty as charged. Mary's things are gone from the house. Guess she finally made a decision."

"It's not all your fault."

"A lot of it is, Slider. First of all, I'm never home. Then, when we talked, it was like neither of us could understand each other, especially after Saudi Arabia and the fallout in Switzerland."

"Everything was wrong with that, Annie. How are you doing? Are you still seeing a doctor?"

"I haven't been, and it's been over three years, but this injury brought back some feelings. After Jack was killed and I was injured, it was almost a relief to be unconscious. I think I'll see a therapist at the clinic a couple of times, a friend of Mom's, just to check myself out. It's not as bad as Switzerland, but I won't lie, I'm wobbly right now."

Rebecca sighed. "So you're dealing with several situations here. Damn your job. Annie. You need someone. Another human being. You've been out there alone too long."

"Volunteering?"

"Want to get slapped again?" Rebecca made a face at her. "And yes, I know there's more to life than just having someone in your life. Accomplishments and stuff."

"Stuff?" Annie gave her a look.

"You know what I mean, and it doesn't have to be so dangerous either. We didn't get to talk the last time you were home. Did you tell your parents about the Saudi-Switzerland thing?"

"I was going to talk with them last October, but the network got me back out there so fast that I didn't have time. I never should have come home and hidden the truth. You and Mary are still the only people who know besides the network and my doctor. What am I going to say? Mom, Dad, I'm sorry, but Mary and I didn't take a vacation. I lied. I went to a party in Saudi Arabia and was beaten within an inch of my life."

"Annie, stop." She reached over and rubbed Annie's hand.

"All right, but you know this is going to hurt my parents or anyone it touches. I've created a monster. And, Slider, talking about connecting with someone, I've only let one person come close to me in three years. Then I backed off before it got beyond a kiss. I stayed with Kerri after the injury, but I'm to the point where I don't even think about it."

"Are you able to touch someone?"

"Yes. Just nothing intimate. I'm not sure it's possible." Rebecca had seen the worst of it when Annie came home from Switzerland three years ago. "I'm dealing with some weird stuff. I picked up more than a piece of concrete in my arm over there."

Rebecca's head snapped up. "Not an STD...no, wait, you just said..."

"Oh hell, Rebecca." Annie groaned.

Rebecca stood and hugged her. "I'm sorry, sweetie. Let me get out of these clothes and into something more comfortable. We'll talk when I come back, but this is what I mean. You can do just about anything, Annie. You have your master's in journalism. You know people, so stop putting your face in front of a gun. Your life scares me to death." She picked up their coffee cups and walked to the kitchen. "Why don't you pick out some wine?"

Annie headed for the bar and took her time choosing a bottle. When Rebecca came back she was wearing jeans and a dark blue sweatshirt. She took the wineglass Annie offered.

"Tell me about the FBI. All you said was that they would be with you tonight."

"The FBI is with me because my name and seven other female journalists turned up on an Iraqi Web site, one that is truly dangerous. It seems unreal to me because I feel they would have made a move over there, not here, but, at the same time, things have happened. The house was broken into when I was having dinner at Mom and Dad's, and the alarm didn't go off, which is not good news. The FBI was working on the loft this morning. That's probably how they got inside."

"My God."

"For the first time, it makes me feel helpless. I was alone over there and handled it. I'm cooperating every way I can, Rebecca, but still, if I was in Iraq, this would hardly get the attention it's getting here." Annie stood. "I think I'll just leave. Get out of town."

"Out of town?"

"Yes, just drive around the Midwest. Look at the states. Do you know how long it's been since I've looked at my own country?"

"You just got home. I know this is pretty ugly, the FBI and all, but wouldn't it be better just to get this settled first?"

"I'm tired of it all, Slider. The war, Jack's death, Mary, my stupid arm, and this situation, whatever the hell it is. I need some down time somewhere. I'd like to tell Mom and Dad about the thing three years ago and then just take off."

"Annie, listen to yourself. What if they follow you, whoever this is? Get all the help you can. Don't take a chance. What can you be thinking?"

Annie frowned, tipped her wineglass back for a healthy drink, and set it down carefully.

"Rebecca, I've had more support from my pantyhose." They burst out laughing. "Okay, okay, you're right, but God, am I tempted." Annie scrubbed her face. "Sarah's right too, and intellectually, I know they're everywhere, but I don't think of them being in my town, or worse, in my home. I always come home and feel safe, but this time I brought them with me."

"Sarah?"

"The FBI agent who is assigned to me. Sarah Moore. She's staying at the house and would be here tonight but has a meeting."

Annie smiled, thinking of the dark-haired woman. "She's the one bright spot in this whole thing. Kind of gorgeous."

Rebecca began to smile. "Not like you, Annie."

"What's not like me?"

"A gorgeous woman?"

Annie laughed. "All right, she's very attractive and great to talk to. We even laugh, and other than you, do you know how long it's been since I've laughed like that with anyone?"

"You used to be the fastest thing on two feet. Well, is she?"

"Is she what?" Annie looked up, confused.

"Is she on your team?" Rebecca started to laugh.

"Oh." Annie frowned. "That's dumb. I don't know. I admit to salivating, but I think I've lost my gaydar. I don't think there's anything she doesn't know about me, and we've talked about her, but somehow I don't think so. In fact, I'm almost sure she's not." She stared into her wineglass, wondering how she could have missed that.

"Annie, you probably just haven't paid any attention. I think we have to work on the fact that you haven't had sex in well over three years."

"We? See? You are volunteering. Anyway, that's nothing. I interviewed a couple that was being punished by their church, and they'd gone over six years." Annie grinned. "They both looked incredibly nervous."

"That's an interesting restriction," Rebecca said. "Give me the name of that church, and I'll see if I can talk David into joining."

"Slider, I could solve that problem for you."

Rebecca leaned back in her chair, laughing, "You just don't quit, do you? You are the most focused person I know. Remember the famous boat incident at your grandparents'?"

Annie nodded. That was a bad moment. The boat engine had quit, and they had almost gone over the dam.

"Here I am screaming, 'We're going over the dam,' over and over."

"Well, we were. You were right."

"I was the only one yelling. You ripped the cover off that engine and started working on it. I swear, you would have thought we were tied up at the pier."

"Rebecca, it was my fault. I was the last one to service the damned thing."

"Yes, but you never looked at the dam, at me, or anything but the engine. You just kept fiddling with it and turning the screwdriver, pulling the cord. Finally, it caught, and off we went, and that's my point. You have the most remarkable focus of anyone I've ever known."

"You are so full of it, Slider. That's not focus. You're confusing it with stubbornness. What can I say? I've been in love with you since I was five. I'm just your love slave." Annie leaned back. "All right, let's change the subject. How's David and how's the job?"

"Ah, okay, that's another world. More wine?" Rebecca got up and headed for the bar. They moved on to more familiar, safer topics, and after three more glasses of wine Annie asked Scott to take her home.

❖

The snow continued to blow in from the lake as Hamel drove slowly past Rebecca's house. He drove past the lights at the gate and pulled over, letting the engine idle. He had followed them here, gone ahead, and turned back. The wind rocked his car gently as he waited for the big black car to pull out of the driveway. Finally, it passed him, taillights fading in the blowing snow. He waited a long time and then turned the car off, easing out the door.

Angling through the old pines, he walked to the back of the house, checking for any remaining lights. Seeing none, he walked through the snow to the back of the enclosed porch. The door was unlocked, and he walked quietly inside. The main door was locked, but he pulled a device from his parka and had the door open within minutes. The dark house was quiet, and he waited in the kitchen, letting his eyes adjust to the darkness. This was just reconnaissance, he reminded himself as he walked noiselessly down the hallway, through each room and then up the steps. Everyone was sleeping upstairs as he quietly opened each door, committing every room to memory just as he had in the Booker woman's home. He was at the back door again and outside in less than twenty minutes, passing through the house like a sigh, an old house creaking in the cold, windy winter night.

CHAPTER EIGHT

Sarah's back was starting to cramp after bending over the table for hours, arranging papers into folders. Don Ahrens, the special agent in charge of the Joint Terrorism Task Force in Milwaukee, looked over at her and grinned.

"Tired?" he asked.

Sarah made a face. "We're supposed to have a paperless system, Don."

The information Annie had provided them had turned them in a different direction and seemed to tie Dr. Majer into the terrorist cell Don had been working on for over two years. It was a name to go with all the activity. Hopefully, the final piece of the puzzle. Sarah smiled at Don with a genuine sense of satisfaction, despite her aching back. He straightened with a groan, looking at his watch.

"Damn, it's after midnight."

"Want some coffee before we call it a night?"

He nodded then grabbed his coat off the back of a chair. "Let's go to the break room. The chairs are more comfortable."

Sarah took a drink as she sat with her coffee and leaned back, letting fatigue wash over her. "There's definitely been someone at the Booker house. Did you see the device from our computer?"

Don nodded. "I told them to look further. Usually, there's at least one more bug. They just put the first one in to distract everyone."

"It's someone who can just walk through our sensors and her alarm system and then bug our computer. Then walk right down the driveway after they were done. Looked like just one person. But it was a size thirteen shoe, so it was probably was a man. Nothing was taken that Annie could find. The only prints found inside were the ones that belonged there, and it looks like he got in through her loft. So, couple that with our bugged computer, it's more than just a break-in. I'm going to move her to a safe house."

"The one on Whitmore's open," Don said and then frowned. "Why aren't you getting her out of town?"

"Her injury. They ran tests today, and we should have the information tomorrow. That's why I've suggested a safe house here. Once they've decided what to do about her arm, we can go anywhere."

"All right, but don't take her out of town before talking to me. This information on Dr. Majer may just break our case wide open, and I want to talk with her. I need to get inside his home without drawing attention to ourselves, and she may just be the person to give us an idea how to do that."

"Probably. And her friend Rebecca teaches with him and knows him," Sarah said. "No wonder the network loves her. She can talk, and her experience is invaluable."

"Such as?"

"I've never had the chance to talk to someone who's actually lived over there like she has. She knows the locals, the families, their customs, how they feel about us. And then there was Saddam. She was there before our troops were and says it's the worst conditions she's ever worked under, but not the most dangerous."

"You're kidding," he said.

"No. In her opinion, Pakistan was far more dangerous. Think about Danny Pearl."

"The organization you were talking about earlier, have you tried finding it?"

Sarah shook her head. "I'm going to do a bit more work tonight, and the FFI was something I was going to look at."

Don finished his coffee. "Let's go to your office and see if we can find it."

"I've spent a fair amount of time on the Information Analysis Center," she said as they walked down the hall together. "I'd like to have the information first, for a change. I'll bet anyone in this country that has to deal with Iraq feels the same way. It's such a different culture, and I always feel like I'm playing catch-up."

"Still, Sarah, the Fusion Centers are the best thing we've devised in this country. It's the best and latest information we have. Best of all, anyone can access it with clearance—military, any of the states, even civilians."

"Is it true we have constructed ten new permanent military bases in Iraq?"

"Ten? Last I heard it was four," he said. While she booted up her computer, he looked at the photos of Annie Booker taped to the cabinets above Sarah's desk. Sarah looked up and followed Don's line of sight.

"Those were taken by a friend over there. An Englishwoman, a photojournalist."

He looked at the first photo, a picture of Annie interviewing an Iraqi man in a uniform, her hair shining in the sunlight. "She's lovely, isn't she? Do you know who she's talking to in this picture?"

"No, I don't remember. She's complicated, Don, and has a bunch of stuff on her plate. I think losing Jack Keegan was a bigger blow than being injured, and someone breaking into the house has really upset her. It upset me, for that matter. Something else she said that I found interesting was that Iraqis often wonder why we don't understand what they're going through, after nine-eleven."

"They view us as terrorists?"

"Not exactly. Annie asked them the same question, and they said while it was true they knew the U.S. was coming, unlike our nine-eleven, they still view us as people attacking them. I saw one of her film clips where the man said they want freedom from what Saddam had been, and from the U.S."

He smiled down at her, saying nothing, and she asked again, "So, it's true, we're building permanent military bases there?" He nodded. "If we're going to leave, what are the bases about?"

"I don't know, Sarah."

"Something else I really didn't like hearing—and I looked at the report from the U.N. today after she told me this—malnutrition in children has nearly doubled since we invaded them, according to the U.N. Human Rights Commission. Annie says when she interviews doctors, they just break down. They can't even talk about it. They don't have food, water, or medicine."

"But, Sarah, wouldn't that stand to reason with interrupted

business and normal food distribution within the country? The lack of medical supplies has been going on for years, and I agree, it's terrible."

"Sure, but nobody organizes like we do. Now that we're there, why don't we just get this done? We're paying for it here anyway." She was quiet for a moment. "No, that's what I would have said before Katrina."

"I don't know, but it seems to me that I heard something was in the works about food and children in Iraq. As a matter of fact, I'm sure I did," Don said.

Sarah swiveled her chair back to the computer. "So many questions, so few answers, right? Annie said the other night that she didn't know what to believe anymore, and I'm struggling with the same thing." She started typing in a search for the organization that Annie had been to in Iraq.

"Here it is," she said, "Freedom First in Iraq, and here's the flyer that she picked up the day the shelter opened." They were quiet, reading the information on the screen.

Don sighed. "Men. You'd think we would have evolved by now."

"This is centuries of behavior and customs in Iraq. It's part of their religion."

"Don't you dare say it."

"What?"

"That some of your best friends are men."

"But they are, and why wouldn't they be?" Sarah said. "My mother, grandmothers, and their mothers fought for most of the things I enjoy today, my rights as a woman. You guys came to this country already in control of your own lives. Women's rights, what a great fight." She glanced back at the computer and was quiet for a moment. "Don, wait. That's a thought. What if it's this? What if it's the FFI that's connecting all these women to the Jaish al-Basca Web site? I'd have gone to see it. Tried to support it if I'd been there."

"Send an e-mail to Josh Palmer. Use my name with yours. Have him check this out and see if all those other women were there. Watch for a response. If we don't have one by tomorrow afternoon, let me know, and I'll go over his head."

Sarah nodded, typing away. "Could it be this easy? Damn. It doesn't explain who's been in her house, though."

"Maybe this is just the first part of the puzzle, Sarah. I'm going home for some sleep, and you should get out of here too."

"I will. See you tomorrow. Since Ms. Booker's already in bed and Mike's at her house, I'll go to my own place and pick up some clean clothes before I see her again."

Sarah stayed on her computer for another hour and finally moved to her couch to stretch out and rest her tired eyes. Nothing was adding up. If it was just a threat as Annie thought, and it would stay over there, not here, why would someone break into her house? The e-mail from Josh with the other women's responses had been the same as Annie's. Not one of them believed it was any more than just what it seemed—a threat. It had to be something else then. Something local maybe.

❖

Sheikha watched as he stepped into her apartment, hanging his coat on the rack beside the door. He went to the desk, turning the small light on. He opened a drawer and took a pad of paper and pen, and began to draw the house that he had just come from.

She stood, just inside the bedroom, and watched him at the desk, outlined in the light from the small lamp. She was as tall as he was and had the same dark hair. She looked at the clock and decided to go back to bed and get some more sleep before she had to go to work at the hospital.

Lying in the bed, Sheikha thought about Hamel, her other half, the man she had helped to raise from the time he was a baby. When they were being trained in Afghanistan, he had been so careful of her. What had changed? He had changed after their father had been killed.

She sighed, wondering why he was so obsessed with the reporter with the strange pale eyes. She had watched her on the news. She was accurate, speaking in a calming voice, but she was also outspoken and forward. The woman would never have survived in her country.

CHAPTER NINE

Sarah drove away from the FBI building the next morning. The new snow made the city fresh, and she turned the car radio on, humming along with the music. She stopped at a red light and impulsively dialed her parents' home number on her cell phone. Her dad's deep voice came on and she said, "Hey, what's shaking, Daddy?"

"Sarah, where are you?" She heard the smile in his voice.

"Up here with the polar bears. Can't play golf yet, but it's not bad. We had new snow last night, and it's actually quite beautiful."

"I got caught in a blizzard in New Hampshire in '67. Couldn't even see across the street. Blew like a son of a gun. That was my first assignment."

Sarah could hear voices in the background. "Do you have company?"

"No, just your mom and sister getting ready for an afternoon with the ladies, and yes, I'm going to the golf course. How's the job going?"

"Caught a break on a current case last night and worked late. Actually, I fell asleep on the couch in my office, and I'm sneaking out for a shower and a nap."

"I don't miss it, honey, but I sure wish you were here. Got a new grip and swing. Cut three strokes off my game. I think I can finally whip your butt and take your money."

"Not going to happen, Dad. Well, if I don't get time on the golf course, maybe. I think I'm going to rust living up here. Time, no time."

"Sarah, you have to take time. I wish I had taken more. Do you have anyone to golf with?"

"I just met someone. Her clubs look expensive and serious."

"Get your game on, kid, and come home for a while. We miss you. Want to talk to your mother?"

"Sure. I only wanted to say hello and check in. Tell my sister that she owes me some e-mail." Sarah's mother came on the line and they talked the rest of the way home.

Sarah wished she were closer and could talk with her dad. He had been shot in Boston, shortly after nine-eleven, and to this day, she didn't know if it had been related to the attack on America.

Sarah pulled some papers out of her briefcase. She separated what she wanted to show to Annie. There was a feeling of isolation around Annie that was puzzling. Or maybe it was just that Annie had said that she was "stunned." And looked like it. Annie probably had been through rougher moments, but not all at the same time.

She got up for more milk and stood at the window, looking out at the snow. She hoped Annie had relaxed last night with her friend. Scott had said Rebecca was "nice" and then added, "pretty." More importantly, he said the two women had laughed a lot together. Sarah grinned, remembering Scott meeting Annie for the first time yesterday. His mouth had opened, but he hadn't uttered a sound. She had that effect on people.

"She's tough," Sarah said. Annie was trying to get through everything, but Sarah felt as if she were watching a slow-burning fuse. When they got the doctor's final report about Annie's arm, she would have to tell Annie that they were moving her. That might just be the last straw. "Can we say explosion?" Sarah said. "How am I going to handle this?" While she was cleaning the table, she had it. *Over a meal.* Satisfied that she had it under control, she dialed Annie's number.

"What did the doctors say?" she asked.

"That there was no stress fracture and everything's healing. They want me back one more time to show me specific exercises I can do on my own equipment."

"So, one more day at the clinic?"

"That's the way it looks now."

"Okay. That's good. How about dinner tonight?"

"Most excellent. Where?"

"Do you like seafood?"

"Love it. Is it informal or…"

"Wear whatever you'd like, Annie." Sarah paused and then said, "Would you do me a favor and keep a bag packed, just in case we need to move suddenly? You know, toothbrush, something to sleep in, a change of clothes, that kind of thing."

"I already have one packed."

She had her bag already packed? Sarah wondered about that as she called Scott and told him to stock up the Whitmore place. They'd meet tonight at the Booker house. Mike and another agent were at the house with Annie right now, but Scott would take over late afternoon. She cautioned Scott not to mention the safe house.

"My God, I finally have an FBI wardrobe. All black and blue." She groaned as she rifled through the clothes in her closet. "Time for more clothes. Wait, I thought this was in Scottsdale," she said, taking a rich brown lightweight leather suit out of the closet. "I might freeze, but I'll look decent doing it." Choosing an electric blue silk T-shirt to go with it, she hung the clothes on the door and headed toward the bed for much-needed sleep. She lay there, thinking about Annie's sleepy face yesterday morning, then she thought of agency rules about clients. She finally fell into a fitful sleep.

❖

Dressed and ready for the tricky evening ahead, Sarah drove up to the Bistro Catering Company to pick up the food. The company was owned by a friend of hers, and she looked forward to talking to Jana again. Mike had agreed to take the food to the safe house ahead of them and was waiting for Sarah. They stood and talked for a moment. Mike said that Annie had looked worn out after her session at the clinic this morning.

A tall, dark-haired woman parked behind Mike's car and Sarah watched her put money in the parking meter, then go into the drugstore. She looked vaguely familiar and Sarah watched her for a moment. She and Mike went into the Bistro, and Sarah lingered, talking to Jana while Mike went ahead to the house on Whitmore. Jana teased her a little because she was being so picky over the food, and Sarah realized she was treating this as if it were a date. She looked down at her clothes. Why had she dressed up? As she paid and turned to go, she noticed the same dark-haired woman watching Mike drive away. *Where in the heck have I seen her?* Sarah wondered. The woman turned and looked at her but then left quickly when she caught Sarah's eyes.

❖

Annie was so beautiful in her green dress that Sarah stared until Annie caught her and she had to look away.

"What?" Annie said. "You said to wear whatever I wanted and didn't tell me where we were going."

"It's a lovely dress, Annie," she said. "We'd better go. Oh, bring that bag we talked about." Annie looked puzzled but went and got the bag without a single comment.

As they pulled up to the house, Annie looked at the old neighborhood. "I know this area. One of my uncles used to own a house a couple of streets over. This is a dinner party? There'll be other people there?"

"No," Sarah said. "This is one of our safe houses that we keep in the city." She braced herself, but Annie said nothing. Scott held the door for them.

Mike had done a beautiful job. There were flowers on the table, and he had even set candles out. The smell of food permeated the house. Sarah lit the candles with a flourish and turned to Annie. "Would you like some wine?"

Annie looked at the table, the flowers, the candles, and then up at Sarah. "Yes," she said.

Sarah hurried about, getting the food on the table, pouring wine for Annie and water for herself. This was going well, she thought.

"Oh, salmon steaks," Annie said and took a deep breath over the food. "And you've got my favorite butter, chive and lemon. What's this? Creamed asparagus and hot bread. You said you couldn't cook."

"I can't, but my friend Jana can," Sarah answered, taking a seat.

"Ah, the Bistro? I know Jana."

Sarah looked up, surprised. "You know Jana?"

Annie took a bite and closed her eyes. "Delicious." She dipped some salmon in the melted butter. "Jana used to date a friend of mine. This is one of my favorite meals that she offers. Did you know that, or was it just a lucky guess?"

"Lucky guess," Sarah said. "I wanted you to be comfortable and relaxed when I told you that we're moving you here for a couple of days until the doctors make a decision." She held her breath. Annie only nodded and ate more salmon. No explosion? She relaxed and began to talk to Annie about the photos and names she had brought home for Dr. Majer.

"These are the names you gave me that came up in our case the Joint Terrorism Task Force is working on. The photos you took will probably be used on forged visas." She held up several of the photos. "This man just happens to be an engineer in Iraq. He now works as a janitor in Dr. Majer's building. We're sure the good professor is involved locally. This is a very big break for us, Annie."

"Forged visas?" Annie leaned forward, scanning the paper.

"Annie, Iraqis have been filtering into our country for years, and trust me, this is good information."

"But look what I did, and have been doing for quite some time. I took their pictures. I helped them make forged documents. Am I in trouble?"

"No, you had no way of knowing, but my senior agent would like you to look at the photos we have at the office. You'd know if it was something you brought home, wouldn't you?"

"I believe I would, but I've been doing this for a while. Where do I go to see the photos?"

"We'll set up a time to have you come to the office. This is the best lead we've had in over a year, but you did mention something that has a dark side. That flyer that you showed me? The FFI has been threatened by Jaish al-Basca, just as you have."

A stricken look passed over Annie's face. "They're on the Web site too?"

Sarah nodded. "We're checking with the other journalists right now. Actually, I hope that's exactly what it is, that you're on the list because you attended the opening of the FFI. Do you happen to know if any of the other women were at that event, the opening, or at the shelter at any time?"

"At least one of them was. We went together. It was the English photojournalist, Kerry, who's still there. Could it be this simple?"

"We can only hope," Sarah said.

"That list, Sarah. I just have such a hard time with it. I don't think it's connected to what happened at my home."

"I agree, but it's what I said. What if this group we're working on has ties to Jaish al-Basca? The break-in at your house just skews everything. It makes it personal. When we get your arm taken care of, we'll move you again, probably up north."

"You mean leave town?"

Sarah nodded, watching Annie's reaction carefully.

"Of course I'll go, if that's what you think is needed." She looked at Sarah, unsmiling. The candlelight played across her already gold skin and darkened her eyes to the color of summer leaves, matching her dress. Sarah hardly knew where to put her eyes.

Annie pushed food around for a moment. "Isn't memory odd? I knew something was moved in my studio, but I still can't remember that man we saw at Sam's store the other night. He's tall, and my memory connects him with Afghanistan. He's just too familiar."

"Do you want to see one of our artists?" Sarah asked. "What am I saying? You could probably do the sketch better then they could."

Annie's face had an odd expression. "I've tried. It's so eerie, Sarah. I get shaky when I try to draw his face, and my mind shuts down. I can't figure this out." She shivered. "Why don't we use one of your artists? You saw him too, and you can help. At least we'll have a drawing, something for your people to work on. If you can get the picture out there, someone might know him, recognize him. Well, maybe this isn't important right now?"

"It's all important, Annie."

"That reminds me, Dr. Majer has invited Rebecca and me to his annual winter dinner."

Sarah almost came off her chair. Here was the moment Don was looking for, the way to get close to the college professor. "That's perfect. We've been trying to figure a way to get in his door without attracting too much attention." She gave a small laugh. "And I have plenty of black for a dinner occasion. Believe me. When is the dinner?"

"This weekend. Saturday night. We could go to the party and then leave town."

"That's more days than I'm comfortable with, but we could always come back for the dinner. It's certainly the perfect opportunity." Sarah was quiet, counting the days. She changed the subject. "Tell me about your arm." She was rewarded with a smile that finally reached Annie's eyes.

Annie leaned back in her chair and told her what the doctors had said. The soft lights turned the dim room gold where it drove the shadows away, and it felt warm and close. Sarah wished this were another time and another reason to be sitting across the table from Annie.

"Can anyone work out at the clinic, or do you need to be a patient or a member?" Sarah made a mental note to drop into the building with Annie in the morning and have a look at it. They could go to the office afterward, talk to Don, and then get out of town.

"Anyone can go there. They even have a daycare center." Annie took a drink of wine and looked at Sarah over the glass. "Have you ever shot anyone?"

Startled, Sarah straightened in her chair. "What?"

"The doctor says the stress I'm feeling after Jack's shooting and the bomb is what law enforcement officers often feel when they've been involved in a shooting, especially a killing."

"No. I've only had to pull my gun a handful of times."

"That's a good thing."

"Are you having problems?"

Annie nodded. "I'm having nightmares again. I got into something about three years ago and didn't want to admit to the symptoms." Annie was quiet for several moments. "This last time in Baghdad was one of the strangest moments of my life. I actually got dizzy because I forgot to breathe." She looked at Sarah with an amused smile. "You expected a little resistance moving me here? Maybe a little temper?"

"Yes, frankly."

Annie concentrated on her plate. "I don't quite understand this, but honestly, you make me feel better. Maybe even secure, and that's a first."

Sarah smiled because Annie had said it like she meant it. She shrugged. "I'm glad I'm doing my job."

"Ah, you save damsels in distress, Agent Moore?"

Sarah felt her cheeks warm. "You know, when they gave me this assignment, I wondered what you would be like. All of us have had some fairly trying experiences with celebrities."

Annie's gave her a look of disbelief. "Celebrity? Who have you been talking to? It's not true. I'm just a hardworking correspondent who takes her job seriously. Celebrity, ha!" She started to laugh. "Well? Did I pass the test?"

"Of course." Sarah laughed too, but stared at Annie's mouth. Definitely intriguing, wide and quirky.

"I know the kind of people you're talking about. I run into them while I'm working, and they're a real pain. They usually just get in the way." Annie propped her arm on the table and rested her chin in the palm of her hand, giving Sarah her full attention. "Didn't you say your dad had been shot while he was working for the FBI?"

Sarah, pulled into Annie's eyes, was quiet for a beat too long and Annie began to smile at her. "Uh, yes, right after nine-eleven. He almost didn't make it."

"But he's fine now?"

"It's like he did a one-eighty with his personality. He changed, became a different person when he came home."

"That makes sense when you've come so close to death."

"I wouldn't know. I've never been injured." She looked at Annie. She was recovering from something that had been close to death. Would it change Annie like it had changed her father?

Annie reached down beside her chair, rummaged about, and put a pen and notebook on the table, flipping the top open.

"Wait," Sarah said, "where did you get that?"

"What?"

Leaning forward, Sarah deliberately looked at the green dress Annie was wearing. "Nope, no room for a pen and paper. Not an inch for anything but you."

"Reporters always have paper and pen. That's in case the electricity, or the memory, fails. If you want to talk 'room,' let's talk about that leather you're snuggled into."

"Believe me, I am way less 'snuggled' than you are."

Annie opened the notebook and shoved it across the table. Sarah picked it up and began turning the pages, looking up at Annie. "Names?"

"The people that I lived with in the hotel in Baghdad during this last trip. Those people went home in just the first two weeks."

Sarah flipped the pages. "What happened to them?"

"They just couldn't handle it or didn't like it, but most were simply afraid. I was too. You'd be dumb not to be. Living in fear is twenty-four/seven when you're in the middle of a war. It gets to be something that you depend on to keep your head on straight."

Sarah nodded and then realized she didn't know about this kind of living. This was new territory.

"Well, super sleuth, where did the intrepid reporter hide the paper and pen?" Annie shot a mischievous look across the table.

"I am not even going to go there." Sarah returned the look, and their eyes held for a moment.

Annie leaned forward. "Coward," she whispered.

"Am not," Sarah teased back. "I am brave and tough, and you should see me catch bullets with my teeth." Annie's eyes were sparkling, and Sarah realized they were doing a pretty good imitation of flirting. Something she hadn't done in way too long, and it felt good

Annie broke the spell and stood, picking up plates. "I'll help you clean up." Sarah watched Annie move away. The dress clung lightly around her lithe body, and she walked confidently She was small-boned but agile, and Sarah swallowed hard as a sudden flush of desire sideswiped her. She picked up plates and followed Annie into the kitchen. Annie was running water over plates, stacking the dishes in the sink. She smiled at Sarah and said, "Tell me something about yourself. Something personal."

"What's to tell?"

"Look how much you know about me, and you've even met my parents."

"You have a point," Sarah admitted. "Tell you what, let's make this interesting. Start from scratch. Take me as you see me."

"Well, you're about an inch taller than me. Five-nine or so?" Annie wiped her hands on a dishtowel and put her fingers around Sarah's biceps. "Look at those muscles, hoo, baby. Can't tell what sport specifically, but you walk like an athlete."

"I play golf a lot. Or did before I moved here. And you know I work out, plus a little kickboxing."

"Golf? Love that game," Annie said. "If I'm in town, you're on this summer, deal?"

"Deal. Let's take you through the house so you know where you're going. I'll get our bags."

They walked through the large, old house and up a graceful staircase.

"Where did you get this house?" Annie asked.

"It used to belong to some DOJ man and his family. He was

transferred to the West Coast and we took it. Some guy with a Greek name that no one can pronounce, so we just call it the George the Greek House, or the Whitmore place." She led Annie into a large bedroom and told her to leave her bag on the dresser. "This'll be your room, and I'm next door." They walked down a long hallway and Sarah showed her the other rooms and the bathroom.

"Would you like to change into something more comfortable?" Sarah asked when they were done. "I'll change too and meet you downstairs. Want some more wine?"

"Love it," Annie said, disappearing into her bedroom.

Sarah was pouring Annie another glass of wine and had found a soda when Annie reappeared at the table.

"Thanks for the flowers," Annie said, picking up her glass. "And the wine."

"I'd like to take credit for that, but it was Mike's idea. I volunteered for Pride weekend three summers ago and ran into him. He had just joined the agency and he was there with his partner, a local guy. I have dinner with them now and then." She looked at Annie's purple Pride T-shirt. "I have a red T-shirt just like that."

"Give me a minute here. I want to talk about you a bit more," Annie said. "You have a master's in criminal science, but also a degree in archeology? That's truly odd."

Sarah was surprised. How had she known that?

Annie put her glass against her forehead and shut her eyes. "Wait, there's more," she said. "You fell out of a tree at age nine, breaking a wrist, left one I think."

"How on earth?" Sarah shot forward in her seat.

"Told you, reporters—the good ones—are intrepid."

"No way."

"Believe in me, super sleuth."

"How?" Sarah cleared her throat.

"I telephoned your mom after you called today." Annie's laugh was soft and teasing.

"You're evil, Booker, you know that?"

"So I've been told."

"Did my mom say…?"

"Perhaps. She certainly loves to talk about you. Oh, something else, you're slow to anger, but watch out if you finally get there. And stubborn."

This *was* beginning to feel like a date, Sarah thought and looked across at a relaxed and laughing Annie. It was exactly what she had wanted.

"Actually, I'm beat, and that meal has me headed for a food coma. I think I'll head off for a shower and bed if you don't mind." Annie stood and walked to Sarah. "I loved the meal." She leaned over and kissed Sarah softly on the cheek. "Thank you," Annie whispered and turned, walking toward the stairway and leaving a nice light fragrance in the air. Sarah could still feel warm breath and lips on her face.

CHAPTER TEN

A thick winter fog hugged the house the next morning, and dry oak leaves skidded across the snow. Sarah stood by the car and surveyed the neighborhood. Scott had just called and said the computer at Annie's house was still not working correctly, so she had him pull the plug and put the whole thing in his car. They couldn't get out of town fast enough for her.

The fog was breaking up as Sarah drove Annie to the clinic.

"I suppose you see this a lot," Sarah said, navigating the streets carefully.

"It's the lake and winter," Annie said, yawning.

"You usually only see this in the higher elevations at home."

"I wouldn't know. I've never been in your home state."

"What?" Sarah teased in mock horror. "You've been all over the world but not to Arizona?"

"Isn't it mostly desert? I've seen enough desert to last me the rest of my life."

Sarah nodded; that was probably true, but that wasn't all the Arizona she loved. She talked about the mountains and mesas, the rivers and lakes in her home state until she pulled into the clinic's parking lot. Scott was leaning against his car, waiting for them, and took Annie into the building while Sarah went to look for Annie's mother.

"Excuse me." Sarah smiled at the young receptionist, laying her ID on the desk. "Is Dr. Booker available?" She took a quick look at the beautiful interior of the clinic while she was waiting.

Sarah followed Annie's mother to her office. The atmosphere was relaxing and comfortable, and they talked about how the building had been designed. They paused on the walkway from the offices to the gym and rehabilitation center as Hannah Booker pointed out the daycare center. "The children we saw in Vietnam were the reason we all began this. We all did at least one tour and came home determined never to see anything like that again." She paused. "But we're doing it all over again in Iraq, aren't we? I don't know how to stop it. War or any of it."

She took several steps and turned. "Call the office, Sarah, I'll set aside time for you, and we can talk about Annie, perhaps tomorrow. I understand that she talked with your mother, so turnabout is fair play, don't you think?" She gave her an impish grin that reminded Sarah of Annie. "Here's the gym and rehab center where Annie's working out."

Sarah spotted Annie immediately. Annie's running shorts and cut-off T-shirt revealed tanned skin over toned muscles, shining with sweat. Where was the soft feminine woman in the green dress from last night? This woman looked like an Olympic athlete. Sarah blinked. There she was, just the right amount of muscle and curve.

"Hey, super sleuth, come on over." Annie motioned at Sarah.

"How's the arm, honey?" Hannah asked, helping Annie off the machine.

"Doc says I'm good to go. This is the last day I have to rehab here. The rest I can do at home. Swelling's down, and my range of motion is good. I'll just have to be careful in the sun until the skin heals." She grabbed a towel, mopping her face and stomach. Sarah could not take her eyes off Annie, following every motion of the towel. She realized both women were looking at her.

"What?" she asked. She'd missed a question.

Annie put a hand on Sarah's shoulder. "Do you have time for a soda, coffee, water or...?"

"Sure, I have time," Sarah said feeling her face heat up.

"I have to go. Nice to see you again," Hannah said to Sarah. "Give me a call when you can, Annie."

"If it's possible, Mom."

"We will when we can, Hannah." Sarah lowered her voice.

"Come on, I'll shower and we'll find some of the coffee Mom always has hidden in her office," Annie said.

"Annie, wait." Sarah caught up with her. "I'm going in with you."

"In the shower?"

"Who's been checking out the showers? Scott?"

Annie grinned suggestively. "For all I would have cared."

Sarah swore softly. "All right, Booker, let me check out the exits, if there are any, and look around. Be done in a minute." They went into the shower area, hearing voices echoing and running water. Sarah knew she wasn't going any farther than the perimeter. She was glad this part of Annie's rehabilitation had been short. She walked up the steps to talk to Scott.

"You should have said something to me about the showers, Scott," she said, keeping her voice even. This was her responsibility, not his, but it was also how he learned.

"I'm sorry, Sarah, it just didn't occur to me." He looked down.

"Scott, that's why you're in training, so you can learn the little things, and that's what always bites us all, the things we take for granted, forget to look at." Sarah put a hand on his arm. "Did you ever finish Annie's local information?"

He nodded. "I sent it to you in e-mail this morning. She's absolutely clean. She was very involved in the community before the network moved her out, and there are a few things about her golf and art."

Sarah nodded and started to leave but remembered the computer. "Scott, wait. Remember to take the new computer to Annie's house after you drop her off at Whitmore. We need to keep things status quo there. Don't go alone. Take someone else with you."

Before they left, Sarah asked to see Annie's artwork that was displayed in the clinic, so she and Annie lingered in the spacious center of the building. Annie talked about some of the pieces, and Sarah thoroughly enjoyed the conversation, asking questions and listening. The paintings ranged from gentle and reflective to high energy.

"As I've told you, I got into a bit of a problem about three years ago and the network gave me some time off. So I painted—canvas, fabric, walls, you name it. I lasted about three months, and then I was pooped. I couldn't pull off one more color or brushstroke," Annie said, taking a seat in one of the comfortable chairs in the large waiting area.

"There's one painting in there, in the first waiting room, the one with all the reds, pinks, grays, and blues. I've never been there, but it has an Arabian feel about it. You only suggested form."

"It is, Saudi Arabia to be precise. Lots of sand," Annie said, tossing her coat over a chair. Her hair, still damp from the shower, swung forward, but not before Sarah saw her face darken.

"You were there?"

"Unfortunately." Annie relaxed, her eyes finding Sarah's again. "What did you think of this building? My dad does the trees and green things. He loves doing it, and I think it connects him to Mom in a special way. They have a unique relationship."

"They remind me of my parents. They lead their own lives but meet somewhere. My folks are in love and have been since I've been old enough to understand. We're lucky to have these people for parents."

Annie looked up at Sarah. "They meet somewhere? Maybe that's the answer to the question you asked me the other night, about hope for either of us?"

Sarah smiled. "Do you believe in chance?"

"Absolutely, I've lived on it for years. But are you asking about karma or fate?"

"Just chance. Can't say as I believe in the others."

"There is a difference, but I do like the 'meeting somewhere' of what you said."

Sarah was quiet for a moment, then said softly, "I love my family, and for some reason, right now, I'm homesick. It's odd." She turned back to Annie. "I have an unusual ethnic background. My grandmother was full Navajo."

"Your mother's mom?"

"Nope, Dad's, and you should see my childhood photos." Sarah chuckled. "My dad had quite a childhood. Do you know about the Navajo?"

"I did a documentary last year on a Navajo Marine in Iraq," Annie said, then grinned. "I read *Laughing Boy* by Oliver LaFarge. Does that count?"

"Are you kidding me? That's a classic, and I think you're the first person I've ever met that even knows about that book."

"My granddad gave it to me on my fourteenth birthday. In our family, a book is a welcome gift. I liked it, and of course, I still have it. I think he knew I was searching."

"Searching?"

"Ah, a long, silly story." Annie shook her head and Sarah watched the gold in her hair catch the sunlight. "When I was thirteen, just a few days before my fourteenth birthday, I asked my best friend Rebecca to marry me, and when she turned me down, mean woman that she still is, I was crushed. I fell into an abyss."

"What?"

"Yes, a big hole. I moped around for days, and the night of my birthday party, in front of grandparents, family, and friends, I announced that I had asked Rebecca to marry me. You should have heard the silence. And when I explained that she had rejected my offer, I burst into tears like the little drama queen that I was. I thought they were all upset because she turned me down. God, can you believe that?" She laughed at herself.

"Yikes!"

"I was the youngest and most spoiled grandchild, but when my older boy cousins laughed at me, I was devastated and clueless. However, both sets of grandparents had serious talks with my parents."

"How were your folks with this?"

"Respectful of my first encounter with feelings while they waded through the mess that followed. They waited a week and then had a talk with me. It was a beautiful discussion. If I'd ever had children, I'd want my parents to talk with them at those moments. They were right about love. The heart does the choosing. The mind tries to steer, but the heart takes over. Ah, young love. How about you, fearless?"

"My sister, four years older, did the honors. We used to spend summers on the reservation with my grandmother. My first girl, well, I was a bit indiscreet. No, I was a lot indiscreet. Nora, my sister, came around the corner at the wrong time, and there was hell to pay. Grandmother was so angry at first." Sarah fell quiet, studying the table.

"And your sister?"

"She just scolded me for not being careful. But she did talk with me. She still does when she feels I need it." Sarah stood and looked down at her watch. "Annie, we have to work on getting you out of town. Scott will take you back to the Whitmore house. Mike and another agent will be there with you, and Scott will go on out to your house. We have to install another computer. That one is still not functioning. I have a meeting with my staff this afternoon, and my senior agent ought to be home from Chicago by then. As soon as you meet with him, we can leave town." Sarah remembered what she had planned to do tomorrow.

She'd have to cancel if they could get out of town. "I'll keep in touch with you and call you after my meeting." She scanned Annie's face. She didn't feel that Annie grasped the urgency or seriousness of her situation. She was going to have to be more firm. Clearer.

"All right. I'll go with Scott."

"Wait," Sarah said, sitting down again. "Now that you're done here at the clinic, we'll have to stay at the safe house."

"What?" Annie frowned at her.

"We have to stay at that house from now on, until we leave. By staying close, we contain the threat."

Annie was still frowning at her. "How am I going to do the exercises they want for rehab at the safe house? Not only that, but I'd like to do a little painting. I don't mind not going out, but..." She trailed off. "Do I get to know where we're going, when we leave town?"

"I'm still setting it up, but I'll tell you when I finalize everything. We'll figure something out for the necessary exercises, but I think the art is going to have to wait."

Annie nodded and kept her expression neutral.

❖

Hamel was parked down the street waiting for Sheika to meet him. Hamel watched the FBI woman get into the car. She had looked right at him and didn't recognize him, even after she'd seen him before. He was just a man in a baseball cap, sitting in a car. The reporter had gotten into her big black car with one of the government men. He smiled to himself. They had found the first bug in their computer but not the second one, and he had easily placed the GPS device on the reporter's car this morning. He could now track her anywhere from his laptop.

The back door to his car opened and his sister got in. Enough for today, he thought, as he drove away in the opposite direction. There is time.

❖

Sheika rode in the backseat, thinking over what she had heard in the gym. The mother and the government woman had spoken to the reporter. Working with weights just two stations away with her back to the three women, she had heard most of the conversation. And what she had heard in their voices made her think about the Booker woman. She heard affection and respect between the reporter and her mother. It made her think of her own mother, their mother, and she glanced up into the rearview mirror, studying his face. She tried to remember the last time she had seen him treat any woman with love or even respect, including herself.

CHAPTER ELEVEN

It had been easy for Annie to persuade Scott to drive her to her brother's apartment. He had also sat patiently while she got her hair done. Her hairdresser had flirted shamelessly with him, making Annie laugh and Scott blush more than once. He hadn't even argued as she'd told him that she needed to paint before they went to the safe house. She stood in her studio now, organizing the painting, assessing the first colors she'd laid on the canvas. One more layer of paint, a few sketches, and they'd be back at the other house. Scott was downstairs, still working on the computer.

Annie had been carefully quiet when Sarah called her on her cell phone, fully aware that Sarah had thought she was talking to her at the other house. Sarah had sounded crabby and unhappy as she told her they would not be able to leave today. After they hung up, Annie thought about what she had done. She had probably just gotten Scott into a world of hurt, and she began to sketch quickly over the canvas. She would get this much done and get back to the house on Whitmore.

Finished, she ran downstairs and changed into a clean denim shirt. She stared at the one packed bag still lying on the closet floor and had a sudden wild urge to leave. It was simple. She could have that discussion with her parents and then just go. She could hear Scott working in the living room and thought of Mike waiting for her at the other house, and then Sarah. "Sarah," she said aloud, feeling the word in her mouth. She sat for a moment, thinking about last night and this morning. Sarah had said they might be able to leave tomorrow. That was a kind of running away.

Annie checked her e-mail as she got ready to leave, looking for something from Kerry, but there was only a forwarded message from Bill Simpson at the network office. Lindsey Kelling at the Baghdad FFI had asked to use the piece Annie had done when they had opened the shelter. Lindsey asked if they could combine it with Annie's piece on the Iraqi custom of honor killings. Annie accessed the actual film while she went to her notes. Squinting at the screens, she finally swore and grabbed her glasses off the desk, then settled in to see if she could put the two pieces together from home. After getting the voice and film coordinated, she sat back and watched.

Her job was beginning to blend with disappointment at the deteriorating situation in Baghdad and the certainty that no one knew exactly what was going on. Usually someone, or some group, had the information. The real story, no matter where she was, was often difficult and usually dangerous. However, discovering the truth in Iraq had become impossible.

Annie concentrated on stories about the people, not the politics. She thought of Jack Keegan and his commitment to those same kinds of stories. She wondered how the network would ever replace him. How would *she* ever replace him? Restless and edgy, she couldn't help the tears that began to blur the film, and before she could stop herself, she was crying.

A hand was suddenly on her shoulder and Scott said, "Ms. Booker, are you all right?"

She shook her head and wiped her eyes with her fingers. Scott handed her a Kleenex just as the doorbell rang. He left to answer it.

Annie followed him and saw her brother Will standing there, frowning at Scott. She grabbed his coat, pulling him inside. "Get in here, idiot. It's freezing."

"I didn't know you meant the FBI had to be in your home," Will said.

"Tell you what, brother, I'll trade your life for mine right now."

"I've never wanted to do what you do, Annie," Will said. "I'm here because I need some help with the recording that I talked to you about."

"The one you promised me a copy of, and by the way, do you need some artwork on it?"

"Good thought. I may just take you up on that. Anyway, our

practice studio overbooked and we need a place. Could we use the bar section in your basement?"

Annie grinned. "Sure, go ahead. It's all yours." She looked at Scott for confirmation, and he nodded.

"Cool," Will said, "let me get them in here. Do you want us to come in through the garage?"

Scott stood beside Annie as people with instruments and amps started coming into the house and Will directed them down to the basement. As the drummer went by, she was certain she could smell pizza. She looked over at Scott. He'd smelled it too and smiled at her

Mike drove up and ran toward Scott and Annie. He drew them off to the side, away from the people trooping into Annie's garage and house.

"Where have you been and what the hell are you doing?" he angrily demanded.

Annie answered before Scott could say anything. "This was my doing, Mike. My brother, Will, is using my basement for a practice session for his band."

"No, he's not. Not with you anyway. We've got to get you to the other house. And, Scott, where's your phone?"

Scott searched his suit coat and then looked at him sheepishly. "It's in my coat, in the other room."

"Do you realize that Sarah's going to shoot both of us?" Mike said to Scott and then he looked at Annie. "Maybe even you."

"Shit," Annie said. "Give me your phone. I'll call her."

❖

The meeting finally over, Sarah walked wearily to her office and flipped on her lights. There was a mailing envelope on her desk and she turned it over. Good. It was Annie's earlier reports from overseas. Even though they were now confident that the Web site threat was tied into the FFI, she wanted to run over this, just in case. *Hell, I just want to look at her and listen to that voice*, she admitted and tossed it in her briefcase.

She scrubbed her face with her hands and reviewed the discussion she'd had with Don Ahrens. He had ordered her to wait to move Annie out of town until after the dinner this weekend at the Majer house.

Sarah had argued vehemently, but Don had simply nodded and told her to put it in her report, to document the fact that he had overridden her decision. This was wrong and dangerous. She grabbed her coat. At least Annie was safety tucked away at the Whitmore house.

Sarah took her anger at Don out on the workout equipment at home, pounding every muscle. She picked up her phone as she walked toward a much-needed shower.

"Damn." There was a message from Annie. "What the hell?" she said, grabbing her leather motorcycle jacket and an Arizona Diamondbacks baseball cap to cover her sweaty hair. She slammed out the door. Twenty minutes later she pulled up to Annie's house. There were at least eight or more cars parked up and down the road. She threaded between two vans in the driveway, swearing aloud, and then realized she couldn't get inside. Everything was locked up. She called Scott and ordered him to open the garage door.

Scott met her at the door, eating a piece of pizza, and Sarah's anger shot up. At least Mike was in front of the computer. The house smelled like beer and pizza, and she heard muted music and laughter coming from the basement.

She was almost speechless with anger and both men knew it.

"Who wants to tell me what the hell is going on?" she said in a cold voice.

"It's my fault," Scott said and admitted that he had brought Annie home that afternoon.

"Home?" Sarah echoed, incredulous. She swiveled to Mike. "And why didn't you call me, let me know they never showed up at Whitmore?"

"I'm sorry. I kept thinking they'd show up," he said, and Sarah could see that he was trying to protect Scott. She studied their anxious faces and understood exactly what had happened. Annie had simply managed the entire situation.

"Dammit. You're both dead and you know it," she said, clenching her jaw. "Who are these people?"

"Annie's brother and his band. They're practicing," Scott answered, his voice rising with nerves. "I thought it would be okay. Ms. Booker was in her office, crying."

"Crying?" Sarah said. She looked toward the basement. Crying?

She turned to Mike, and he swore that Annie identified everyone that walked into the house.

"And what would you have done if someone walked up and she said she didn't know them?" She glowered at him, hands jammed into her pockets.

"I wouldn't have let them inside."

"Point being, it would have been too late. They would be there, in front of her." She tapped him on the head and exhaled. "I'm trying to get her out of this house, this city, and Don wants to wait until this weekend. Between you two and Don, I'm banging my head against the wall." She walked to the refrigerator and grabbed a soda. "I'll deal with you tomorrow. Let's go look at the basement. We'll watch from the steps."

❖

Annie was thoroughly enjoying herself. They had remodeled this part of the basement into a bar, but Annie hadn't used it in a long time and she couldn't stop smiling. About twenty people were crowded inside as the band ran through their songs. It hadn't taken Annie long to figure out that Will had set this little pizza and beer party up under the guise of a practice. She poured herself another beer, sitting with people she had grown up with. No secrets with this group. She'd known most of them since high school and would have given anything to have Rebecca here. This was fun.

Will started playing a reggae tune, and a hand grabbed Annie's, pulling her up to dance. She grinned at Tori and leaned into her. Tori had been an exchange student from Norway who had stayed in Milwaukee and finished college. They had met on the golf course, and Tori had become Annie's first lover. Three years later, Tori had found the woman now playing saxophone in Will's band, but she and Annie had remained close friends.

❖

Sarah watched a tall, fit woman with a punk blond crew cut take Annie out onto the floor. Annie's form-fitting jeans and white T-shirt under the blue denim shirt showed her agile body off perfectly, and Sarah took a long drink of her soda. The two women moved apart as Annie danced in front of the blonde and started to unbutton her shirt suggestively, causing the crowd to laugh. Despite her arm, she got it off in a flawless maneuver, never missing a beat, and the blonde pulled Annie into her body, moving easily with her. Annie's hand went up into the air swinging the shirt over her head, finally letting it go, and then she settled against the woman as their friends whistled and clapped.

Damn. Sarah took another drink, her insides clenched. She watched the blonde's large hands run slowly down Annie's ribs, caressing her slim hips and ending up on that cute little backside she'd admired this morning. Sarah almost groaned out loud. Taking another drink, she gripped the bottle so tightly her hand hurt. Annie's body was free as air with the music, her face against the woman's shoulder. Finally, the song ended, much to Sarah's relief. Her body was on fire.

❖

Annie sat down and reached for her beer as Tori bent over and kissed her. "Whew," Annie said, fanning her face with her hand, laughing with her friends. A dark-haired man picked Annie's shirt up from the floor and walked back toward her as she was happily talking with the people at the table. Two hands clamped down onto Annie's shoulders, and her beer sloshed down the front of her.

"Stop it," she said, looking up. A man she'd grown up with, a neighborhood boy once married to her cousin, was staring down at her, handing her the blue shirt. Or were they still married? Foggy with alcohol, she couldn't remember. "Hey, Link," she said, wiping herself off with a napkin.

"Glad to see you too," he said, pulling his chair next to her. "Home for a while?" She nodded. "I suppose you heard I'm no longer in the family?"

Annie made a face, glad she had one brain cell still functioning. "I thought I heard, and I'm sorry, but it's still good to see you."

He tipped his chair back on two legs. "Well, it's not your fault, although she did go off with someone you know."

"Who?"

"That big girl that used to play first base on your softball team."

Annie's table quieted, and she looked at her friends. This was news, but no one had told her, including her cousin. She laid a hand on Link's arm. "I didn't know, and I am sorry. You had kids, right?"

"Bet your sweet ass we did. A boy and a girl. You're not to blame, Annie, but it's your kind that are, and the damned courts gave her the kids. God will judge all of you." Link's face was red, and several people at the table stood. Annie felt her face grow warm as she stared back at him.

"Link, I didn't know about her. No one told me a thing, but if she's still the same person I grew up with, she's a good mother," she said as firmly as she could manage.

His chair slammed down, and he was inches away from her face, about to say more when Will put a hand on his shoulder. He shook it off and stood, kicking the chair into a group of people standing by the bar. There was a moment of stunned silence, and then all hell broke loose as the group at the bar came at him. Annie's chair was shoved over backward, but it was caught before she hit, and suddenly, she was looking up into Sarah's face. Sarah pulled her up, putting her body between Annie and the fight, and pushed her away.

Will separated the angry men and jerked Link toward the stairs. Sarah and Annie followed them up in time to see him take Link out the door. The music had stopped in the basement.

"I didn't know you were home," Annie said, looking at Sarah's faded jeans, black turtleneck, motorcycle jacket, and baseball cap. She stared for a moment and then grinned. "Cool clothes."

"I just got here and was sitting on the steps with Mike and Scott when the fight broke out. You looked like you were having fun," she said sarcastically.

Will walked back in the door and said that a friend was driving Link home. Annie just shook her head and introduced Will to Sarah.

"I'm sorry about this," he said to Sarah. "Annie looked like she could use a little company, and so I organized this. I'll pack up the party and get everyone out of here."

"I think that's a good idea," she said.

❖

Sarah left them standing there and walked to the back of the house, giving them some time to get the place cleaned up and quieted down. As she went past Annie's office, she noticed the lights and the computers were on. Papers were scattered over the desk. It looked like material on the FFI. She reached over and hit the refresh on both computers. Annie was interviewing a short young man dressed in a suit on one screen, while the text ran on the other. Sarah read a bit of the text regarding the FFI and then spaced down. She saw Annie's piece about honor killings that she had seen the day Annie had come home. Scott poked his head into the office.

"I'm leaving, and, Sarah, I am sorry." He looked genuinely contrite.

She shook her head and turned her back to him. "No. You're not leaving. You're staying here tonight. I'm taking Mike and Ms. Booker back to the other house but I want you here, watching that computer and this house. And, Scott, you'd better think about what you're going to tell me tomorrow."

She walked into the den and sank down on the couch, leaning back and thinking about Annie's dance. Not only was the entire event unacceptable, but damned if she wasn't feeling a little jealous. She reached up and turned the light out just as Annie came in and sat on the couch next to her.

"I've had a bit to drink, but I'm not totally out of it," Annie mumbled, kicking her low boots off and pulling her legs up under herself. The room was dark except for the triangle of light from the kitchen outlining Annie's profile. "This is too bizarre. I survive Iraq and come home to crap like this." She was quiet for a moment. "This is all my fault. Are you really angry?"

"Yes, I am. With all of your experience, you should know better."

Annie sighed and they sat in the dark without speaking.

"I'm really angry, Annie. If you don't value your own life, I'm not certain I can help you. You were careless, and what about Scott? You could have gotten him hurt or worse. I can't believe that you don't recognize how dangerous this is. I thought you understood that last night." Sarah stood. "We're not leaving town until after Majer's party. Put your shoes back on. We're going to the other house. I've already sent Mike."

Annie sat up, picking up a shoe. "I was working on some film and notes in my office when Will came by and asked to use the basement for a practice session. Of course, he brought beer and pizza."

"Your computers are still on. I was in your office."

"I'll shut it all down before we leave. My interview with the FFI is on there. I should show it to you."

"Who was that tall Norse-looking woman?" Sarah asked.

"Would you believe, my very first?"

No wonder they looked like they knew each other's bodies so well. They did. "What's she up to now?"

"Married to that good-looking woman playing the saxophone. They're one of the best couples I know. We've been friends over twenty years. I met her when I was sixteen."

"Let's go." Sarah helped Annie up. "Don't forget your computers."

Annie fell asleep on the drive and left Sarah with her own thoughts. Driving through the snowy streets, she looked across at the sleeping woman and her anger slowly drained away. Had Scott said she was crying? Once home, Annie immediately went to bed without saying a word and Sarah stayed downstairs, talking with Mike. She got a calmer and more accurate story about the afternoon. When they were done, she went upstairs for a shower.

Sarah stripped down to a T-shirt, inserted the network disc into the DVR, and crawled into bed. She looked at the dates, noticing the reports began well over three years ago.

Propping another pillow behind her, Sarah settled in. The film showed a different image of Annie. Her hair was longer, less streaked, and she looked more rested and fuller in the face. Sarah froze the frame and looked at it carefully. Age had made Annie's face more interesting and beautiful. She was interviewing a diplomat in Pakistan, a pudgy fellow with a yellow tie. Annie was wearing a light pink top, and Sarah watched the man's eyes. Yep, he was staring right at Annie's cleavage with a big smile on his face. "Dirty old man," Sarah muttered and then smiled. She'd been guilty of the same thing with Annie.

The film ran for a while, and then Sarah sat straighter, pushing up in the bed. "What the hell?" Annie was changing right in front of her eyes. She clearly looked more stressed, tired, and her smile had lost the jauntiness of the first part of the film. But it was her eyes that Sarah stared at. They had grown older, and there was an odd preoccupation around them. It was almost haunting. It was the look of isolation that Sarah had been fussing about. She stopped the film, checking the dates of the last reports. It was over two years ago. She turned the disc off and looked out into the room. "What the hell happened to you, Annie?" she asked trying to remember what Annie had said today at the clinic. The network gave her time off when she ran into a little trouble? It wasn't little, Sarah thought as she turned out her light.

❖

The sound of crows woke Sarah in the morning, and she had a moment's disorientation. She pulled on jeans and crossed to Annie's bedroom. The bed had been made. It was only seven thirty, and she walked downstairs barefoot. Sarah looked out the back door and saw Annie walking back to the house through the snow, hands in her parka pockets, her bare head down.

She swore under her breath. Annie shouldn't have been out there alone. There was a freshly made pot of coffee on the counter along with a stack of photographs on top of a large brown envelope. She picked them up, turning them over to look at the back as well. The enlarged photos showed enormous mountains and a snowy road beside steep drop-offs. They were the tallest mountains Sarah had ever seen. More photos peeked out of the envelope. Sarah poured two cups of coffee and put them on the table. Fresh cold air came in with Annie, and she looked at Sarah.

"Morning. Are you still speaking to me?"

Sarah pointed at the coffee. "I want to ask a favor. No, this is an order."

"What?"

"Don't leave the house like that, without me or one of the team, Annie, please."

Annie slipped out of her boots and hung her parka over a chair. "I'm sorry. I just don't think about it."

"I have to do something FBI-related this morning. Since you're so restless, would you like to go along?" She looked at Annie's windblown hair and red cheeks. Christ, she was lovely. "You don't have to dress up. Jeans and whatever will be fine. Heavy socks and warm shoes."

"We'll be outside?" Annie asked.

"Not exactly. But you will need warm clothes. Let's eat breakfast and go. What are those photos?" she asked.

"Something odd that I found in the office yesterday afternoon, and I brought it with me last night. Jack had given me these to hold on to the day before he was shot. The first photos are a mountain pass in Afghanistan. A French photographer that I used to hang out with took these." Annie handed the first two to Sarah. "Aren't those huge?"

"I don't think I've ever seen anything so desolate. Were you with the photographer when these were taken?"

Annie nodded and pulled more of the photos out, handing them to Sarah in sequence. "He was killed in Iraq over a year ago."

The next photo was a jeep filled with some bags and a person at the wheel, a man. Sarah's breath caught. Someone was running, their arms and legs blurred. It was Annie. The following one was Annie half out of her coat, and then another as she was bending over a woman covered in what appeared to be blood. In the next, Annie was down to her T-shirt and jeans, on her knees in the snow. The final picture was Annie, blood on her arms and the white T-shirt, standing with her hands at her side, looking down at the bloody woman in the snow. Sarah looked up from the photos. "Did this woman make it?"

"No." Annie shook her head. "We were following a small unit of Marines. They let them go by but shot at us."

Sarah stacked the photos and then laid them on the table so she could look at them again in sequence.

"She has blood all over her," Sarah said again.

Annie nodded. "She took the first picture, the one of him in the jeep, and that's when they shot her. They were a team, lovers actually, and I had met them in Kosovo. We were less than a quarter mile behind the Marines, and they sent three men back to help us, including a doctor. They knew we were back there and heard the gunfire."

"These are terrible photos, Annie."

"I keep these to remind myself."

"Remind yourself?"

"Of where I've been, why I do what I do. When people ask me why I do this job, and they always do, I talk about Jack Keegan, his dedication. I'd really like to include moments like this too, but I don't. That isn't why I'm showing them to you. Look at these." She handed the rest of the photos to Sarah and sat down across from her. There were three large photos of men, sitting in what appeared to be a living room, but the décor was sparse and certainly not American. Each photo had at least six or seven men, and one of them looked distinctly familiar to Sarah. She looked up at Annie.

"What is this?"

Annie pointed at the man that looked familiar. "I don't know and I have no clue where Jack got these. He mentioned that they had been left for him at the bureau in Baghdad, and he told me to take care of them until he went home. Sarah, it's him." She tapped the photos again. "The man at Sam's."

Annie was right. It was the man they had seen at Sam's little grocery store over a week ago.

"Are the mountain photos connected to these men?"

"Not at all. I've never seen these photos before."

"Could I have them? I'll have Scott take them in to Don."

Annie left the room for a shower, and Sarah studied the photos. Finally, she got up and took some bowls out of the cupboard. Cereal would do this morning.

Forty minutes later, they were driving to the small private airport the FBI used in north Milwaukee. "So, you're still not going to tell me where we're headed, are you?" Annie's voice had a bit of the old teasing tone.

"I have to blindfold you and—" Sarah started, but Annie interrupted.

"No one blindfolds me. The only broken bone I've ever had, unlike someone sitting across the table from me, was during a high school prank involving me wearing a blindfold, and I broke a tiny little bone in my foot. It kept me out of a golf match, and I'm still punishing Rebecca for that one."

"All right, cranky, no blindfold, but it sounded like fun." She parked the car. "Ready? I have twenty minutes to get my bird in the air."

Annie looked surprised. "You're a pilot, Sarah?" Annie almost skipped as they walked to the hangar, eyes shining. The plane was ready for Sarah as she introduced Annie to the crew. *After last night, this is good*, Sarah thought and climbed in, tossing the folder behind the seat.

Sarah talked to the tower until they were clear, then flew along the Lake Michigan shore. The little blue Cessna angled north as the sun splintered the sky into rainbows through ice crystals in the cold air. Sarah handed Annie a pair of headphones so they could talk and explained that she made this trip whenever possible, carrying information too sensitive for fax, telephone, or computer to a tiny office in the northern town.

Annie asked how she began flying, and Sarah explained that she had been part of a high school flying class, then private lessons, and had continued into college. The FBI used her services when possible, and that helped keep her rating up.

"So, that's how many years?" Annie asked.

"If you include high school, it's about nineteen years."

"And that makes you how old?"

"Thirty-five."

"Okay, so I'm the old-timer here, at thirty-eight. You're just a kid, Moore." She stared out the window at the passing landscape. "I love flying," she said and began to tell stories of all the crazy flights she had taken in her life. Her face was animated, and Sarah smiled, once again the beneficiary of Annie's stories.

"Why didn't you learn to fly?"

"I didn't dare get involved because I knew it would keep me and hold me forever. I just would never land."

Sarah smiled at Annie. "I understand."

Approaching Green Bay, Sarah trimmed the flaps, reduced air speed, and talked to the tower, letting Annie listen in. As they taxied down the runway, a car drove up, and a tall redhead got out, waiting in the cold sunlight.

Sarah reached behind the seat as the plane shut down, and she opened the window. She looked down at the figure striding toward the plane. "Hey, Rosy, how've you been?"

A Southern drawl laced with some pretty healthy cussing came floating into the cabin.

"What?" Sarah grinned and cupped her hand behind her ear as she dropped the envelope. The woman asked where she'd been and Sarah pointed at Annie. The redhead grabbed the struts and crawled up to take a look as Sarah did the introductions.

"Looks like a darned good reason to me. Are we going to see you soon? Allison says you still owe her for that last poker game." She grinned, took another longer look at Annie, then raised her eyebrows suggestively at Sarah.

"Let me get back to you. Maybe this weekend," Sarah said and Rosy got down, walking back toward her car. The woman stopped and took her phone out of her jacket, talked and looked back at Sarah. She began walking back toward the plane and held her phone out.

"It's Don, for you. Something about photos?"

Sarah talked with her boss for a few minutes and then handed the phone back to Rosy. She watched her walk away, saying nothing, thinking about Don's information.

"Good friend?" Annie asked.

"One of the best. She and her partner, Allison, have lived up here for about two years. Allie's a nurse, a darned good one, ex-military out of Iraq, but she won't talk about it. We'll probably come up here, to her house, when we manage to get you out of town." Rosy drove away and Sarah put the headphones back on, talking to the tower and checking the weather for the trip back down.

"Didn't you say we're not leaving Milwaukee today?" Annie asked. "I mean, here we are. Why don't we just stay?"

"If I had my way, we would. My boss says not until after the party." Her mind grumbled at Don again. He hadn't really given her any reason, and that just angered her all the more.

Once in the air, Annie watched the lake and rubbed her arm.

"What's up?"

Annie smiled. "I'm working on a painting, and sometimes I just space out, working it out in my mind. That's what I was doing yesterday, painting, but I forgot to do my exercises."

"Do you let people see it before it's done?"

There was a long silence and then Annie answered cautiously, "Maybe." She looked at Sarah. "Are you asking?"

"Yeah, I guess I am. My days are so busy that it's wonderful to think about something that's not life and death. Well, you know about that."

Annie nodded. "When I'm into a painting, sometimes I can hardly stand to be away from it. I value my gift. It's like dreaming on canvas Right now it's the only thing that makes sense to me, but it needs more work before it can be seen." She tightened her seat belt and looked at Sarah.

Sarah caught Annie's quirky expression.

"Did you bring me along just to keep an eye on me today?" Annie said.

"Maybe. I still can't believe you did that yesterday."

"My head just won't straighten out. Trust me not to do that again?"

Sarah nodded and looked out into the blue sky that surrounded them. This felt so good to her. "Annie, I watched some of your early reports last night."

"You did? You watched my old films?"

"You're in Pakistan to begin with on this tape. You're fun to watch. I always learn something too."

Annie smiled at Sarah. "Thank you, schmoozer. Did the FBI teach you that, or is it just something you've learned in the bars? You know, all those women, so little time?"

Sarah laughed. "Would I really tell you if I had?"

They laughed at each other, and Sarah hated to lose the moment. "Back to the film. I noticed something as I was going over it last night."

"Like what?"

"Well, it's like you changed in about a year."

"What do you mean?"

"I felt like you…" Sarah stopped, searching for the right words. "It was like you lost your sense of humor."

Annie gave a sad little laugh. "That's interesting." She looked out of the window, away from Sarah. "I've had that time described a lot of ways, but never quite like that."

Sarah waited for more, but Annie added nothing. The sound of the motor filled the silence. "Listen, if it's personal, I'm sorry, but it really was noticeable on the reports."

"Only if you look closely. And you do. You look at everything."

"Now who's schmoozing?"

"Sarah, you do notice things. There was some serious trouble at that time, but the only people who know about it are Rebecca, Mary, and some doctors. I promised myself, even before the injury in Baghdad, that I would come home and talk about it, especially to my parents."

Sarah reached down for the thermos she'd brought along. "Here, pour us some coffee."

"Don't you have anything stronger? We can share."

"If this is too personal, you don't have to say any more."

Annie took a drink and held the cup out to Sarah. She was gripping the thermos lid so tightly that her fingers were white.

"I need to tell Mom and Dad first because Mary and I weren't exactly forthcoming when we got home."

The plane was nearing Milwaukee, and Sarah held her hand up. "I have to check in. Hold on, okay?"

Annie nodded and then said, "Wait, can you fly over the house? I've never done that." Sarah banked the plane right as she talked with the tower.

"Sarah, look at that," Annie said on the second circle around her house. "See the tracks into the woods? And look, tire marks in the snow just off the road."

Sarah banked the plane again, giving herself a good look. Annie was right. There was definitely a trail in the woods to the north of the house, but there were also car tracks in the snow. She didn't remember seeing that in the report from the team.

❖

Hamel climbed the stairs to Sheikha's apartment above the garage. He had a bit of time and wanted to check his laptop to see if his electronics were still working. Pausing at the top of the steps, he looked out at the lake just as a cold wind caught him. He took her keys out of his pocket and opened the door, thinking about the warmth and dryness of home. He hated this cold.

He booted up his laptop and keyed over to a page, then shook his head. His relay to the FBI computer in the Booker house was not working. He smiled. Perhaps they found the second virus he had installed. It didn't make any difference. The GPS on her car would do the job. He changed pages on his computer. There it was, but why was she north of the city? He frowned. The car was close to a small private airport. Majer had assured him that she would be at the party this weekend, and he would check her position later. He needed those photos. His contact in Iraq wouldn't wait much longer. He wouldn't miss her this time.

CHAPTER TWELVE

Sarah called Scott on their way home from the airport, describing what they'd seen from the air. It looked like a lot more than just one visit last week. Scott would go over their notes, talk with the rest of the team that had checked out the woods, and meet her at the house. Sarah also called Hannah Booker to see if she had some free time today.

"You just want to get even because I called your mother," Annie teased.

Sarah shook her head. "Did you ever think about kids? I mean, having your own?" she asked.

"What on earth? What made you think of that?"

"When your mother was showing me the clinic's daycare center, she talked about her experience in Vietnam and the children there. My grandmother organized something like that on the reservation, and I worked there in the summers. Your mother reminded me of that."

Annie concentrated on something on the console of her car. "With my job, it's not a good idea, and Mary would never have considered it anyway." She turned, looking out at the lake. "How about you?"

"I've always wanted kids." Sarah said, surprising herself. She'd never revealed that to anyone. They pulled up to the safe house and Sarah hit the garage door opener.

"By the way, where did that airport come from?" Annie asked. "I've lived here all my life and never even knew it was there. Talk about lake effect."

"It was a private airport in the beginning. After nine-eleven, all of the local law enforcement got together, and I mean all, and sort of commandeered it. Makes it easier to protect, like what we're doing here with you. Did you notice that almost everyone was in some sort of uniform?"

Annie nodded. "You know, I could write a book on 'while I've been away' and sell it without any problem."

"It's changed a lot. What's lake effect?" Sarah asked.

Annie laughed. "I'm sorry. That just popped out. That's something people on the Great Lakes say when the lakes snow on them. It often comes as a surprise."

"The *lakes* snow on them? How does that work?"

"The wind changes direction suddenly, and all the land around the lake gets snow, usually a sizable amount. If you drive inland, even as little as five miles, it's not snowing, and sometimes the sun's out. It's unexpected. Sort of like my life right now, right?"

❖

Sarah changed clothes, and they waited for Scott together at the kitchen table. "I wanted to show your mother that network film and discuss it with her," Sarah said.

Annie worried her bottom lip. "We'll talk about it when you get home tonight. I promise. I just haven't talked to anyone here, especially family. I have to correct what Mary and I said when we came home, and I'm not certain how I'll do this."

She looked unsure, just as she had in the airplane earlier, and Sarah changed the subject. "So, do I get to see the painting you're working on?"

"No, it's not ready for showing. Sarah, my studio is at my house. How am I going to work on the painting? How am I going to do those stupid exercises? I can't do either if I'm supposed to be here." She got up and disappeared upstairs. She reappeared moments later with a baseball cap, handing it to Sarah.

"Oh no, not a Milwaukee Brewers cap. No way."

"Oh yes, no D-Back hats allowed in Milwaukee. I brought this with me last night."

Sarah gave her a look and a fake sigh, putting the hat on. "Have you been to the new stadium?"

"Nope." Annie shook her head. "Almost made it once, but

Mary and I got into one of our wars and missed the game. You like baseball?"

"Love it," Sarah said, adjusting her new hat.

"I always buy season tickets, and it's a dome. If it's raining and golf is out, we'll go to the ballgame. By the way, I liked your outfit last night. Great jacket with the faded jeans and the black turtleneck. It lent…uh, ambience."

Sarah made a face at Annie. "I got your message after my workout and hadn't even showered."

"So, you're a biker?"

She shook her head. "No, I just ride horses, but that jacket is my pride and joy. I bought it from the real deal at the motorcycle races north of Phoenix when I was twenty-five. It's been with me ever since."

"You don't have a bike?" Annie teased. "Just advertising?"

"Actually, oh hell, you're going to laugh, I wear it when I ride the horses." Annie shook her head, laughing. Sarah glanced at Annie from under her eyelashes. *Two can play*, she thought and raised her eyebrows at Annie, "So, you like the butch look?"

"Sometimes."

They heard Scott at the door. Sarah just grinned and said, "I'll head over to the office when I'm done at your mother's, then come back here. Thanks for this morning, Annie. I enjoyed it."

Before Sarah left, the three of them looked at the reports. The footprints the night of the break-in were consistent with the ones the team had found in the woods. As Sarah put the information in her briefcase and left, she thought about something she hadn't mentioned to Annie. They had talked to neighbors within a two-mile radius around the house, but no one had seen anything out of the ordinary. All they had were footprints of the single intruder and tire tracks. Otherwise, zippo. No, she corrected herself. Now they had the photos from Jack Keegan and the man they had both seen. It was *something*. Don had called her because they had a lead on two of the men in the photos and had sent copies out to every agency he could think of. However, there was nothing on the man she and Annie had seen.

After parking at the back lot of the clinic, Sarah sat in the car for a while, trying to decide how to approach Annie's mother without the film. If Annie was going to talk with her parents about a personal matter, Sarah didn't want to interfere.

Hannah was on the phone and waved Sarah to a big chair. Sarah first updated Hannah about the Web site, showing her copies of the FFI flyer that Annie had brought home. She explained that they had verified that each reporter had been to the organization within a month of its opening.

Hannah read the flyer and then handed it back. "Annie's job is so public, but I assume you've gone over this with the network or with local officials. What I'm driving at is that it's not a stalker or one of our domestic groups."

Sarah nodded. "We have. Right now our main focus is the break-in at her house."

"She certainly is less resilient than I've seen her in a long time."

"Hannah, she's tough, but I think it's just everything happening at once."

"Is she doing any painting?"

"As a matter of fact, that came up today. I might get to see what she's working on right now."

"What? You must be kidding. She never, and I mean never, lets anyone look at her work until she's ready."

"But she did paintings here, didn't she?"

"Well, yes, but most of them were done in her studio. Except for the times at night. Sometimes she'd paint all night and I'd see her when I came to work in the morning just as she left." Suddenly she looked across the desk at Sarah and was quiet. "She was like she is now, only more so."

"What do you mean, Hannah?"

"About three years ago Annie went to Saudi Arabia on her way to Iraq, but something happened and she ended up in Switzerland. She told me that she changed assignments at the last minute."

"What happened?"

"I'm not sure, actually. She wouldn't talk about it. Mary went over there and they said they just took a little vacation. Annie stayed at Rebecca's for a time, and Mary went to the house alone when they came home. I didn't even see Annie for at least a week, maybe more. Honestly, we thought they were having some problems, just going through something. They both looked so miserable."

"Has she always used humor as a defense?"

"Yes, since she was the most picked upon, teased, and otherwise just plain crucified by her brothers and sister. The youngest child thing."

"I'm the youngest. Believe me, I know."

"Did she always follow the rules?"

"Heavens no. She was the first to break rules, but honest about it if you caught her. Annie has never been a devious person. At least around the family."

"Did she always want to be a journalist?"

"No. She was always such an exceptional athlete I thought she'd go that way, but her mind and that incredible curiosity won."

Driving to the office, Sarah thought about the time period that Hannah had talked about. Annie had said she hadn't told her parents everything. So she had hidden something and wanted to clear the matter up, needing to talk with her parents first. Saudi Arabia and Switzerland, Hannah had said. Sarah wondered if she could track Annie's passport.

❖

Finally, Sheikha thought. Hamel was going to discuss his plan. The apartment was too cold, and she turned the thermostat up. She could hear the neighbors coming up the stairs, going into their apartment. She hated the cold weather here and would have preferred to work on their business back in Baghdad, but he said he couldn't trust anyone but her to take care of the American side of the business. At first it had made her feel valuable, but then she began to suspect that he had just wanted her away from him. He had been gone for over four months this time, and when she had complained, he had quoted "Inshallah," *it is God's will*. He never answered her.

Hamel's dark hair was short and his new beard trimmed. He looked handsome, and she felt her heart warm. She remembered when they were children, his sweet eyes and smile. All this, she thought, for the American reporter with the strange pale eyes.

"It's more than the reporter," Hamel explained to her. "Someone took photos of the group that included Amer, and somehow Ms. Booker's associate got them. The night we killed him we would have taken her, but their soldiers were too fast. I looked through her office when I was in her house but had to hurry because of the FBI. We need them back, Sheikha. Majer has promised she'll be at his party, and I will find them then."

They stood at the table, looking down at the floor plans of the house that he had been in and of Majer's home. Shiekha listened carefully, understanding what it was that he needed from her. She nodded and he went to the coat rack, putting on his parka. They would meet again this weekend. "*Allahu Akbar*," he said as he left. *God is great, and Allah decides our destiny.* Listening to his footsteps clatter down the steps, she sank back into the chair, staring at the papers he had left with her.

CHAPTER THIRTEEN

Annie did her rehab in her basement. Checking with the four agents, she happily escaped to her studio, grabbing a bottle of water on the way. Two of the agents sat on the stairway talking while the other two walked the house. Upstairs, she moved the easel into the light and was lost to the painting, leaning into the canvas with her brush, painting steadily. Much later, backing away, she took a deep breath and cocked her head. The canvas was only three feet tall and five feet long. Just right. She took a few more steps away, walking slowly in an arc in front of the easel, thinking out what she had just added. The phone rang, scrambling her concentration, and she knocked several things off the table trying to reach it. "Damn," she said, finding the noisy object under several paint rags.

"You won!" were the first words she heard. She recognized her producer's voice.

"Bill, good to hear your voice too. Is there money involved?"

"Huh?" He started to laugh. "Dummy. You won the International Correspondents Award for the story last November."

Annie tried to remember which story he was referring to. "Was it a report, a doc, or what? Oh, I know, the story of the Marine, the American Indian?"

"You have to come in for this one, Annie," Bill said, and she could hear voices in the background.

"Bill, is the big cheese right behind you?"

"Yes, and the award is this Friday night. We're carrying the program anyway, but, oh man, Annie, you won, for the idea, the writing, and the presentation. This is so great for all of us. That means I win too. The whole crew wins on this story."

The awards would be the day before Majer's party. "Well, I'm honored, but the credit goes to you and the crew." She caught an echo. "Wait, am I on speakerphone?"

"I just put you on," he said. "You have to be here for this one, Annie. It's the first one in over three years, since you and Jack blew everything away."

"Ms. Booker," an older, deeper voice came on, "you'll stay in the network suites. Come in today, and we'll get the promos shot and taped."

Annie unconsciously straightened a bit at the voice. *More work, exactly what I don't want,* she thought. "Thank you. I couldn't have done it without my producer and crew, but then, you know that." She cleared her throat. "What about the FBI?"

Silence followed and Bill kicked her off the speakerphone. She could hear them talking. "Annie, just bring them along."

"Well, someone better notify their office there. Will you do it from your end? Call that young guy, Josh something. I can't remember his name."

"Palmer," Bill finished for her. "I'll call him as soon as you and I hang up."

"Can I bring my Milwaukee agent, the one that's with me here?"

"Absolutely. By the way, how's your arm?"

"I'm healing, but the rehab is a daily grind I could do without. Did they tell you my house was broken into?"

"Yes, they did. I talked with Josh Palmer last week. Do they know any more than what they did then?"

"Not about the break-in, but I think they're making some progress on another part of what's happening here. I'll call my FBI agent when we hang up. Get back to me with the times. Oh, what do you want me to wear for the program?"

A woman's voice came on the line. "Whatever you darned well please. Just no boots, buddy."

Annie laughed at Bill's direct superior, Ellen Kennedy. "I wasn't even thinking of boots. Although, now that you mention it, they'd probably be a lot more comfortable than those killer heels you had me in the last time we did this."

"Yes, but if I recall, you loved my choice of dress," Ellen said. "Why don't you let me do it again? Feed my love of shopping and save you the trouble?"

They laughed. The last award had been with Jack, and Ellen had dressed her in one of the most revealing dresses Annie had ever worn, before or since.

"Okay, deal, but don't forget about my arm and the stitches, or we could turn it into a trendy tattoo. Anyway, I'm a little older, so less skin would probably be in order, don't you think?"

"Have you seen what women are wearing?" Ellen asked. "Next to nothing. It's crazy. We'll get back to you with ticket information and what else within the hour. Talk to you later, sweetie." She hung up.

Annie pumped her fist and whispered, "Yes! This'll make Jack so—" She went quiet, remembering, and walked to the big windows, gazing out at the lake. Walking around the studio, she looked at the locks on the windows, checking each one of them. The familiar shiver of fear ran through her. *Damn, in my house.* She wondered how they had opened the windows from the outside. She felt it again, the urge to run, to get out of here, then she stopped herself. What was she thinking? Her flight left for New York in less than three hours. She was *getting out of here.* She turned to the painting of Sarah. The work could be seen at this point, but did she want Sarah to see it? She reached out and traced the outline of the body, almost feeling the skin, the clothing, her hands in the black hair. It made her tingle, and she stepped back, surprised. It had been years since anything on her body had done that. She pulled the cover over the painting and clattered down the steps to her office.

❖

Sarah was on her computer, looking at the history on Annie's passport, coming in and out of the country. It had taken her quite a while to gain access, but she was rolling now. She scrolled backward and found the time both Annie and her mother had spoken of. About three years ago there had been a three-month period where she had been in the United States, then she left for Japan. Sarah scrolled down and saw that Annie had been accurate. She generally was out of the country for three to four months and then back here for three to four weeks. Her trips had been steady for almost ten years with the exception of this three-month period. Annie wasn't kidding. The network had her on the fast track. Sarah leaned back in her chair just as the phone rang.

"Okay, what did my mother tell you?" Her voice had a smile in it.

"Me first. What did my mother tell you?" Sarah said.

"Not going to talk, huh? All right, how would you like to join me for tonight and three days in the Big Apple?"

"New York City?"

"Last I heard they were still calling it that."

"What's the occasion?"

"There's a network award program I have to be at Friday night. The boss himself was on the phone to let me know that this is not an option."

"I have to clear it with my guy here," Sarah said. There was no way would they let her go and she knew it. They'd hand Annie off to Josh Palmer. "Annie, let me call you back." She got up immediately and left for Don's office.

"No," was Don's first response. "Sarah, you know the drill. Josh will pick up on that end. How long again?"

"She leaves today and returns Saturday, in time for the party at Majer's." Sarah tried to keep a professional tone as she looked across the desk at her superior. "Josh is too new, and this is not what I had in mind when I said I wanted to get her out of town."

"You know the new rules. We have to hand the client off to the next available office. You're right about Josh, but they'll team him up with experienced people." He picked up the phone. "But we won't know if we don't ask, right?" Ten minutes later he gave up and set the phone down.

"No dice, girl, sorry. But still, she's out of town."

Sarah got up to go back to her office. "Right, but what if this turns out to be domestic, or whoever it is, and they just plain *follow*? I appreciate your effort, but I swear, if anything happens to her out there, I will go to New York City, whether the agency wants me to or not."

Sarah slammed into her chair in her office, knocking it back against the wall. Damn, if it wasn't one thing it was another. It should have been simple. Just take Annie to Green Bay. *Now she's going off to New York City and I can't even go.* She called Annie.

"What?" Annie said. "Why not?"

"Because, post nine-eleven, things just go from office to office in the FBI. I think you'll probably get Josh Palmer."

"That kid is so green he looks like an alien," Annie said with a disappointed laugh. "It would have been so much fun. Will you take me to the airport today and pick me up Saturday?"

"Wouldn't miss it. What time?"

"Now. I have exactly three hours."

"I'll be there. I'll call Mike's house and explain what's going on."

❖

Unlike the night Sarah had first picked Annie up, the airport was jammed. They battled their way through the crowd, and Scott put the luggage out for security. Sarah talked to the U.S. marshall that would be on the flight and introduced Annie. Cleared, they walked down to the gate where Annie would be boarding. "Will you watch the show Friday night?"

Sarah turned, hearing a whisper of shyness. "You shouldn't even have to ask," she said softly, away from Scott's ears. The airline announced the flight, and Annie picked up her backpack.

"Here I go again. Thanks for bringing me, and I'll see you Saturday?" Sarah's heart clutched. She'd miss her and was afraid for her.

"You know I'll be here, and you know how to reach me, Annie."

Annie turned to go but stopped, coming back to Sarah. She dropped her bag and hugged her. "I'll miss you, Agent Moore," she whispered in her ear and then was gone. Sarah stood at the window until the plane took off. She could still feel the warm brush of Annie's breath on her ear. Scott had waited with her, and they walked silently together back to the parking enclosure.

"I don't like not going with her," he finally said.

Sarah just shook her head. "She'll be back." She waited until he got in his car and left.

Driving away from the airport didn't feel good to Sarah. The Milwaukee sky had turned cloudy, and the lake that had been so blue this morning was now gray. At an intersection where she would normally turn to drive to the office, she turned the other way, driving out of the city and into the surrounding country. It was a good day to go to the stable and see how her horses were doing. She called and left Don a message that she would be out the rest of the day but would leave her phone on.

Rainbow's End sat on a corner, a bright yellow house with yellow barn and stable. Sarah parked then knocked on the back door, but no one answered so she walked toward the stables.

As she came around the corner, she could hear Sherry whistling, and despite her mood, she started to smile. "Hey, there," she said into the stable door. Sherry spun around and dropped her brush.

"Dammit, Moore," she grumbled, "remember how old I am. You'll give me a stroke." But she hugged Sarah. "I think I've lost my touch."

"Old FBI agents don't lose their touch," Sarah said, "just their fingerprints." She looked down the stable to see if she could see her horses.

"They're out in pasture," Sherry said. "You're not dressed to ride anyway." She cupped her hand under Sarah's chin. "What's this I see?"

"I just put someone on an airplane, and I'm going to miss her." Sarah looked down. "You've known me too long."

Sherry gave a disgusted snort, "Yes, we've known each other a long time, but that's a good thing, isn't it?" She tossed a brush at Sarah. "Here, help me finish this bad boy, and we'll go to the house."

Later, in the kitchen, they sat over a cup of coffee and talked. Sherry's partner owned a computer firm in Milwaukee and would be home soon. It didn't take much to persuade Sarah to stay for dinner. Sherry had retired from the agency four years ago and bought this farm about the same time Sarah had been transferred to Milwaukee. Sarah was helping set the table when Nina came in, smiling when she saw Sarah.

"Look what I found, Nina," Sherry said. "Someone claiming to be from the FBI."

"Thank God it's not you anymore," Nina said, giving both women a hug. "I wondered whose big black SUV was in our driveway. You're driving those these days?"

"No, that car belongs to someone else, not the agency." Sarah had driven Annie's car to the airport.

"Nice car," Nina said.

They caught up over dinner and settled into the living room over coffee.

"What's up, youngster?" Sherry asked, putting her arm around Nina. Sarah watched them and wished Annie was beside her.

"Just wanted to see you," she lied, "and the horses. If I'd thought of it, I'd have dressed for a ride. Bet those guys are a ton overweight."

"We ride them all the time, and you know that." Sherry lifted her eyebrows. "You didn't answer my question."

"Well," Sarah started and then stopped, realizing it had been just a little over two weeks. "I've got an assignment. A woman's name on a terrorist Web site, and they've assigned me."

"And?" Nina gave her a smile.

"And," Sarah echoed, "she's kind of fascinating."

"And," Sherry prompted, grinning, "you'd like to know her a bit better?"

Sarah felt her cheeks grow warm. "All right, you two, yes, I'd like to know her a bit better, and I think the feeling's mutual."

"Do we get to know who this is?" Nina asked.

"Sure, it's Annie Booker—" Sarah started, but Sherry interrupted.

"The correspondent from Iraq that just won the award today?"

Sarah nodded, surprised Sherry knew about the award.

"It was on the radio station that I was listening to in the stable. She's local and well known," Sherry explained.

"God, Sarah, she's gorgeous," Nina finished for Sherry, "but the word around town is that she's been tied up with some doctor for a long time. Wait, wasn't she injured there?"

"They've split, and the doctor's with some other doctor. I know a little about why, and I'm being careful of it. Still, they are definitely over. And yes, she was injured, a car bomb." She looked at both women, frowning at her. "What?"

"We've known each other for a long time, and you've never brought this kind of, well, whatever it is, you've never brought this to us."

Sarah gave a little shrug, uncertain how to explain.

"It's the look on your face," Sherry said. "You look almost, what, Nina, reverent? That struck-dumb look, and I've never seen you look that way, even around that blonde, what was her name?"

"Patricia."

"Heard from her lately?"

"Long time ago. This woman is different." Sarah finally said what her heart had been messing with since leaving the airport. "First of all, you know the agency's rules about clients, not to mention my own rules, never get involved. Then, there's the fact that she's good at her job, well known, as you said, and will probably go back to Iraq."

Both women sitting across from her laughed. "This is a first, Sarah. Usually you're out here, hiding from someone. I'll be darned, Sherry. You're right. She's been struck." Nina laughed again as she said it.

Sherry gave her an encouraging smile. "Tell us about her."

"She's incredible." Sarah knew she was blushing but forged on. "Best sense of humor, and brains all over. You're right, Nina, she's gorgeous, but she doesn't seem to notice, and she laughed at me when I called her a celebrity. She didn't even tell me that she'd won an award. One of my agents told me. I've met her family, and I swear they've cloned my parents. Her mother is a psychiatrist at the women's clinic downtown, you know the place, and her father has a huge nursery business."

Sarah stopped talking, seeing her two friends staring intently at her, then she babbled on. "And she plays serious golf and likes to fish. What are the odds?"

"Charlene's Angels, right?" Nina said and Sarah nodded. "I do their computers, Sarah, and I've met Hannah Booker. Neat lady. No kidding, that's Annie Booker's mother? I never even thought about that. Well, that's just crazy because I know her sister too, Molly."

"Don't you agree Hannah's a cool lady? I haven't met Molly."

"Sure is, but I don't know the reporter, other than seeing her on TV. This is kind of a big deal, I agree." Nina looked at Sherry. "They're good businesswomen and down to earth. They actually listen to you when you talk to them."

It occurred to Sarah that Annie did that too. Always listened, really listened, when they talked. Her heart thudded a bit.

"I'm not sure what to do," she said softly.

❖

After two twelve-hour days with the network, Annie was tired. Her suite at the hotel was littered with papers, clothes, and empty coffee cups. She wandered around, putting things where they belonged and throwing trash in the garbage. She spoke to the FBI agent sitting in the larger room in the network's suites and walked back to the kitchen, picking up a bottle of wine. Everything was ready for tomorrow night, and she looked at her dress hanging on a door. Finally, she headed for the shower and decided against clothes when she got out. She grabbed a blanket off the bed, wrapping it around her, and went to the table in the suite's bedroom. She collapsed into a comfortable chair and sat in the dark, staring out at the clear, cold sky. She counted the different countries where she had sat and stared at the night sky. Her arm ached from today's workout, and she missed her home, the lake, and something else. Sarah.

Annie had called Rebecca and then her parents earlier, but she'd waited to call Sarah. She called her own house, wondering if Sarah would stay there, but no one answered. Annie reached for the wine bottle, poured half a glass, and then moved her laptop across the table. Sarah's card was in the top pocket, and she pulled it out, looking at all the numbers listed. She hitched the blanket up over her bare shoulders and called Sarah's home phone.

It rang twice before it was picked up, then dropped with a loud thud, more noise, and then a voice said, "Moore."

"Hey, super sleuth, what's up?"

"Who's this?" a sleepy voice answered, but Annie could hear the smile.

"Someone who misses talking to you," Annie said with a soft laugh, twisting the stem of the glass around on the table.

"No one I know. What're you up to?"

"Around five-foot-eight." Annie shut her eyes, seeing wavy black hair and beautiful black lashes over brown eyes.

"Sorry about dropping the phone. Are you ready for tomorrow night?"

"I've done two days, twelve hours straight, shooting promos, fighting over the speech, clothing, and a zillion other things that won't amount to anything after our few minutes on live television. I'm ready for it to be over with, but I get to play tomorrow. I'm going to have lunch with my producer's wife and then spend some quality time at the art galleries. Ah, heaven." Annie pulled the blanket up around her again. "What are you doing?"

"I fell asleep over one of your books on Islam. Pretty exciting stuff, right? How's your arm?"

"Fine, but thanks for asking. I've been faithful to my exercises in the hotel gym, but it's a pain. Just for the record, Josh Palmer lost me for the whole afternoon yesterday, and I sent security after him." Annie laid her head on her arms.

"Annie, other than that happening, anything I should know about? He's just at the beginning of his career. Is there someone else working with him?"

Annie heard the change of tone in Sarah's voice and was quiet for a moment. "No, all quiet on the eastern front. Two older men have been with him, except for yesterday. Sarah, he's just untried. I'm sorry. I shouldn't complain."

"Yes, you should. I'll be at a friend's house tomorrow night to watch you on television."

Annie's head came up and she sat straighter. A friend? "You have a friend? Oh wait, Sarah, I mean I'm glad you'll be at a friend's house tomorrow night." She gave a little laugh. "God, did I really say that?"

Sarah laughed with her. "When you get back, we'll get together. I've known these two women over ten years. One of them was my instructor when I was in training. It's the ranch where I board my horses. Her partner has a business in Milwaukee that does work for Charlene's Angels. She knows your mom and your sister Molly."

"Really, Mom and Molly? Who is she?"

"Nina Webster, owns her own computer business."

"I've actually seen her. Tell her to remember the ad that Molly did for her, about the bears. I did the artwork. She'll remember, Sarah, and I'm sure we met when she came in to review the ad. Attractive lady."

"What time do I pick you up Saturday? And we have the party at Majer's that night."

"Around noon, Saturday," Annie said, wishing it was Saturday already. "You'll still be at my house that night, right?"

"Absolutely, and you know what you forgot? Do I get to see the painting?" Sarah joked just before they hung up, making them laugh.

Annie finished the wine and checked out the moon one last time before she pulled the drapes and got into bed. She lay there, thinking about her painting. At first, she had considered doing the face in a half shadow, giving it a little intrigue. On second thought, she wanted the face fully into the viewer's eyes. Those eyes and that mouth. She smiled. Yeah. That face should be seen completely.

❖

Sarah watched Annie's show with Nina and Sherry.

"Did you find that crow statue?" Sarah asked Sherry.

Sherry chuckled. "Yes, it's in the kitchen in the box on the counter. Don't forget it tonight."

"It's for Annie. What are the chances we'd both like crows?"

Sherry groaned. "Crows, God."

They quieted as the show started. Sarah's throat was tight as she watched. *This would be a perfect moment for something to happen, people coming and going. You wouldn't want obvious crowd control on television.* It was bad for public relations. She wondered who was with Annie tonight, who would take her home and stand watch at the hotel. Her mind fretted as she watched images float across the screen including the promos for Annie.

The network had won five awards, three connected to Annie's story. When it was time for Annie's award, she looked every inch the professional she was, but also the woman Sarah knew. She wore a revealing pale yellow dress with transparent yellow sleeves flared at the wrist. Sarah would have bet the sleeves were to hide her arm.

"Beautiful dress, but, oh baby, fashion today certainly doesn't hide much." Sherry chuckled.

"Look how bright she is," Nina said.

Annie's speech was short, beginning with thanks and recognition of fellow correspondents that had been murdered while they were in Iraq. More than any other conflict in modern times. She also talked a bit about the desperate conditions in Iraq, the deteriorating situation, and loss of control. She ended with a few obviously heartfelt words about Jack Keegan. Before Sarah knew it, Annie was walking back toward her group with the statue in her hand, handing it to them, laughing. Sherry was right. That dress didn't hide much. Sarah wondered if the FBI was even there. Her stomach clenched.

"Your mouth is open, Moore," Sherry commented dryly.

"I'm trying not to drool." Sarah laughed with her friends. "Have you ever seen her artwork? Stop into the women's clinic and look at it. And she's an award-winning author, but did I mention—" She looked at Sherry and Nina grinning at her. Damn. "Okay, enough. I'm babbling."

"She gave a nice speech," Nina said. "Drew very little attention to herself."

"Want to help me put the barn away for the night?" Sherry raised her eyebrows at Sarah.

Sarah nodded and stretched. Work would get rid of the energy she'd been accumulating. She hugged Nina, thanked her for the evening, and looked for the box with the carving of the crow.

Later, finishing the barn, they sat on the tack box talking.

"Well, when do we get to meet her?" Sherry asked.

"We have a party to attend tomorrow night, and the minute it's over I'm taking her away from here. Going up to Rosy's in Green Bay. Could you get away and join us up there?"

"Maybe. I'll ask Nina, but her schedule's pretty full. Still, it would be fun. I love that wild poker they play, and both of us really enjoyed that weekend."

Sarah nodded. "You've seen me be a lot of things, Sherry, but never this. Just for openers, I've never even considered stepping over the line with a client. I just can't settle down."

"You never break rules." She shook her head. "You know this may not be possible. She looks as if she's just hitting her stride, and it appears she's going to be recognized for what she does. The rest of her talents may just be what rounds out the person."

"She seems to be watching me, interested, and I'm certainly watching her. Something's happening between us."

"You're at the beginning. Stay in touch with me as this goes along, but right now, just enjoy. I assume she'll go back to Iraq when she's recovered and the case is resolved. By the way, what's the level of danger?"

Sarah shook her head. "A lot more than she'd like to believe, but when you've been where she's been, I understand her attitude. She showed me some pretty raw photos from Afghanistan the other day, and tonight she mentioned the people who were killed who worked with her. I've never been involved with a client who has come out of such a perilous situation into this kind of threat. That man, Jack Keegan from her network, shot right next to her, and then the bomb. She just shakes her head at me when I talk about it. She's so used to living around fear that she's not your average citizen, but she definitely doesn't like it in her home. Who would? And you're right, Sherry, she probably will go back to Iraq. Although, God, did you hear what she said about journalists becoming targets?"

Sarah stopped talking and watched her breath in the cold night air. That's exactly what she felt Don was doing, dangling Annie out there, like a target.

"In her home?" Sherry asked.

"There was someone in her home who knows how to get by her very sophisticated alarm system and trash our first computer. I spent this week running down leads from our domestic terrorism group in Virginia and came up blank. Truthfully, we're pretty much spitting in the wind right now. Well, we have one lead." Sarah thought for a moment. "Something else. She's restless and feels kind of isolated to me. There's a sort of fight-or-flight kind of thing around her. You've worked with veterans. Wouldn't this be similar?"

Sherry nodded. "Is she seeing a therapist?"

"I think she has, the first week she was home. In the beginning, before the break-in, she certainly didn't want the FBI around her either. I'm not sure she does now." She told Sherry about the day Annie had manipulated Scott to take her around the city and the party in her basement.

Sherry chuckled. "Nina would have done something like that. You've always had good instincts, Moore. That's one of the reasons that I recommended you for profiling. But throw personal feelings into the mix, and it's a mess. Remember, this is how I met Nina. She was my client, and I'll never regret it, although I almost lost my job over it."

"Don and I argued—really fought—over getting her out of here. He doesn't want to tip our hand. I'm about ready to jump out of my skin."

"Don Ahrens? Haven't thought about him for a while." She tossed some tack onto the shelf and sat down next to Sarah. "You'll do what you have to. After it's all said and done, it really doesn't matter."

Sarah stood. "She matters. A lot."

CHAPTER FOURTEEN

The next morning, Don and Sarah drove around the Majer home before Annie's plane came in. The home, north of the university campus, sat back from the road and was surrounded by trees. They took photos of the grounds surrounding the house to go with the maps and structural blueprints they had posted in Don's office.

"How can he afford this on a professor's salary?"

"I was just thinking the same thing," Sarah said as they made one last pass at the property. "I know you've had his bank records pulled."

"Sam has the information, and when we meet tonight, you'll get a look at all of it. You're on your way to the airport?"

Sarah nodded, feeling a little rattle of excitement. "A lot of this feels wrong about Majer, doesn't it? Or maybe it's family money. Something he brought into the United States."

Don shook his head. "Not according to the records we have. By the way, those photos from Ms. Booker are creating quite a stir. Everyone believes that one of the men in the photos is the anti-American cleric Amer al-Sadr and two of his pals. They still haven't identified the man you both saw that night, but they're working on it. The thing with Amer is powerful and I wonder how Jack Keegan got those photos. Sarah, it may have been what got him killed."

"That man we saw might be connected to Amer? Christ, Don. What does Homeland Security say?"

"They haven't told us one damned thing. As usual. Where are you taking Ms. Booker after tonight?"

"Up to Green Bay, to Rosy's house." She looked at him, not hiding her unhappiness with the situation. "I feel like we've put her out there like a target, and you know it."

"Maybe. But I couldn't see any other way to do this. This is two-plus year's work, and I know we're going to nail them tonight."

"That doesn't make it right."

"That's why I had you document my position on your reports."

"Great. I get to be right if something happens. That's not much consolation, Don. I'll be glad when tonight's over. My instincts are screaming."

Don sighed and turned the car toward downtown Milwaukee. "There's something going on, and it's not the Web site. I think it's the photos and they're using the Web site like a big neon light, broadcasting her name out there. They'll blame Jaish al-Basca for whatever they want to do."

Sarah was quiet, thinking of the three-to-four-month gap in Annie's life that she'd been working on. "There is something else, Don, three years ago. She didn't say any more other than there was some serious trouble. I checked it out. Even talked with the network, but all they would say was that she was 'off assignment,' and I mean that's all. Apparently, it's personal, but I'll ask her again tonight."

"No, Sarah, don't ask. *Get* the information."

"I got the search as far as her going into Saudi Arabia but couldn't find any documentation of her leaving the country. Then I caught up with her entering and leaving Switzerland about a month later, but I can't find out where she was while she was there." Annie was not deliberately hiding information. She just hadn't realized how important it might be.

The airport was as crowded as the day Sarah had put Annie on the airplane. Sarah looked down the concourse as she held her badge at security once again. Walking down to Annie's gate, she saw TV cameras and news reporters. How did they get back here, to this part of the airport, she wondered, looking around. You couldn't do this without some kind of security clearance, and her adrenaline shot up.

People were already coming off the plane, and when Annie came through Sarah started toward her, but cameras and news people made a wall around Annie. *Damn, I should have had one of the team here with me,* she thought. Feeling more frustrated with each passing minute,

Sarah swept the crowd with her gaze and then saw a familiar face, a tall woman with dark hair. She tried to move for a better look, but the woman disappeared into the crowd and Sarah lost her. Pondering the face, she looked at Annie again. Annie moved off to the side so other people could get by. She was answering questions, laughing, and obviously, she knew most of these people. Her gaze connected with Sarah's, and she had a heartbeat's silence. Then Annie looked away, answering another question. Twenty minutes later, the crowd broke up and Annie moved to Sarah.

"Sorry, I wasn't expecting that."

Sarah took her backpack. "It's hell to be famous, right?"

Annie stopped and gave Sarah an even stare. "Don't say that to me. It's not true."

"Many more awards like that, with national TV coverage, and it's going to be, whether you like it or not."

"Just the locals, wanting their moment. I've known many of them for a long time, worked with some of them. It's just a professional courtesy." Annie leaned over for her other bag. "Come on. Let's get out of here."

Sarah frowned. The slip in security could have turned into an ugly scene. She paid the security office a visit on the way out of the airport.

They stopped at Annie's favorite deli downtown, picking up lunch to go. Scott and three other agents were waiting for them at the house and they helped with the luggage. Finally, the two women sat down at the big oak table in the kitchen.

Annie dug into her food, watching Sarah, finally asking, "What do you have to do now? I have some time before the party to unpack or whatever."

"Go home, change my clothes, and have a quick meeting with the group that will be with us tonight. This is so important to the investigation. If we can get evidence, any evidence, we've got them, thanks to you."

"Then you'll come back, pick me up, and we'll go together?"

Sarah laid her fork down and looked at Annie, taking a deep breath before she spoke. "All I want to do is get tonight over with and get you away from here."

Sarah finally smiled at her and Annie's eyes lit up. "I missed you, gumshoe."

"Annie, I'm sorry I'm cranky. Scenes like that at the airport make me crazy. There's no way to protect you. It was just me, without backup." She remembered the dark-haired woman's face in the crowd and thought about it for a minute. "I enjoyed the awards, but the network didn't send us the film, and I'd really like to watch it."

"It was a longer format, a documentary, so it wouldn't be in my regular reports. You didn't get any of my specials?" Sarah shook her head. "They're in my office, the shelf above my desk. Bill sends me a copy of them, and also I'll get a disc of this ceremony. Anytime you want to see it, just take it off the shelf, but I warn you, it's like the Annie Booker marathon. You'll get tired of them."

Never, Sarah thought. "I'd appreciate it, especially the one you got the award for, about the Navajo. Also, very pretty dress and nice speech." She paused and then grinned. "As a matter of fact, that dress, Annie…"

Annie started to laugh. "Oh, don't even say it. Ellen Kennedy, one of the senior producers, always does my shopping. More 'me' than dress, right?"

"Are you tired?"

"No, I'm used to this. Always on the go."

"All right, don't get too unpacked. We're leaving right after the party tonight. We'll come home and change, then we're off. I'm going to be very strict with everyone, most of all you. We have to be very careful, please."

"Sarah, I just can't connect Jaish al-Basca or its Web site here in America, but if it's not them, who is it?" Annie looked upset. "I feel as if I'm back in Baghdad." She gave an exasperated sigh. "However, I promised myself in New York that I will do whatever you think I should. Let's get this over with."

"I need all the help you can give me."

Sarah hung the yellow dress in the closet, surrounded by Annie's light scent. She took a deep breath, then carried a small bag into the bathroom, spotting the gold statue sitting on the counter. She walked into Annie's office, holding it out to her.

Annie looked up. "Sorry. I meant to bring it in here. Just put it up there with those other things, please." She pointed to a shelf where some plaques and statues were arranged. Sarah put it on the shelf and paused to read the awards.

"Look at all these things," Sarah said, "and golf trophies in the basement."

"Does that impress you?"

"No, but you sure do, and I have to get going or I'll miss the meeting. Scott and the others will walk the house and stay until we're ready to go." Annie smiled. "I left something on the kitchen table for you. It was stored at Sherry's, and I thought of you. I want you to have it, please. I'm glad you're home. I'll be back in less than three hours."

❖

Annie left the luggage out on the big bed, unpacking most of it into the dresser and into the closet. She stood and looked at the small getaway bag and repacked it into one bigger bag before finally wandering out into the house.

Annie talked to Scott and the agents for a bit and then made coffee. The box that Sarah had left felt heavy as Annie carried it down the hall to start a bath. Sarah had written the word "Survivor" on the top of the box, and Annie slit the tape to open it. The business card taped to the inside of the flap said Rainbow's End. It was where Sarah kept her horses, her friend's business. Carefully pushing the packing aside, she pulled out a large carved wooden crow poised to fly, black with blue highlights. The wings were enormous. The delicate details on the bird were so realistic that Annie touched one to see if it was a feather. It was just like Sarah. Unusual.

She stretched out in the bath water and she closed her eyes. While in New York, she had run into Karin, the woman who had given them shelter in Switzerland after the hospital. They had talked for more than two hours over food and drinks, and Karin asked about Mary. Her kind eyes had asked more as Annie had explained the emotional tangle when they returned, and Karin had nodded and said, "I thought as much."

"But, Karin, Mary stayed there even when I wanted her to go. It would have been better to have ended it right then, not drag it out for three more years."

"She felt responsible for you, Annie. I could see it. I'm not sure she wanted the responsibility, but she couldn't stop it."

"I should have ended it right there."

The last thing Karin had said to her was, "If you're still thinking about Mary, put yourself in her place. What would you have done?"

Annie let her body sink completely under the warm water, and she exhaled slowly, blowing bubbles up to the surface. *Karin was right, she thought,* sitting up in the tub. *I would have done the same thing, tried everything to make it right and make it go away. What's a little cement in my arm, compared to that?* Closing her eyes, she remembered the hospital. Mary's blue eyes, always wet with tears. The delicate lavender walls. Every day she had memorized the cracks and marks in the plaster, just trying to hold on. The color had melted with the drugs as each day was just another breakdown. They had locked the doors behind them as they left.

Annie shivered in the warm water. She had to talk with Sarah. Tonight, on the way to Green Bay, would be a good time. She pulled in a ragged breath. Glancing up at the crow, she thought of the media crush at the airport today. She had enjoyed herself, until she had seen the unhappy expression on Sarah's face. *I'll bet my life upsets her, just like it does Mary and Rebecca. I'm not making her job easy. This job is my choice, but it's pulling everyone around me into it. Maybe it's time for me to pull away from the job. Jack always said never duck the truth, look it right in the eye, but how can you look it right in the eye when you can't see it? He never saw the people who shot him, and they didn't care about his truth. Their truth is terrorism and how much money they could make off this war.*

She thought of the possibilities. *It's not the Web site. The FBI doesn't think it's anyone local, a stalker, and they don't think it's involved with the car bomb.* She went through the last years in her mind. Almost every single piece she had done could be interpreted as controversial, especially the series she and Jack had put together two years ago. Sarah said the FBI had gone over every report that had generated feedback to the network, as had Bill Simpson from New York City. They even had a group on the East Coast working on domestic terrorism. *Then what the hell is this?* She groaned and clenched her fists.

She sat up, opening the tap for more hot water. *This is crazy. I'm not going to give up my life for this, whatever it is. Bring it on, boys, I will win. I know fear as well as you do. It's like breathing.*

Annie reached up and angrily grabbed the shampoo, ducking under the water, soaking her hair, and then scrubbing it, hard.

❖

Sheikha hung her clothes in the closet, trading them for a dress. She pulled it out and hung it in the bathroom. She had gone shopping with her mother when she had bought this. It was the last contact she'd had with her mother, the last time she'd been able to talk with her.

Smiling, she turned the shower on. Sheikha missed her mother's warmth, her bright mind. She missed her two little sisters. She adjusted the temperature of the water, then stepped inside. At least this country had dependable water and food. She worried about her family and knew they hadn't been getting the food or care they needed. They had tried for several years to get them out of Baghdad, but because of their father, they could not get a visa for the family. Finally, they had found a way. She would see them soon. The plan was already working.

The reporter had looked so happy at the airport this morning, and she thought about the government person that had spotted her. She wondered if she'd remembered her from the meeting on the street or the clinic. They'd probably have to kill her as well. She and Hamel had discussed involving the government in this directly. She wasn't as confident as he was, but if they could get their hands on the photos they could get on with their life and their business.

CHAPTER FIFTEEN

S arah slid into her chair at the meeting, her mind focused on the evening ahead. Don had merged the illegal immigration with Annie's case so they could all work together tonight at Majer's party. Sam Coates, her counterpart on the illegal immigration case, nodded and slid papers across the desk toward her. She read over the financial information on Dr. Majer, every muscle in her body feeling tight and tense. Rolling her head to stretch her neck and shoulders, Sarah finally straightened, exhaling slowly. She trusted Don Ahrens as much as anyone she worked with, but this still felt dangerous to her and she thought about the trip out of town after the party.

"How many people inside with me?" she asked

"You're the point on this one, as you'll be with her most of the time, and there'll be four other people inside with you. Everyone got that?" Don looked around to make sure everyone understood. "Scott will be shadowing you, and I'll be outside. I'm sure some of the core people involved with our problem are going to be there." He took a long drink of coffee, "Okay, that's five people inside and four cars at the exits."

Don held up his hand. "Two things. This is not only our opportunity to get the evidence we need to finally shut this group down, but it's also a dangerous moment for Ms. Booker. Some of you have seen the photographs that tie her to a large player in Iraq, but we have to wait for Homeland Security to confirm. Whether they confirm or not, we know someone's out there, been around her, so be vigilant. Everyone." He pointed out the exits marked on the maps. "If you get the word from anyone, seal everything immediately. No one leaves, and I don't care who it is, they stay. We've all done this before, so just be smart."

He turned back to Sarah. "Tell the agents at Ms. Booker's to wait for me at the Majers', all right?" Sarah nodded and followed the others out of the room.

❖

Annie heard Sarah yell hello down the hallway. Still in her stocking feet, Annie walked from the bedroom. She caught Sarah's reflection in the big French doors. Annie stopped, unable to move her eyes. Sarah's new light gray suit, blended silk threaded with silver, shone in the light. The fabric held her fit body splendidly, black hair a perfect counterpoint to the lightness she created. A white silk top under the coat gleamed, and silver sparkled at her ears as she turned. Annie stood, spellbound at the sight.

"Am I early?" Sarah asked.

"No, I'm just not ready." Annie finally took a breath, walked toward her, and turned. "Will you zip me up, please?" Everything in her wanted to turn to Sarah and fold into her.

"What a pretty color, Annie," she said.

❖

The bit of moon that had hung in the midnight blue sky earlier was covered by dark clouds as they drove to Dr. Majer's. A powerful wind battered Annie's car. Blowing snow made driving slow. Rebecca was sitting in the back giving new meaning to the term "backseat driver" as Sarah negotiated the city streets. Annie thought about the drive to Green Bay after the party, wishing she didn't have to talk to Sarah and tell her what she never wanted to talk about.

"Slider, Sarah knows where we're going," Annie grumbled.

"What did you call her?" Sarah asked.

"Nothing, she didn't say anything," Rebecca said, poking Annie in the back.

Annie grinned at Sarah. "It's just a nickname, *Slider,* but she won't let me tell her kids about it."

Rebecca started pulling on her gloves as they neared the house. "You can tell them anytime you want, Annie, but I warn you that Shelly would love new bedtime stories."

"Is this, what did you call it, lake effect snow?" Sarah asked.

Rebecca and Annie laughed. "No, this is the real deal, a good old-fashioned fast blizzard out of the northwest. If it was lake effect, it would be coming in from the lake," Annie explained. "This has been predicted for two days. I saw it on the news in New York City."

"How do you people cope with this every year?" Sarah said.

"It's just part of Wisconsin," Rebecca said. "When you grow up with it, you respect it but live with it."

Sarah pulled the SUV in behind a line of cars and cut the motor. "All right, let's run over the story." The wind rocked the car briefly and snow melted down the window in silver streaks.

"I'm a friend of Annie's that you've just met, right, Rebecca? And, Annie, I work for the government but was just transferred to Milwaukee, and you're not sure what I'm doing now. How's that? If anyone presses, just have them talk with me."

"I could tell them that you catch bullets with your—" Annie started to say, but Sarah put her hand over her mouth.

"Don't even think of it, Booker," she said.

"Well, I for one would like to hear that story." Rebecca chuckled, getting out.

Annie and Sarah followed, both laughing. The snow pelted them as they struggled to open the door against a sudden hard gust.

The house was a warm contrast to the storm raging outside. It was filled with a low hum of voices mixed with music and a pleasant aroma. The professor and his wife greeted them, and Annie handed over the folder from Baghdad. The FBI had gone over each scrap of paper before they'd given it back to Annie. Sarah looked around, reviewing the background she had on the Majers. The financial report had shown money, lots of it, but just as it came in every month, a lot went out. *He's just like a big bank, distributing money to terrorism in America*, Sarah thought. He'd been a respected professor in Iraq, then Germany, and finally here in the U.S., but nothing that earned this kind of opulence. He and his wife were gray haired, and Sarah knew their children were grown and gone, all into professional lives in the United States. She watched Dr. Majer disappear into a side room with Annie's folder and return moments later without it. The surveillance made Sarah feel more assured, but she was flooded with edgy adrenaline, wishing the evening was over and they were on their way out of town.

They passed a trio playing classical music as they made their way to the bar. Sarah asked for a sparkling water, but Annie and Rebecca were drinking something amber.

"What is that?" Sarah asked, pointing with her chin at Annie's glass.

"Something very Wisconsin." Annie held her drink up. "Brandy."

Rebecca moved to Sarah's side and said, "Would you like me to point out people that I know or teach with?" Sarah nodded and watched a tall, distinguished man come out of the crowd toward Annie. "That's our university chancellor." He shook Annie's hand and they talked for a moment. "I hope he's trying to talk her into teaching here next year. We have an opening at a high level in our journalism school, and I'd like to see her consider it." Rebecca took a drink and looked at Sarah. "She's ready for a break. What do you think?"

Sarah studied Rebecca, remembering Annie's marriage proposal story. She shook her head. "The network loves her, Rebecca."

Rebecca frowned. "Her head's on sideways from the car bomb and the other thing. She's scattered."

"What do you mean?"

"It's like she's running in another gear. She's usually relaxed and low key when she gets home, but not this time. I understand that the injury and her house being broken into is not the most calming thing to come home to, but it's more than that."

"Rebecca, I don't know what to say. She's excellent at what she does and has quite a future. You should hear what the network says to us, and now the award. Have you ever seen her like this before?"

"I just want her to consider getting away from the danger. She's always been talented, and not just in this field. She could be every bit as good in another field."

Sarah turned to check Annie's whereabouts, but she couldn't see her.

"Did you see where Annie's gone to?" she asked Rebecca and they looked out at the crowd. Thinking of the slate blue suit with the pale yellow top that Annie was wearing, Sarah moved quickly toward the large living room, past tall candles burning in metal holders sitting on the floor. They left a delightful scent in the air as Sarah walked by, but they were practically the only lights in the room. She walked behind a long leather couch and took a sip of water, heart racing. *Where the hell is she?* She scanned a group close to the fireplace and found her, speaking to a group of men and women. Sarah watched Annie morph from casual to professional as she talked about Iraqi politics, choosing her words carefully. What a talent Annie had, the ability to get attention immediately just by speaking. Sarah watched the people listen and lean toward her.

"Intriguing, isn't she?" a soft male voice said behind her, startling Sarah. She glanced over her shoulder. The accent was foreign and its owner was a somewhat familiar handsome young man. Sarah nodded at him.

"I saw you come in with Ms. Booker and Dr. Larsen," he continued. "Are you here in an official capacity?"

"Pardon me?" Sarah turned toward him.

"I am asking, what is it you Americans say, are you Ms. Booker's caretaker?"

I wish, Sarah thought, holding out her hand. "I don't believe we've been introduced. I'm Sarah Moore."

The man ignored her hand but bowed slightly. "It is inappropriate where I come from to touch a woman's hand, or any part of her body, particularly when she is unattended. My apology."

"Unattended?" Sarah asked.

"Women in my country do not leave the residence without a male."

Sarah turned slightly away from him, looking back at Annie, who was now looking at her. "No, I am not her bodyguard, just a friend."

Annie said something to the group and started toward them.

"Have you met Prince Abdel?" Annie asked in a voice as cold as the wind outside, sending a tingle up Sarah's spine.

"We were just talking," Sarah said, unconsciously moving slightly between Annie and the man, into the unsettled air about them.

"Ms. Booker, we meet again, and it is my pleasure." He bowed again.

Annie wasn't smiling as she turned to Sarah. "The prince and I met several years ago in Saudi Arabia." Sarah felt as if she could touch Annie's hostility.

The prince cleared his throat and said, "I wonder, could I have a private word with you?"

"Shoot." Annie lapsed into slang, never taking her eyes from him.

He looked pointedly at Sarah. "We can talk in front of Sarah," Annie said in the same distant, low voice. "We're friends."

"Ah," he said and repeated "friends" with a different emphasis. Annie put her hand firmly on Sarah's shoulder. Sarah watched the play of emotions on his face. "Very well, I wish to apologize, Ms. Booker."

Annie's hand on Sarah's shoulder increased its grip and Sarah looked over at her. Annie's face was remote, quiet, as if the prince had not spoken.

Finally, he spoke into the accumulating silence. "My mother has made the trip with me. Would you join us for dinner? She is over there." He gestured at a woman across the room. Annie and Sarah looked through the low lights just as a tall, attractive woman looked toward them, nodded, and smiled. Sarah immediately knew the face. It was the woman in the airport this morning, but also, from somewhere else. The young prince was certainly shorter than his mother.

"Thank you, Abdel, it's not possible." Annie abruptly broke the silence. "Please excuse us."

She turned her back to the man and spoke to Sarah. "Let's boogie, girl, I'm hungry." They moved to the dining room, and Sarah raised her eyebrows at Annie.

"I'll explain later. It's part of the story about Saudi Arabia that I didn't get to tell you earlier this week, and it's not a nice story. He is about the last person I would expect to see in this house, and if I'd ever thought he would be here, I'd have talked with you about it. When we leave tonight, I promise to tell you," Annie answered Sarah's unspoken question. "Have you seen Rebecca?"

Sarah shook her head, and they looked at a tempting display of food before them. They filled their plates and moved to an unoccupied table.

Sarah noticed Annie's hands were shaking. "That man, Prince whatever, certainly looks familiar to me."

Annie grimaced. "When I was in New York City I heard that his photo was in several news magazines last month. And his mother looks familiar to me."

"Damn," Sarah said, "I remember now. The French girl that he supposedly assaulted over there. I thought he was in prison. His mother looks familiar to me too, Annie, from the airport, this morning. You've seen her too?"

Annie swung her eyes to Sarah. "Yes, but I can't remember where I've seen her. He's not in prison because it happened over there, and men get away with anything. It honestly doesn't make any difference that he's a prince or a Saudi, he'll never be prosecuted," Annie said, her face bleak. "Let me assure you, Sarah, he's deadly. Personally, I loathe him." She was quiet for a moment. "What I can't figure out is why he's here, in this house. Politically, he and the good doctor ought to be sworn enemies, not to mention their religious differences."

Sarah nodded, thinking of her research she'd been hammering away at all week long. She looked around the room for her surveillance.

"Is it possible it's not political? That it might be personal?" she asked.

"I don't know. You might be right. What else could it be?"

"This is a long shot, but what if it's family?" Annie raised her eyebrows in a question, so Sarah continued, "I mean, do these families marry one another?"

Annie shook her head. "Very unlikely. I've never seen or heard of it. Or to put it another way, it would be a sort of Romeo and Juliet kind of thing."

"But not impossible?"

"Nothing's impossible, just unlikely." Annie leaned closer, the familiar impish smile on her face. "But it wouldn't hurt to check it out, and while you're at it, check out the prince's mother, for both of us."

Sarah grinned back. "And so, since you have designated me your 'friend' to the prince"—she held her fingers up, making quote marks in the air—"what would you like me to do?"

"I'd like you to be resourceful. For example, background on the prince and his mother. Look at all the resources at your fingertips. We've almost been living together. Doesn't that make you at least a friend?"

Their eyes locked for a moment, and Sarah thought, *Lord, no wonder you're successful.* "And, I suppose, share this information with you?"

Annie grinned again. "Of course, but wouldn't this come under collecting data anyway?" She reached out to touch her and said, "Sarah—"

"Well, here you are." Rebecca's hand fell on Annie's shoulder, causing her to jump. "I suppose you ate without me?"

"Yes, and try the beef, it's wonderful." Annie's face turned up to Rebecca.

"Did you see the prince?" she asked, and Annie gave her a sudden look. Rebecca hesitated, the smile leaving her face. "I met his mother, and what a surprise she is."

"What do you mean?" Sarah asked.

"Well, she works in Germany, not your-stay-at-home Saudi mother for sure."

"Germany?" Annie frowned. "How does that work? Saudi wives and mothers don't work out of the country. Did she introduce him to you? She certainly looks familiar to both Sarah and me. I swear I'm losing my memory. First the man at Sam's store, and—" Annie stopped. "That's it, Sarah. The man at Sam's, that's who she is."

Sarah was confused, and they all looked out into the crowd in the dim light, trying to find the woman they were talking about.

Sarah saw her first. "There she is, by Dr. Majer. I don't know. She looks like a woman to me."

"What have you been drinking besides brandy tonight?" Rebecca teased.

"All right, you two, I know this is crazy, but I'm telling you, that is the twin to the man I saw at Sam's."

"Fine, a twin. That's different," Sarah said. Annie was right. The woman looked a great deal like the man they had run into at Sam's. She frowned. Where on earth had she seen the woman other than the airport this morning?

"Anyway, she didn't introduce me to the prince. She just pointed him out, across the room," Rebecca said and then looked at Annie again. "I'm starving, but I need to wash my hands first."

"Ms. Booker?" a woman's voice said and all three women turned. A short, gray-haired lady was smiling at Annie.

Annie stood quickly. "Nyalia. My goodness, it's Dr. Majer's sister, the one I just interviewed in Baghdad, Sarah. The photos, remember?"

"How nice to see you," the woman said and reached for Annie's hand.

"I am surprised to see you, Nyalia." Annie took her hand with a smile. "How did you get out of Baghdad?"

"Prince Abdel and his family helped us. I brought my two daughters as well."

"That is wonderful." Annie introduced Sarah and Rebecca to her. "Have you eaten yet?"

"No, I was just going to wash up first and then join my brother and his wife. Will you walk with me?"

"We were just going that way," Annie said and they moved through the crowd to a quieter part of the house. There were several women standing in the hallway, waiting to get into the bathroom, so they fell into line as well. Annie talked to the woman about her trip. Sarah walked away and checked in with her surveillance, then walked back to the line, listening to the conversation. Rebecca went in as the line shortened, and Annie asked about Prince Abdel and his mother.

"How did you happen to know him?" she asked.

"He came to the house and offered his help," Nyalia said. "I had never met the man before, but he had known my husband. They made all the arrangements, and it was a lovely trip. I am so relieved to be finally away from there safely. Isn't this a beautiful home?"

"I'm happy to see you here," Annie said and told her to go ahead as Rebecca came out of the bathroom. After the door closed Annie turned to Sarah. "I can't believe that. Why would someone of the prince's stature bother with an engineer's wife? An Iraqi engineer's wife?"

Sarah shook her head. "Annie, you're certain they're not related?"

"No, but how could they be?" The conversation ended as Dr. Majer's sister came out. Annie looked back at Sarah and raised her eyebrows in a question as she entered the bathroom.

Rebecca's stomach growled and she grinned. "I'm hungry." Sarah looked at her watch, then at Rebecca.

"She'll be out in a minute," Rebecca said and then added, "I'm going back for my food. See you in the dinning room."

Sarah nodded as Dr. Majer's sister walked away with Rebecca. Hearing the wind howl outside, she moved to the window, watching the snow for a few moments, and then she stepped back to the bathroom door, rapping lightly. "Annie?" She looked at Scott, who was watching her, standing at the edge of the crowd.

Nothing stirred, so Sarah knocked again and tried the handle, but it was locked. "Annie, are you all right?" When there was no response, she put her body against the door and quickly broke the lock. The bathroom was empty, the noise of the winter storm echoing inside. Annie was gone.

CHAPTER SIXTEEN

Within five minutes, the FBI was in control of the Majer household with all exits sealed. Sarah isolated Dr. Majer, his wife, his sister, and the prince with his mother in the dining room. Don had warned her that the prince and his mother had diplomatic immunity, and Sarah went out of her way to be courteous as she spoke to them. The mother sat at the far end of the table, away from her, but Prince Abdel stayed close as Sarah paced with barely restrained anger.

The prince pointed a finger at Sarah with a sly smile. "I knew you were a government person." He paced with her.

"But I am also her friend, as is Dr. Larsen," she said, and turned to Dr. Majer's sister. "I know where you were at that time, but where was everyone else?"

"My wife and I were walking toward the kitchen to check with the staff about the food," Dr. Majer said, and his wife nodded.

Sarah looked at the prince. "And you?"

"We were going toward the dining room, through the crowd," he said, looking down the table at his mother.

Sarah looked at Dr. Majer's sister. "Where are your daughters?"

"Upstairs, asleep I hope."

"I meant to ask you earlier, do you have other children?" Sarah said.

"Yes, as I said, my husband, an engineer, was killed four years ago in Afghanistan. I have an older son and daughter that were with him when he was killed."

Sarah walked down the length of the table. "Where are they now?" she asked, but before Nyalia could answer, Sarah's phone rang. She swore softly, unclipping it and answering.

"Sarah, it's Don. No one was outside, but we have thermal imaging in the basement. Whoever or whatever it is, it's alive."

"Get someone in here to cover me, and I'll meet you," Sarah said, shutting her phone. Sarah asked the professor about the basement and turned toward the other end of the house.

❖

Annie woke and tried to move, but her body was unwilling. "Where...?" she mumbled, her voice echoing in her ears. Turning her head slowly, she knew she was on her back and her head hurt. Too cold, not Iraq. She willed her eyes open but could only see darkness. Unable to concentrate as a dreamy feeling washed over her mind, she lay still and then thought she might have been in another car bomb. Suddenly, a hand fumbled with her clothing, but her eyes wouldn't open. She could hear someone's ragged breathing, felt the warmth of another body and felt herself being lifted into someone's arms. *My mouth tastes terrible,* she thought, falling back into sleep and the cold covered her like a metal blanket.

❖

Sarah met Don coming down the hallway, and they ran to the basement area their imaging had locked onto. Guns drawn, they slowly pushed the door open, quietly stepping into a cold, dark room. Don fumbled for a switch and they stood, transfixed by the sudden small light amid crates and boxes. Sarah took the aisle on the left and Don took the other side. She could hear his steps as they shuffled down lanes created by the boxes into the semidarkness. Just as she got to the back wall, she stumbled over something and fell into the boxes, knocking several over. Straightening, she saw Annie's body.

"Over here, Don," Sarah called. She knelt, putting fingers to Annie's neck. She felt a pulse. "She's alive!"

"Annie, oh no," Sarah said as she felt the cold skin. Pulling her own suit jacket off, she covered Annie's bare legs. The pale yellow top that she had zipped up for her earlier was gathered up from her skirt, revealing a few inches of stomach. Sarah pulled it down gently and looked at the rest of her clothing. Everything seemed in order. Don was talking on his phone as he ran toward her.

Sliding his gun back under his coat, he said, "I called an ambulance. Damn, is that blood?" There was a dark swatch inches from her own knee.

"It's so dark down here. I'm not sure, but I think you're right. Do you have a flashlight?"

"No, but I think there's one back by the lights." He went to look. Sarah gently moved Annie's jacket aside, checking for injuries. She examined both of Annie's hands and thought there was blood on one of them. She saw a small cut that was bleeding on her lower lip, and there was an odd odor around her face. Annie's eyes fluttered as Sarah turned her head to get a better look.

"Annie, baby, can you hear me?" Sarah spoke softly, pushing the hair back. There was blood on Annie's neck and ear. She recognized the odor as Don came up with a flashlight. "She's been drugged with something like chloroform. The smell's all over her."

He was down on his knees on the other side of Annie's body as sirens wailed in the distance. Footsteps followed by a huge crash sounded from the other side of the room, and they both stood, guns drawn again, staring and listening in the direction of the noise. The lights went out, and they were plunged into utter darkness again. Sarah went to one knee across Annie, the other hand feeling for the flashlight. The storm outside ripped at the house as Don moved quietly away from her. He was soon lost in the inky blackness. Sarah heard the scuff of a foot to her right and turned, but not in time to avoid the bullet that knocked her backward beside Annie's quiet body. The noise and the pain were shocking as Sarah aimed her gun at a dark shadow moving away. She fired three times, just as the lights came on. The smell of gunfire hung heavily in the air, and she scrambled back onto one knee across Annie, gun still up. Suddenly, Don was in front of her.

"Did you get him?" Sarah could barely hear him speak as her ears rang from the shots.

"I fired. I'm not hearing very well, Don, and I think I've been shot." Sarah sank down beside Annie. "I'm sure it was a man, but check her for me. Did he shoot her too?"

❖

Sarah and Don watched as Rebecca climbed into the ambulance with Annie.

"In all the things I've seen, I've never seen a person disappear like that," Don muttered grimly. He and Scott had searched the basement room while the medical technicians worked on Annie and Sarah. They had found blood where Sarah had fired, but the person had simply disappeared.

Upstairs, he and Sarah looked into the dinning room at the people sitting at the table. The most they could do with the Saudis was to hold their passports for forty-eight hours.

Sarah had her jacket back on, covering the blood. "Sarah, go to the hospital," Don said.

She shook her head. "It's just a flesh wound," she lied. "I'll go after we've finished with these people."

"We have the lab people down there now, collecting anything they can find."

"I thought of something downstairs. Let me run with this."

Nodding, Don followed her back to the dinning room. She stood at the head of the table. "We'll need DNA and fingerprints from each of you."

"No," Prince Abdel's mother responded. "Certainly you don't believe that we had anything to do with this?"

"No, not really, but it will eliminate you from any suspicion or questions about what has happened here tonight. You certainly saw Ms. Booker."

"No, I talked with her friend, Dr. Larsen."

She looked at the prince. "How about you?"

The prince stood and looked at his mother defiantly. "I'll be happy to give you that thing, what is it? A DDA?" Sarah took a closer look at him and wondered if she'd misjudged his age.

Don spoke. "All right, we'll have our people in here in just a bit, and I appreciate your cooperation, everyone." Sarah sat across from the prince's mother.

"Thank you for your cooperation," she said, keeping her voice low and calm. The woman gave her an angry look, and Sarah took a closer look. This close, despite the low lights, she could see that the woman was almost too young to be the prince's mother. An older sister, perhaps, but his mother? She didn't think so, and Sarah was certain she smelled a chemical odor.

"How long will this take?"

Sarah glanced at her watch. "About twenty minutes and you can go. We appreciate your patience." She reached for the coffeepot, watching her own hands shake as she poured. The liquid was hot, but she couldn't taste it. She looked up and saw the woman across from her notice her shaking hands and tried to calm herself.

"Ms. Moore," Dr. Majer said, and Sarah looked down the table. He had taken his tie off. The top shirt button was open, and he looked tired and disheveled. "Did you find Ms. Booker?"

Sarah glanced up at Don and let him talk. She watched the others carefully as he explained where they had found Annie. With the exception of Prince Abdel and his mother, they all looked shocked when he explained that she had been found, unconscious, in the basement of the house. Sarah was sure the young prince and his mother had known where she was all along.

The idea she had in the basement found its way through her cluttered mind, and she stood. "Dr. Majer, would you and your wife come with me for just a moment?"

She led them to the bathroom and closed the door behind them. "This is where Ms. Booker was last seen. Since there are no windows, where is the door?"

Both looked confused.

Sarah continued. "This is a large bathroom, double shower, commode, wash basin, and this door that was locked from the inside. However, there has to be another way out of here. Would you show me, please?"

"We had this bathroom installed when we purchased the house. It was formerly an office," Dr. Majer said, walking around the room. Sarah walked with him and looked at his wife. She was frowning, looking at the shower.

Sarah opened the glass shower doors and looked at the tiled walls inside. "There," she said, "step inside and pull that sideways." She looked for an indentation in the wall. Dr. Majer pushed on the wall, but nothing happened. "Move it sideways, push sideways," Sarah said, and as he did, the wall opened to reveal darkness behind.

"I've never seen this," he said, looking at Sarah. "This room is for guests only."

Sarah picked up one of the lamps on the counter, shining light into the blackness and revealing an inside wall.

"Ah," the professor said, "What is this?" He gave Sarah a puzzled look.

"I think it's a passageway, stairs leading to your basement." Sarah believed it was the first time he'd seen this concealed door and steps. She looked at his wife. "Would you ask Agent Ahrens for his flashlight?"

❖

The hospital emergency room was busy when Sarah walked inside. She had driven Annie's SUV from the house through the dark winter storm, often slowing to a crawl on the treacherous roads. She parked in a doctor's parking place and stopped at security to report the car and show her identification. Spotting Hannah Booker ahead of her, Annie spoke her name and Hannah wheeled around.

"Sarah, thank God."

"How's she doing?"

Hannah backed off a step and looked at Sarah. "They said you were shot."

"How is Annie?" Sarah repeated.

"Come with me," Hannah said, taking her hand and leading her into an office. "This is my office when I'm on call, so put your coat over there. Did you drive Annie's car?"

Sarah took off her coat and sat on a couch. "How is Annie?"

"She's going to be sleeping this off for quite a while, and she'll be sore. It looks as if she was hit, hard, on the back of the head."

"Did they do an assault kit?"

Hannah's head jerked around. "Why?"

"It's pretty much procedure."

"Let me check that out. You stay here."

Sarah leaned back and closed her eyes, heart beating heavy.

Moments later, Hannah was back. "You were right. Procedure. They'd already done it." She shook her head. "This is why you let other doctors treat your own family. Where did you get hit?"

"On the left side. I must have moved just right. Should have hit me right between the eyes, Dr. Booker. I think he was shooting at Annie."

"It's Hannah, and let me have a look." She lifted Sarah's jacket. "You're going to have to stand up for this, I'm sorry." She helped Sarah to her feet and tugged the shirt out of her slacks. "They've done a good job, but I want to see it better. Why don't we walk across the hall and I'll put you on the table? Can you tell me anything about what happened?"

Sarah sat on the table in the examination room, talking about the events that led up to Annie's disappearance. When she got to the shooting, she said, "I shot back and it appears I hit him, but we lost him."

"It grazed you. It's not a long wound, but it's deep," Hannah said, gently probing the track of the bullet. Sarah sucked her breath in sharply. "You're going to need a couple stitches, or it'll tear." Hannah reached for a gown and a blanket. "Here, put this on. We'll do it right now." She looked out the room and said something to a nurse. They got her shirt off, and as she lay back on the table, the room spun a bit.

"You're a psychiatrist. You do stitches?"

"We all did just about everything in Vietnam, and I've stitched up kids for years." She smiled down at Sarah. "Careful what you say. I'm the one with the needle."

A nurse peeked in the door. "Dr. Booker? Dr. Williams is asking for you."

"Tell her to come down here." She gave Sarah several shots around the wound. "Let's see what Kilie has to tell us about our girl, so listen with me, will you?"

Sarah smiled at hearing "our girl."

A slender blonde woman entered the room. "Hannah, you can see her now, but I need to talk with you first." She put a hand on Hannah's shoulder and then looked at Sarah with a question on her face.

"It's okay," Hannah said. "This is Sarah Moore, the FBI agent on the case. She was injured trying to help Annie. Sarah, this is Annie's personal physician, Dr. Kilie Williams."

"Well, you still remember how, I see," Dr. Williams said, watching Hannah work on Sarah.

"What did you find, Kilie?" Hannah never stopped working.

"Concussion, but not severe. I put some stitches in her head, but she'll be fine once the drug wears off. Thank God they didn't re-injure her arm. Whoever it was, Hannah, they weren't trying to kill her. They wanted her alive. That's a new drug, like a synthetic chloroform." She walked to the other side of the bed. "FBI? Annie's talked to me about you." She looked at Sarah thoughtfully as she hung a stethoscope around her neck.

Hannah pulled her gloves off. "You're done, and here's what I want you to do." She put a hand on Sarah's shoulder. "Get back in here tomorrow and get these checked."

Dr. Williams smiled at her, "She did a good job, but she's right. Have someone check these tomorrow. Here, let me give you a hand up."

Sarah found her shirt and held it up. "Well, this is shot," she said and then realized what she had just said. They laughed. Hannah went to the sink to wash up just as James Booker looked in at his wife. He raised his eyebrows at the laughter.

"Hannah," Dr. Williams said, "why don't you and James go down and see Annie first. I'll finish with Agent Moore." After they left, Dr. Williams said, "Sarah, I work with Hannah. Why don't you come to the clinic in the morning and I'll look at your wound?"

Sarah stood, and a wave of dizziness rolled across her. Dr. Williams helped her to a chair and pulled a stool over in front of her. "Okay?" she asked.

"I was just off balance for a minute," Sarah said.

"No, you've been shot and your body is adjusting." She took the stethoscope from around her neck and held it against Sarah's chest. "Let's see what's going on here." After a moment's silence she draped the instrument back around her neck. "You're settling down. Need some help with the buttons?"

Sarah shook her head and began working on her shirt.

"I need to talk with you, and I promise good coffee and bagels tomorrow morning." She smiled as she stood, holding on to her as Sarah tucked her clothing back into her slacks. "Let's go see Annie."

Rebecca was sitting on a chair pulled up to Annie's bed, her head in her hands. She didn't even look up when Sarah came in with Dr. Williams. Sarah hesitated and then walked over and whispered her name, putting her arm around Rebecca's shoulder.

Rebecca lifted her head, tears in her eyes. "Sarah, she's asked for you." She stood and leaned over, kissing Annie's cheek. "Here, sit here. I have to make a call. How could this happen, right in front of us? My God."

"She was conscious?" Sarah asked.

"She was mumbling, saying something about talking to you, Sarah," Rebecca said, wiping her eyes with a tissue again. She turned to leave, and Dr. Williams walked her out with an arm around her waist. Sarah took Rebecca's chair, pressing Annie's hand to her cheek.

"Annie," she said to the still body amid the beeping machines. "I let them hurt you," she whispered.

❖

Sheikha locked the door behind her as Hamel stretched out on the table in the basement room of the hospital. They'd had angry words in the car as he tried to blame her for his failure with the reporter.

This time she had spoken up. She was not to blame and had done exactly as he'd instructed her. She'd taken the reporter down the steps to the basement where he'd been waiting. She had been surprised how little the woman had weighed as she'd lifted the unconscious body. She talked with her mother tonight, and now it had seemed wrong to be doing this. For the first time she felt like disobeying Hamel.

She walked to the table, pulling gloves on, and then turned, taking a suture kit from its sterile wrapping. She could feel his still-angry eyes burning holes in her back. *Let him hurt*, she thought. She didn't have any painkiller, so he was not going to enjoy this. She took some satisfaction from this knowledge.

Turning, she stared at him, not moving.

"Hurry up, I'm bleeding," he said, and she moved to the table, looking at the wound. She wondered if the bullet from the government woman was still lodged in the muscle in his leg. She didn't care that he screamed when she poured the disinfectant on the wound. If he had done what he said he was going to—take the woman outside immediately—he wouldn't have been shot. She drew her hands back and stared at him.

He growled at her through clenched teeth. "I'm supposed to meet Adnan right now with the reporter. I'll be fortunate to be alive after he sees that I failed. Hurry, what are you doing?"

"Nothing," she said and put another stitch in the torn flesh, listening to him swear at her for hurting him.

CHAPTER SEVENTEEN

The machines in the emergency room cubicle beeped rhythmically, almost lulling Sarah into sleep. She shook her head and got up to check the agents standing outside the curtains. After talking with them, she returned to the chair beside Annie's bed. They were going to move her to ICU until she regained consciousness.

She picked up Annie's hand again and took a deep breath. "Dammit, I should have just taken you. To hell with Don. Screw the rules. All the rules." Her mind went back over the Majers' party, and she stopped at the memory of Annie looking at her with the prince, just before she'd walked over and introduced him. What was that look? Fear? No, it had been shock and surprise, and she certainly had not wanted to be near him. She brought Annie's cool hand to her mouth and studied her face. With her eyes closed, it was a different face. Annie's energy was hidden.

The curtains were pulled back and Hannah came in with a tall woman dressed in jeans, stocking cap, and a big coat. Hannah introduced her oldest daughter, Molly, who immediately hugged Sarah, thanking her with typical Booker family warmth. Molly leaned over the bed, kissed Annie, and brushed the hair back from her forehead.

"Here we are again," Molly said to Hannah.

"It's been a while," Hannah answered with a quiet laugh. "The last time was rollerblading, or something with wheels. She didn't break anything, but she had a heck of a bump on her head."

"Did you get Rebecca off?" Sarah said, realizing she was still holding Annie's hand.

"Yes, Jim gave her a ride, and she asked that you call her tomorrow."
Hannah looked at Sarah. "How are you feeling?"

"What happened?" Molly pulled her stocking cap off, revealing
dark hair like Hannah's.

"She was shot," Hannah said.

"What?" Molly stopped unzipping her coat and stood very straight,
alarmed. "Shot? With a gun?"

"And you should go home, Sarah. Go to bed. Those injections are
going to wear off soon," Hannah said.

Sarah laid Annie's hand carefully on the bed, reluctant to let go.
"Thanks for the doctoring, Hannah. We have two agents outside, and
they'll stay with her, wherever they move her. They'll make sure no
one but family is here, so if anyone else is coming in, you'd better alert
them."

She looked at the two women, wanting to make sure they
understood, and took a deep breath. "This is serious. Remember what I
said the first night, Hannah? People forget we're at war. These men are
instructed to use their guns if they have to. You've met them, Hannah,
and make sure Molly meets them. The hospital staff, including Dr.
Williams, has been briefed. I hate to sound so grim, but be careful."

❖

Sarah drove directly to her office to update the case before going
to Annie's house. She turned the light on over her desk and booted up
her computer. She felt restless and uneasy, the night stringing through
her mind. She hadn't wanted to leave Annie. Coffee, she thought and
headed to the lounge. Don Ahrens was pouring himself a cup as she
walked in.

"What are you doing here? You should be at the hospital, or home
in bed."

"Been to the hospital, all taken care of." Sarah reached for a cup.

"Just made coffee. No one can say I don't let my feminine side
show." He grinned. "Come on, let's go into your office and you can tell
me what the doctor said. Oh wait, let me pour your coffee and then you
can say nice things about me when Human Resources checks me out."

Sarah could feel him try to ease her down. "How's it going with the Majer kitchen staff?" she asked, sipping the coffee as he sat down in one of her uncomfortable chairs, across from her.

"You know, same old, same old. Language barriers, no one has their papers, and the list goes on." Don pointed at her computer with his chin. "Check out the Web site that Ms. Booker's name's on."

Sarah swiveled carefully to her computer. The injections that Hannah had given her were wearing off, just as she'd said. She raised her eyebrows and looked at Don.

"Damn, they've added names, all women. This has to be connected to that organization, the FFI."

Don had his eyes closed and opened them a bit, squinting at her. "How's Ms. Booker?"

"She has a concussion, but the doctor said the drug that was used is new, like a synthetic chloroform. She was still out when I left, but her family is there and I met her personal doctor. Whoever did this didn't want to kill her, and they didn't re-injure her arm, thank God. Do you want to do the debriefing?"

"Let's not," Don said, dropping his feet to the floor with a thud. "Go home, Sarah, and go to bed. This will all keep. The posted guards at the hospital are all we can do until she regains consciousness. The lab work won't be done until tomorrow, and I've got everyone assigned. Let's meet at two o'clock. Wait, tell me again what they said about you."

"Annie's mother, Dr. Booker, put a few stitches in me, and I have an appointment with Annie's personal doctor tomorrow morning. Maybe she'll have more information for us." She glanced across the desk at him. "Did you find anything in the basement?"

"Everything. There's box after box of material. This is exactly what we were looking for, and I have people there now. We'll work around the clock until we're done. Tax dollars at work for counter-terrorism." He studied her. "I'm going home. My God, Sarah, where did you get these chairs? They're awful."

Sarah gave him a tired smile. Who said guys were insensitive? She turned back to her computer and began to document everything she could remember from the night. It helped, setting it all down, word by word, moment by moment. She could edit it later, but right now, during this quiet moment alone in her office, Sarah wanted it all there.

The winter storm had moved away over Lake Michigan, but it was still snowing lightly. She hit the garage door opener at Annie's, surprised to see another car inside. She opened the door carefully, hearing women's voices. The kitchen that had been clean just a few hours ago was now cluttered. She shoved the keys in her pocket and looked again. Pots, pans, and boxes sat on the counters and the floor. "What the hell?"

"Stop, I've called nine-one-one," a low female voice ordered her from behind. Sarah whirled in a fluid motion and dropped to a low squat with her gun drawn, pain from her side taking her breath away. The phone fell from a blond woman's hands, clattering sideways on the hallway floor. "My God, don't shoot."

Sarah stood slowly and holstered her gun. "Mary?"

Two women stared at her with frightened faces.

"Who are you?" Mary asked.

"Sarah Moore, FBI," she answered, pulling her ID from her pocket and holding it up. "If you really did call nine-one-one, at least let me call them back and cancel. I'm staying here for a while."

"FBI? You're staying here?"

Sarah nodded, asking again if they'd called 911, and Mary answered, "No, you just scared the hell out of us. I'm Mary Iverson and this is still my house, but apparently you know that." She moved aside and introduced Meg.

"I'm sorry I frightened you two," Sarah said. "Things have been moving pretty fast, and I didn't think about you coming home. I'm here with Annie until we get this thing settled."

"That explains the clothes in the guest room, but where is Annie? And what *thing* settled?"

"Just a minute," Sarah said and went into the living room to check the computer. She came back to the kitchen and eased into the closest chair. "Let me tell you what has happened."

The three women sat at the table until all the questions had been answered. Mary put her hands over her face when Sarah stopped talking.

"We haven't been here that long. I'm packing up what I have left in the kitchen. It's the last bit of anything I want to get out of here." She stood and paced. "Damn, now she's brought the danger into the house. I can't believe she did this. God, this makes me mad." She sat back down, looking at Meg. "We can't stay here tonight. It's not safe." She looked at Sarah, who nodded in confirmation. "Wait, did you say something about a Saudi prince?"

Sarah nodded again.

"If it's Abdel, he's hurt her before, and I want to stop this, now."

Sarah's sat up straighter, all senses fully alert as Mary continued. "I'm going to tell you about it. It's time someone did. We've been quiet too long."

Much later, Sarah helped the two women put boxes into Mary's car and watched them drive away. "What a night," she mumbled, trying to force her numb mind to wrap around the Majers' party. Little pieces of memory of Annie, the prince, and others kept floating around in her memory. She saw Annie lying unconscious on the cold cement floor and then the flash of gunfire. Mary and Meg appeared in her mind, and she irrationally grinned at the memory of both frightened women in front of her gun. *Not very professional*, she scolded herself, *but wait until I tell Annie that story*.

Taking a soda from the refrigerator, she drank some of it while standing under the hot shower, no longer able to keep Mary's hurtful story out of her mind. The incident in Saudi Arabia three years ago. The horrible beating.

Mary had grown quiet as the memory caught up with her. "I'm sorry," she said, "this is still hard. They beat her so badly, almost to death. Annie doesn't know that I came home and saw a therapist as well. It still hurts to talk about it." Sarah had listened, nausea creeping across her stomach. Now the words would not leave her alone as she turned the water off. Swearing aloud, she took a quick breath, tears gathering in her eyes as she leaned against the shower wall.

She was certain this was the time period Hannah had spoken of, the three months Annie had done the paintings in the clinic. No wonder Annie wanted to talk with her parents. She and Mary had stayed in Switzerland until Annie's face and body had healed, but neither had told anyone other than Rebecca and Annie's doctor. After a year with the therapist, Mary had decided to separate herself from Annie's danger, and Sarah wondered how they had made it through the last years together.

She picked up the packet of pills that Hannah had given her for pain and shook one loose in her hand. There was a place in Arizona where she used to park her old pickup. The stars were beautiful from that mesa, and she ached for the deep peace she had always found there. Crawling into bed, she wished she could go home, to Arizona, if just for a while and take Annie with her.

CHAPTER EIGHTEEN

The next morning was so bright and sunny that Sarah's eyes hurt. The house seemed wrong, empty, without Annie. The pain pill and exhaustion had held her tightly for the first six hours until she'd begun to dream of Annie and the events of last night. She'd finally gotten up, disgusted, sore, her head pounding. She dressed slowly for her meeting with Dr. Kilie Williams, still thinking of her dreams.

Sarah had called the doctor as she left Annie's house. The clinic was closed for the weekend and the doctor was waiting for her at the front entryway. Sarah had immediately envied the doctor's comfortable tan shirt over a white turtleneck, jeans, and well-worn cowboy boots.

Dr. Williams first looked at Sarah's stitches and changed the dressing on the wound before doing anything else, joking that Hannah should have taken up surgery.

"How do you feel this morning?" Kilie asked. "Any more dizziness?"

"No, just a little sore, but I'm all right. Thanks for looking at the stitches."

"I don't envy you your job, Sarah."

"What do you mean?"

"Terrorism and the war. Sometimes I wonder if we understand that we're at war. It's so distant and unconventional that it seems unreal. Our neighbors...Annie's neighbor too...just lost a daughter over there two days ago. I haven't had the heart to tell Annie, but I will." She tapped her pen on her desk. "Hannah said you're working with a local terrorist group that may tie in to Annie?"

"Yes, a very well-organized group, and the information Annie provided may have opened it up for us. I'll know more today when I get into the office. Kilie, I don't think Americans are uncaring. I think we're confused and maybe sad that it's come to this." She was quiet for a moment. "I had a little surprise last night. Mary was at Annie's house."

"Ah," Kilie said. "With Meg?"

Sarah nodded.

"And?"

"She told me about Saudi Arabia and the prince."

"All right," Kilie said, leaning forward on her elbows, face neutral.

"Mary said you know about the attack, but Annie's mother doesn't?"

"Hannah isn't aware of any of this, and it's been difficult for me, working with her. She's going to be very angry at first. I flew to Switzerland with Jack Keegan and Bill Simpson, Annie's New York producer. That was complicated because I had to say I was going to New York City and not mention Switzerland. A lie of omission, I guess, but not a comfortable one. I'm glad I went, however. Annie was in terrible shape, and honestly, Sarah, I wasn't sure we'd ever get her back."

"Does anyone in the family know?"

Kilie shook her head. "I've known the Bookers over twenty years and this is going to be very hard on all of them. Annie has told me that she's going to tell them and asked me to be present for some of the conversation with Hannah. I'm not looking forward to this."

Sarah looked out at the sunshine on last night's fresh snow. "Dr. Williams, the incident last night may be tied to what happened before, and the prince apologized to her in front of me. Do you know if they found any kind of physical evidence when she was in the hospital in Switzerland? We did prints and DNA last night."

Kilie Williams narrowed her eyes, thinking. "No, I don't. Why don't we find out?"

"You can access that information?"

Kilie nodded and handed several sheets of paper across the desk to Sarah. "Here, I ran this off before you got here, but I'll call the doctor now." She picked up the phone while Sarah began to read. "Sarah, give me your information, and I'll have Dr. Hatawabe deal directly with you."

Sarah handed a card over and went back to her reading. It was all there, the nature and extent of the injuries, the name of the hospital, the dates and the doctors, even their notes on the case. "My God," she said quietly as she heard Kilie leave a message.

"She was in a session but will return my call. Ironically, when Annie came back injured this time, I called this doctor, just to touch base. That woman is extraordinary, and I will always believe she personally saved Annie. I was totally in over my head."

Sarah pointed at the papers she held. "This is hideous."

Kilie closed her eyes for a moment. "Some of us are stronger than others, but still, Sarah, it lingers in Annie. Because of that, there are some things I would like to discuss with you."

"Please. I can use all the help that you, or anyone, can give us."

"First, you'll have all the information from Switzerland, but there are some personal things I'd like to talk to you about. Would that be all right?"

Sarah nodded.

"Hannah guided Annie my way when she was almost seventeen. She was out to her family and friends but had just become involved with her first woman. She had questions."

"The tall blonde? I saw her at Annie's house."

"Yes, and thankfully, a very careful person," Kilie said. "My partner and I got to know them well that summer."

"Partner?" Sarah smiled.

"We have a horse ranch not far from Annie's. You've driven by it every time you've gone to her house. Nicki had just had our first child and Annie became our first babysitter."

"You have kids? That's great."

"A boy and two girls." She handed Sarah a framed photo off her desk. Sarah studied the photo, smiling.

Kilie cleared her throat. "Actually, Annie's talked about you quite a bit. I don't think she's even aware of how much she's said. She's talking about you like she used to talk about Tori."

Sarah straightened in her chair, surprised. "What about Mary?"

"No. In the beginning, I think it was genuine, but then it merged into a sort of business relationship. I work with Mary and Meg every day, and frankly, I am seeing something much more comfortable and real between them than it ever was with Annie. After the injury and Switzerland, it was agonizing to watch."

"Annie said she was gone too much and too long."

"Yes, she was gone a lot, but what I saw was that she didn't even notice, and that's not like her. Annie's a caring person."

"She's a new experience for me. In the first place, there's her appearance. Sometimes people just go speechless in front of her."

Kilie laughed. "Isn't it amazing?"

"The oddest part, to me at least, is that she doesn't seem to notice. And you don't dare call her a celebrity. Hannah told me that she was shy, but I have a hard time believing that."

"Oh, but she is, and that causes all sorts of interesting personality characteristics. You have no idea how much courage it takes for her to speak to a crowd. When it's television, it's fine. That's just a camera and perhaps the person or people she's interviewing. However, a crowd makes her sweat bullets. Did you see the presentation award last Friday?"

Sarah nodded.

"Did you happen to notice her left foot? It was tapping about ninety miles per hour."

"My observation skills must be deteriorating. I missed it."

"Looking at the dress, huh? Or lack thereof?"

"How could you not?"

"Don't feel bad. You should have heard Nicki. Ha!" She laughed. "All of this, the person that Annie is, kind of threw Mary."

"She was jealous?"

"No, it made her competitive and still does. But she was very helpful when they got back from Switzerland. She tried to do everything she could."

"She certainly was angry last night."

"I imagine she's just worn out with it. The same is true of Annie, now that's she's been injured again and Jack Keegan was killed. She's just sort of dazed. So it is very hopeful to hear her talk about you so enthusiastically and with humor. Actually, at this point, any humor with Annie is good."

"At first, she felt isolated to me, and something else, like she might run at any moment."

"That's why I'm talking with you," Kilie said. "One hundred years ago I would have been her father asking this."

"Her father? You're asking me to be careful? No. You're asking about my intentions." No one had ever asked her that question. "Kilie, agency rules are so strict that I'm not even supposed to notice she's a woman. One hundred years ago? All right, my intentions are honorable."

❖

Promptly at two, Sarah sat across the desk from Don. She looked up to see his eyes on her, and he suggested she call the hospital. Sarah nodded and left for her own office to make the call. She locked the door behind her, wanting some quiet, uninterrupted time.

Annie's mother picked up the phone in ICU, answering in a tired voice. "She's just about to surface. I don't want her waking up alone."

"Have you been there all night?" Sarah asked, catching the weariness in Hannah's voice.

"Yes, but Molly stayed. She just left."

"I'm going into a meeting now, but I'll be by as soon as we're done," Sarah said.

"I would appreciate it." Hannah was quiet and then repeated, "I just didn't want her to wake up alone."

Sarah heard the worry in Hannah's voice and looked out her office window. A few lazy snowflakes floated by, but the sun still shone brightly. "Hannah, as soon as I'm done, I'll be there."

"Wait, someone's coming in." Sarah could hear voices. "It's Mary, Meg, and Dr. Williams. Now we have four doctors in here." Hannah laughed a little. "A bit of an overkill, huh?"

"I'll be there before five. I have clothes for Annie. Can you think of anything else?"

"She'll be starving. How about some fried chicken with a vanilla malt? There's a great chicken and ribs place close by the hospital with real malts."

"I know the place."

Sarah started to leave for Don's office but changed her mind, easing back into her chair. She dialed Rebecca and discussed the conversations with Mary and Dr. Williams. Rebecca told Sarah about the first weeks when Annie had gotten home three years ago. After hanging up, Sarah entered parts of Rebecca's conversation into Annie's case file on the computer.

Don looked up with a smile as Sarah came back into his office. He held papers out to her. "How is she?"

"Her mother's still there, and her roommate just came in. She's about to come around," she said, taking the papers. "What's this?"

"Some very interesting DNA results that I managed to sneak through the lab at warp speed."

"What the hell?" Sarah blurted out, looking at the results.

"That's what I said. This is the blood from the basement and the DNA we took from the group in the dining room. The preliminary lab report says the shooter is a male and at least a brother to the woman who said she was the prince's mother. By the way, nice job with her. That woman didn't want to do this."

"Did you run it through the database?"

"Sure did, but nothing in the U.S., so it's overseas now as well as in Virginia with the photos. I bet we get something there. And here's something else you might want to see. The results from Dr. Majer's sister."

Sarah looked at the paper, shaking her head. "I just don't believe this. She's the mother to the shooter in the basement *and* the woman claiming to be the prince's mother? Damn. She said she had two older children, and I forgot to come back to that."

"This is just preliminary, but at first glance, it appears that's what it is. What the hell is going on here?" Don shook his head.

Adrenaline shot through Sarah. "Don, in the first place, that woman, the prince's so-called mother, is a question mark. She didn't look old enough to be the prince's mother. Secondly, she was familiar to both Annie and me. The man we saw in the store, the man in the photos, could be her twin, so perhaps they are siblings. Then look at the prince. He's not related to anyone."

"This is a long way from a Web site."

"Last night, at Majer's party, when Annie introduced the prince to me, he apologized to Ms. Booker for something. Annie's roommate is home, and I talked with her at their house last night. She told me that Prince Abdel had been involved with Ms. Booker before, three years ago. Then, this morning, Annie's personal physician gave me the entire story. While Annie was at the prince's home in Saudi Arabia on her way into Iraq, she was beaten so badly that her doctor said she didn't think she'd make it. I know she didn't expect to see him at the Majers' or perhaps anywhere."

"All right," Don said, "that's the prince. Maybe that's Ms. Booker's only connection to him." He held up the sheets of papers. "These connect Majer's sister, the shooter, and the so-called mother. Not the prince."

Sarah nodded. "Majer's sister, Nyalia, said the prince arranged for her transportation over here from Iraq. Annie questioned that immediately. She said it seemed odd, unusual. There's nothing involving any of them in your investigation?"

"No, they're new players in our terrorism group here. I'm sure one of them has to be connected to those photos and Amer al-Sadr. So why don't we do this? We'll have Sam Coates concentrate on Dr. Majer and his sister. I'll take her two adult children and the prince."

"What about me? Where do I fit in?"

"You have Ms. Booker, but truthfully, Sarah, you've been involved in a shooting plus being injured. You'll have to go on limited duty as soon as we get this straightened out. First, you have to see the folks in Internal Affairs and then the department psychiatrist. Then I'll just have you stay with Ms. Booker, take her out of town."

Sarah waited, making sure he was finished. "What about the basement at Majer's house?"

"That's a different story. The boxes in the basement are loaded with information, visas, photographs, and more. It'll take us quite a while to get through it all, but he's nailed. I have an appointment with him this afternoon."

"When we were in the bathroom last night and found the door to the basement, I believed him, Don. I don't think he knew that was there. I think he knew something was coming down, as did his wife. He just didn't know what."

"His sister seemed genuinely shocked."

"Yes, but I think everyone there had some knowledge of something about to happen. How do we follow up with the prince?"

"I'm talking with State. I'm going to have to bring them in on this. We have to find him before he leaves the city or the country. Maybe Majer will know where he's staying."

"The FFI was organized less than a year ago, and Ms. Booker's injuries in Saudi Arabia were over three years ago. I just can't believe they're connected. I don't believe her injury has anything to do with the Web site threat."

"I think you're right, but the prince is our only lead."

"After I finish here, I'll talk to Annie about the prince if she's able," Sarah said, feeling tired already. She looked at the bright sunlight on Don's desk and thought of Annie in the yellow dress the night of the awards.

CHAPTER NINETEEN

After Sarah gave a formal statement to the guys from Internal Affairs regarding the shooting and then did it all over it again with the FBI psychiatrist, her mind was swirling. Rubbing her forehead, she made her way back to her office with a fresh cup of coffee and some ibuprofen. "Christ," she mumbled, shuffling through her computer notes from the meeting with Annie's personal doctor this morning, trying to concentrate and failing. Kilie Williams had added the finer details to Mary's story from last night, and as much as she needed this information, Sarah felt like ducking and hiding from some of the words.

Sarah pulled up to the hospital in Annie's SUV with a bag of chicken and two malts. The temperature on the console registered ten degrees, and she could see her breath when she stepped out, feet crunching on the snow. Sarah stood for a moment, spotting a slice of moon starting to rise over the lake, the same as it had last night before the storm had moved through.

Sarah identified herself to the agent guarding Annie's room and asked her about visitors. The last visitor, Annie's brother Noah, had left about thirty minutes ago. Sarah braced herself to enter.

There was only a dim light against the darkness in the room as Sarah walked quietly to the bed. She set the food on the bedside table and hung her parka over a chair. She had changed into jeans and boots, comfort for what she was sure was going to be a long evening. Pulling the chair close to the bed, she propped her elbows on the sheets and watched the sleeping woman.

"Where are you, Annie?" she whispered. The expressive mouth

was relaxed but still tipped up at the corners. The cut on her lip was already healing. Her eyelashes were long and thick, curling up at the ends, and Sarah idly wondered why she hadn't noticed them before. *Probably because Annie's eyes always overwhelmed you, caught your attention before you had a chance to look further*, she thought. She picked up one of her hands and thought about Kilie's unspoken question this morning. Intentions? She laid her forehead on the bed next to Annie, worn out, and feeling tears sting her eyes.

Suddenly, there were fingers in her hair, sliding down her face, and a sleepy voice said, "Do I smell chicken?"

Sarah's head jerked up and she looked right into Annie's sleepy green eyes.

"I left you a message on your phone."

"I turned my phone off." Sarah straightened and looked away, shy at being caught with tears in her eyes. "Ready for food? Listen to my stomach."

"Don't they feed FBI agents?" Annie asked. She fumbled with the buttons on the bed, bringing herself to a sitting position. "My God, I am so hungry." She rummaged in the bag, and soon a piece of chicken was on its way to her mouth as she reached for the malt.

Sarah grabbed a piece of chicken, and the other malt, and joined the feeding frenzy with a happy sigh. Finally, with greasy hands and slurping malts, both sat back and looked at one another. Annie patted her stomach and gave a discreet burp.

"I don't think I've ever had an eating experience quite like that," Annie said, hitching her body up in the bed. She peered down into the bag. "There's only three pieces left. We'd never make it as chicken farmers."

"I'm glad you like it," Sarah said, heading toward the bathroom to wash her hands and face. "Do you want a washcloth? By the way, I'm still driving your car." She splashed hot water on her face and scrubbed her hands. "Annie," she asked again, "do you want a washcloth?" Not hearing an answer, she peeked out the door. Annie was bent over, holding her stomach, head on her knees. Sarah grabbed the wet cloth and went to the bed. "Annie, what's the matter?"

"Nothing, just give me a minute," Annie choked out, shaking her head.

"It's something, or you wouldn't be doing this. Are you going to throw up? Shall I call a nurse?" She put her arms around her, holding her tightly.

Annie shook her head, finally easing back into Sarah's arms. "I'm sorry," she said, "the pain pills. I'm not supposed to eat for a while. I forgot." Annie looked up. "That chicken was worth every bite." She pulled Sarah's head down, kissing her on the forehead. "Mmm, you smell like the outdoors and fried chicken."

Sarah bit her bottom lip. "Annie," she mumbled and leaned closer, unable to stop herself. A sudden knock on the door made them jump, and Sarah let go of Annie, turning as a nurse came into the room with a tray.

"I need you to leave for a few moments," she said, looking at Sarah, who was blushing to the tips of her fingers. "Are you okay?" she asked as Sarah fled.

Sarah stood outside, pushing so hard against the wall that it hurt. "What the fuck was I doing?" she said, heart thumping hard. A familiar voice said her name and she turned to see Hannah and James Booker walking toward her. Sarah stared at them, certain they both knew exactly why she was blushing.

"The nurse is in there," she said.

"Yes?" Annie's dad asked, looking at her expectantly.

"Are you feeling all right?" Hannah asked, feeling Sarah's forehead. "Well, no fever, just a case of the blushes, huh?" She raised her eyebrows. "Why don't we go to the doctor's lounge and let James have a few moments with Annie? I need to talk with you." Sarah followed her to the room at the end of the hall, collapsing into one of the comfortable chairs.

"Kilie said she looked at the stitches," Hannah said.

"She said you should have taken up surgery."

"She lied." Hannah gave a short laugh. "Have you found out anything more about what you and I talked about last week?"

"Did Annie say something?"

"Sort of. I mentioned therapy this afternoon, and she did something I haven't seen her do in years. She threw a little temper tantrum, complete with some pretty explicit swearing. She said she'd had all the counseling she could ever use three years ago." She looked expectantly at Sarah. "If you can't talk about it, I understand, but I could use a little help here."

Sarah looked down at her boots. "I brought the chicken, and we had just finished eating when the nurse came in. The food made her sick to her stomach."

"I forgot about that. You can't eat for a while after that medication. Did she actually vomit?"

"No, but I thought she was going to."

"Well, that's a miracle, and speaking of that, the assault kit came back negative."

"We do have some concerns about the DNA that we collected last night, Hannah, but confirmation will be slow. When I give you information, I want to make sure it's correct." Sarah gave her the look she would give her own mother. "Hannah, I was hiding something when you and Mr. Booker walked up, but I need to talk with Annie first. Is that a good enough answer for right now?"

"You have the same look on your face that my kids get when they don't want to talk."

"If I ever need a psychiatrist, you're my doctor," Sarah said, relaxing and grinning. "We have some leads but are nowhere near answers right now. We need more information and evidence."

A man stood beside the bed with his back to them, talking to Annie and her father as Sarah followed Hannah around the bed. Annie introduced Bill Simpson, her network producer from New York City, and he stared at Sarah for a moment. "FBI?" he asked.

Annie's eyes caught Sarah's and wouldn't let go, patting a spot on the bed beside her. Sarah hesitated and then finally sat next to Annie. A warm hand soon covered hers as the conversation flowed around them, but Sarah could barely concentrate. When the producer finally looked at her again, Sarah could see that he was angry, and she didn't blame him.

Later, only Bill and Sarah were left, and he was getting ready to go. He told Annie that he was putting her officially on leave, not to worry about assignments and to just get better. He put his coat on and looked at Sarah and then Annie.

"Does she know your history with the prince?"

Annie looked at Sarah. "I understand Mary talked to you last night? And Rebecca and Kilie today?" Sarah nodded, and Annie continued in a soft, tired voice. "Then it's done, and if I'd ever thought I'd see him again, I would have told you in the beginning. You should have had this information." She lay back in the bed, her hand finding Sarah's again. "Now what? Am I never going to get away from this person?" Annie's voice was angry and there were tears in her eyes. "Bill, think back, I was drugged the last time too, but the only person I can remember is the prince. What if it's not him? Or if he has a friend?"

Her grip on Sarah's hand had increased and Sarah looked across the bed at Bill. His face changed, and he leaned over, pulling a handkerchief out of his pocket and dabbing at Annie's face. Sarah looked down to see tears on Annie's cheeks and repressed an idiotic urge to knock him away but got up instead. Bill straightened up with a look that felt like a gunshot, and Sarah unconsciously took a step back.

"Did I understand, Ms. Moore, that you had surveillance at that party last night?"

"That's correct."

"Bill, stop it. It's not Sarah's fault."

"Oh, yes, it is, Annie. This never should have happened, and she damned well knows it." His eyes were accusing and unflinching.

"Yes, I do," Sarah said but kept her eyes locked with his until he turned and looked at Annie.

"I'll see you tomorrow before I leave. Have a good night's sleep." He kissed Annie on the cheek. Without looking at Sarah again, he left.

She leaned over and looked into Annie's wet eyes. "I think you know what I'm about to say," she said. Annie closed her eyes. "Your boss was right. It never should have happened, and I need to apologize."

"Not for that. I don't ever want to hear you say that, Sarah. For as long as you may know me, don't ever say that to me again. This is not your fault. I think you made him hurry and not do whatever else he had in mind. Bill is just angry at the situation. I chose this life, and it's my responsibility."

Annie looked genuinely angry, and Sarah leaned over the bed, cupping her chin. To hell with the rules, all of them.

"All right, take responsibility for your own life, but right now, I'm part of it, and I have to take my share." She bent down, gently kissing Annie's soft mouth. Sarah took a quick breath, shocked at what she'd just done, but she kissed her again. Then Annie's arms were around her, pulling her down and kissing her, hard.

They both stopped, looking at each other, surprised and trembling.

"Annie, I have to stop, my legs are giving out." Sarah sat down abruptly on the bed, legs shaking. "My God." She let her head drop. "I'm going to be struck dead for this."

Annie pulled Sarah's face up so she could see her.

"It's against agency rules, even my rules," Sarah said with a deep breath and then bent in for another kiss because she couldn't stop and because Annie tasted so good. "We'd better talk about last night, because I'm not going to stop kissing you."

"I'd rather talk about the last few minutes." Annie's face was so sweet that Sarah kissed her again.

"Oh," she whispered. She bit Annie's bottom lip softly, tasting her tongue and sliding her hands up the warm skin of Annie's back. She wanted to just lie down and put her arms around her, but somehow she sat up instead.

"All right," Annie said. "Since I can't lure you into my bed, then the very least I can say is thank you for almost shooting Mary last night, something I certainly have considered."

Sarah laughed. "I should be ashamed, and I shouldn't laugh, but I could hardly wait to tell you. You should have seen their faces."

Annie made her describe the whole scene, laughing, but finally, she lay back in the bed, looking genuinely exhausted. "Did you think to bring the beer?" she asked, the corners of her mouth turning up.

❖

Annie woke up in the middle of the night drenched in sweat. It was the same dream, her nightmare, careening through her mind, but for the first time, Sarah appeared in the dream, trying to help. The hospital was still and dark, like a morgue, and she thought of Jack Keegan.

She had told Sarah what she could remember about the attack in the bathroom. Someone came up behind her as she closed the door, then the familiar smell of the drug and bits of memory of waking up in the basement. Someone had been fumbling with her clothing, and she had heard breathing close to her. But that was all she could remember until the hospital.

She took a drink of water and thought about asking for another pill, but then decided against it. Annie turned on her side and tried to look out the window. She thought about the hospital in Switzerland, the depression and anger. *I'm still angry, it still makes me cry, and here I am, back in a hospital*, she thought. *If you killed a person's spirit, would it be called murder?*

Annie ignored her hurting head and put her hands to her lips, remembering Sarah's mouth. She wiped her eyes with the sheet. God, those surprising kisses, but at last, it felt like more. Annie realized that Sarah had looked surprised as well. She pulled the covers up to her chin, closing her eyes. Sarah's arms around her had made her entire body shiver, and she wished she were here, beside her now.

CHAPTER TWENTY

The phone was ringing as Sarah got out of the shower. Don Ahrens growled at her. "What the hell, Sarah? Where are you? You missed our ten o'clock meeting this morning. Are you at home or at Ms. Booker's?"

"I came home last night. I was just too tired to go out to the other house. I'll check it out before I go anywhere else."

"Prints are back from Majer's house. Abdel's so-called mother, and the shooter's, are all over that basement room, plus Ms. Booker's, of course. Oh, and the boxes are the mother lode. This is the end for that group."

"Wait, is there any more information? Does the woman have a name? I mean, other than trying to pass herself off as the prince's mother?"

"Not yet. When I talked with Dr. Majer last night, he claimed he'd never met her before or seen her previously, but obviously, if she's his niece, he's lying. I had Josh Palmer check with the embassy in New York City, and no one there's heard of her, seen her. Nothing, nada. But I think you're right. I believe him too about that crazy wall in the bathroom."

"I spent the night in Annie's hospital room. Her boss is in from New York. I want to give you a heads up because that guy's really angry at me. He's right. It never should have happened."

"I've already spoken to him this morning. Yeah, he's mad, but I think he's just angry at the situation. I took him through the whole evening. I even let him listen to a bit of our tape, especially when you were waiting outside the bathroom for her. He backed off. He didn't know you'd been shot, and I'll bet Ms. Booker doesn't either."

"He was really angry last night."

"He talked about the beating, and I pointed out that drugs were used again. He didn't have much to say after that. He just feels bad, Sarah. Those two have worked together a long time. He and Jack Keegan went to Switzerland when she was injured, did you know that?"

"Yes, and also her physician, Dr. Williams, the woman I spoke to yesterday. Don, check Annie's file and see what I've added. I also spoke to the woman who was the attending physician in Switzerland, and she's e-mailing me Annie's file from there."

Don was quiet, as if he was going to say something, but then he changed the subject. 'You know, I've never seen a hidden door like that. It's like something out of Sherlock Holmes. How in hell did you happen to think of it?"

"Ironically, Annie and her brother built two into her house, one that goes upstairs to the loft, her painting studio, and the other in her bathroom. That's new for me too."

"The mother and her two kids, the brother and sister, or whatever they are, all of this is going to take some sorting out. Whatever, you've done it by the book so far, so we're not going to talk guilt, right? Besides, it was my decision to have her at the party and still in town." There was a moment's silence as Sarah refused to respond. "I have people at the airport as well as the prince's hotel right now."

"You've located him?"

"Should have known, of course. He's at the DuMont, downtown. If you'd been at the meeting, you'd have known this."

"Enough."

"Where are you headed now?"

"To Ms. Booker's house, then on to the hospital. She said they are going to release her today. Don, where do you want me?"

"Right where you're going. Stay close to Ms. Booker, but I'm thinking about paying the prince a little visit."

"If they do release her today, I'm taking her to Green Bay tomorrow, to Rosy's. There's no reason to keep her in town."

After she dressed she checked her e-mail. There was nothing new from Josh Palmer, and she leaned back in her chair, finally letting her mind remember Annie last night. She could still taste her mouth.

She shut her eyes, rubbing both temples with her fingers. *I've never broken this rule in over ten years, but I'll do it again if I get the chance. Would they fire me over this*, she wondered. "It was just a kiss," she said into the silence and then recognized the lie. It was a lot more than a kiss. She felt it to the bottom of her soul. "Damn," she said, knowing full well she couldn't keep her hands, or her heart, off Annie Booker. Sarah rapped her hands lightly on the chair's armrests. Kilie Williams's conversation made her wish for time to think this through, but no matter what happened, the important thing was to make sure Annie was safe. Everything else would have to be sorted out later. But still, the taste on her mouth lingered.

She pulled a box out of her dresser drawer. She sifted through letters, photos, odds and ends until she found what she was looking for. Her bankbook. Two more years and the ranch would have her name on it. Then would come stock and horses. This was her retirement plan after the FBI. *In about twenty years, if I live that long*, she thought. She'd never talked about this with anyone, not even her family. Sarah stared out space. When this was over perhaps she could take some of the vacation she had coming and show Annie the place. Unless, of course, Annie went back to Iraq.

❖

Sarah looked at the city, driving the snowy Milwaukee streets. The city was old and small, but she loved the quaint buildings and the lake. This city had more parks than any city she'd ever lived in. Sarah decided that she could probably live here, despite the snow. She would just have to get back into skiing. There had been snowshoes in Annie's basement, and she wondered how hard that would be. She thought about Green Bay. Maybe she and Annie could do some cross-country skiing if Annie was able.

The day was sunny but cold. A beautiful winter day, if there was such a thing. Church bells rang out across the city, as they did every day at this time, and a frigid wind whipped snow across the sidewalk. In the hospital gift shop Sarah impulsively bought an armful of hothouse lilies for Annie. Speaking to the agent on duty at the door of Annie's room, Sarah told her to take a break, go get some coffee, and bring enough for two back with her when she finished.

Sarah locked the door behind her when she entered. Annie was sitting at a table reading a book. She looked up at Sarah and smiled. Sarah pulled the flowers out from behind her.

"Oh, they're beautiful," Annie said, getting out of the chair.

"Don't stand, Annie," Sarah worried out loud, walking toward her, but Annie was already in front of her, taking the flowers and burying her face in them.

"Do you have any idea how long it's been since anyone brought me flowers?"

"When I saw them I thought of you." Sarah felt fifteen all over again.

Annie looked at Sarah over the flowers and hugged her, kissing her cheek. Sarah put her arms around Annie, closing her eyes with happiness. "Why are you up?" she murmured.

"Just let me hold you, Sarah. I haven't wanted to hold anyone for a long time." Annie leaned into her. Neither woman said a word, until she pulled back. "You'd better tell me about those rules you were talking about last night, or I'm liable to get you in a bunch of trouble."

Sarah grinned at the impish eyes, glad to have Annie back. "Your mom surprised me and asked about the agency's client rules."

Annie started to laugh. "My mother, the matchmaker. What did you say?"

"I said there were rules about clients, but I didn't have to like it. Annie, I do have to be careful about this, and they're very strict." She took a sudden breath as Annie moved back into her body, arms inside her coat, snuggling even closer. "That feels good," Sarah said softly against Annie's ear.

"I have to warn you, I am a notorious rule breaker. Damn. Now *my* legs are shaking." Annie pointed to a chair beside the bed. "Pull that over here beside me so we can talk. As much as I'd like to, I won't jeopardize your job."

Sarah sat down with some relief. "Could we talk about this tonight?"

Annie nodded and pulled a blanket off the bed, tucking it around her. "This has been such an emotional day. I talked to Mom this morning. For two hours I told her everything I could think of, pretty much destroyed her day and maybe her trust in me. Kilie came in for a while to add some details that I wasn't aware of. I am so angry at myself about the way I've handled this. I've never seen Mom so quiet as she was this morning. I'm ashamed."

Sarah moved the chair closer. "Annie, your mother will understand."

"My mom and dad expect honesty. This is the first time I've broken that rule in such an important way."

Sarah reached for her hands, rubbing them with her thumbs.

Annie sighed, looking at their hands, together. "That feels good," she said. "Thank you for the flowers. I was in the hospital in Switzerland the last time anyone gave me flowers, and I love them. I love them in my house and I love to grow them. Kilie released me to go home today. Take me home?"

"Are you sure you're ready to go home?"

"She says I am, and that's all I need. I want out of here."

"I feel like your mother saying this," Sarah made a face at Annie, "but how do you feel inside? You know, bad dreams, that kind of thing?"

"Yes, I have them, but I've never wanted to talk about this. Even though I've had tremendous help, I still have my moments of anger and...dead low tide."

Her voice was so low that Sarah scooted her chair closer as Annie continued. "Sarah, I am not going to live in fear. I won't live this way. Let's find these people and get this over with." She swiveled toward her. "And why didn't you tell me that someone shot you?"

Sarah groaned and let her head fall forward. "Honestly, I thought you knew. And don't ask me how you were supposed to know. Osmosis, I guess. Things have been moving so fast, and besides, my mind was somewhere else last night."

"No one said a word to me, and that is just wrong. Guess how I found out?" Sarah shook her head, and Annie pulled her chair as close as she could. "Scott."

"Scott Frazier?"

"It was nice of him to come and see me. He seems to have the greatest admiration for you."

"Ah, he's my new guy. A little under a year."

"Uh-huh," Annie teased. "He said you were shot when you went to one knee over me?"

"Something like that, but—"

"No, not something like that, and you know what?" Annie interrupted and leaned over, whispering, "You are my hero," and kissed Sarah. Not a little kiss or a thank-you kiss, but a kiss that made Sarah's entire body respond.

Neither heard the knocking at the door until Sarah remembered the guard and the coffee. She went to get the coffee, and when she came back, Annie was shaking her head.

"Rebecca must never know this."

"What?"

"That I've been in a locked room with a gorgeous woman and a bed."

"You're right. Rebecca doesn't need to know this." Sarah shook her head, but she glanced at the bed.

Annie was quiet and Sarah looked back at her. She'd lost her smile again.

"All right. What can I tell you that Mary and Kilie haven't said already?" Annie said. Sarah took a notebook from her coat, bracing her knees against Annie's.

"Kilie put me in touch with Dr. Hatawabe, and she sends her regards."

"I wish you could meet her, Sarah. She is a wonderful person."

"I've got the information from Switzerland, but what caused the attack?"

Annie straightened. "A little over three years ago, I was on my way into Iraq, on assignment. It was a very critical time, and we went in through Saudi Arabia. The French journalist that took the pictures you saw at my house invited me to a party at a Saudi palace, Prince Abdel's." Annie stopped talking and looked at Sarah. "Truly, I never thought I'd see that man again. When I saw you talking with him at the party, my heart stood still. You know how people say, 'my heart stood still'? It's true. Mine did. I swear I'd never experienced hate before. Anger, yes, I've been known for that. Just ask." She turned with a wry grin. "Or has someone already told you that?"

Sarah shook her head and waited.

"I got into an argument with one of the prince's friends, a Saudi diplomat, and some other men at the party over the American presence in Iraq. Or at least, that's what it began as. It morphed into a full-blown stupid debate about religion and even a man's place in society. We were all drinking, and no one really had any control over where the conversation was going. This was around the time Amer al-Sadr was organizing his army militia and recruiting anyone he could. We argued over that too, and I finally went to the patio to get away from them." She stopped, swallowing. "I remember someone grabbing me, the fear and the smell of the drugs. The French photographer and the men with him stopped them before it became more than just a beating."

Sarah could hear the tears in Annie's voice, but was afraid to interrupt. They needed this conversation. "Do you really understand why that damned Web site, even concrete from a bomb, seems small?" Annie cleared her throat and gathered herself. "I've had people say to me that I am tough. I don't think I'm tough. I think I just don't have a choice. Dr. Hatawabe is a bit of a Zen person, you know. Stay in the moment kind of thing, the one who got me into reading those books at my house, among other things. She taught me a lot, Sarah, but most of all, how to keep the darkness away." She took a drink of coffee, thinking.

"So I'm angry and hurt. First the attack, then Jack's killed, then the explosion, and now this. I also understand that I've made the decision to put myself in this position." Annie looked away and crossed her arms. "What's left? Death? There are so many things worse than death, and one of them is fear. That's worse. It kills your mind, your hope, your soul. It made me so angry that I just went back over there, to hell with all of them. What else could they do to me?" She was quiet again, sitting very straight. "Is there any other information you need?"

Sarah's heart was pounding. "Is there anything else that might help me?"

"No. I think I just pissed whoever he is off, by going back to Iraq. I let him know that he doesn't frighten me. This whole thing's about fear, isn't it?"

Sarah was staring at Annie, going back over the conversation. "What?"

"Did you say Amer al-Sadr?"

"Yes, he was there with a bunch of scruffy-looking people, like he'd just come in from the—" She stopped abruptly, staring back at Sarah. "Oh, my God, the photos. Sarah, the photos that Jack Keegan gave me to keep."

"Yes, the photos. Some of our people thought it was him."

"Shit," Annie said quietly under her breath. "I'm reacting, not thinking. I know what's different. That's the only time he didn't have a beard. I know very well what he does." She had tears in her eyes when she looked up.

Sarah immediately put her notebook back in her pocket. "I want to get this information to the office, Annie. As I said, we did fingerprinting and preliminary DNA on the Majers, his sister, the prince, and his mother. By the way, that woman is not his mother."

Annie looked startled. "Who is she?"

"Remember the man you saw at Sam's? Right now, the evidence is telling us that the woman is his sister. And I thought I knew her also. I'm sure I saw her at Jana's Bistro, and she was in the airport the day you came back from New York City." Sarah reached for her hand. "That means they've been around you. Probably a lot more than we know."

Annie shook her head. "This is unreal."

"That's why you have a guard here at your door. And it's locked. Right now, I'm going back to the office, and when I'm done, I'll come back here and pick you up. Tomorrow, we're leaving town. Or, if you're up to it, we'll go tonight."

Annie nodded and got up. She padded back to the bed and stretched out, pulling the covers up. There were dark smudges under her eyes, and she looked as if she could sleep.

Sarah gave Annie a hug, holding her tightly. Annie's eyes had tears in them once again, and Sarah put her fingers on Annie's lips. "Go to sleep. Let those pills do the job, and I'll be right back. We'll get you home tonight and maybe up to Green Bay, away from all this." She bent down for a quick kiss and then kissed her harder. "You taste so good. Sleep," she said as she left.

❖

Sarah was parking Annie's car in the ramp when she saw Don Ahrens getting into his car. He gestured for her to get in with him and started the engine.

"Where you able to find out anything from Ms. Booker that might help? You and I both know that if Ms. Booker, or the network, had given us this information in the beginning, we might have handled this differently."

"True, but I can understand why she didn't want to talk about it. She told me today that she thought she'd never see him again, and I believe her."

"Yes, that's probably what she thought, but as I told her boss this morning, we can't protect someone from something that we have no knowledge of. We all know they play by different rules over there, but still, someone should have said something right from the moment she got home. We needed that information."

Sarah took a deep breath and hauled out her notebook. "All right. Here's what Annie told me this afternoon," and she told him about Saudi Arabia and Amer al-Sadr.

CHAPTER TWENTY-ONE

The DuMont Hotel was one of the best to be found in the Midwest. Sarah and Don got out of the car and headed across the street. Scott Frazier was waiting inside the lobby.

"What's the status?" Don asked him.

"There's six people there now. Altogether there have been eight people in and out. All men. Haven't seen any women at all."

"Fine. Scott, give your electronics to Moore, and you go to the car." His face fell, but he gave Sarah the microphone. Don chuckled. "I just ruined his day. Soon he'll be glad to sit in the car. By the way, nothing we've found so far at the Majers' implicates Prince Abdel. I'm just not sure where he fits into all of this."

Sarah adjusted her communications as they walked toward the elevator. She mentally shuffled her information on the young Saudi and prepared for the interview.

Midafternoon, the hallway was flooded with sunlight as they walked toward the suite. Don knocked, and a young Arabic man, perhaps in his early twenties, opened the door. Don asked to speak to Prince Abdel. He closed the door, and they could hear voices inside as Don leaned against the door, listening. The prince opened the door and smiled when he saw Sarah.

"Ah, the caretaker," he said with a smile. "Is this an official visit?"

"No, just talk, if you have a moment?" Sarah had a relaxed smile on her face and let it sound in her voice. "This is Don Ahrens from my office."

"Come in, come in." The prince stepped back. He was wearing a white T-shirt and jeans with nothing on his feet. "I apologize," he said, catching her looking at his clothes. "I was sleeping."

Don and Sarah stepped into the suite. The TV was on and four or five young men were watching a soccer game. Fast-food containers and sodas were scattered on the table. Sarah thought these were probably bodyguards, but reviewing their body posture, she and Don didn't seem to pose much of a threat.

"Sir," Don began, "we would like to speak with your mother as well, if that is possible."

"She is not here," Abdel said, looking around at the other men in the room. "She left some time ago to do some much-needed shopping before we leave." That was a major slip on the prince's part, and Sarah quickly took a second look around the room.

"That's fine," Don said in a reassuring tone of voice. "We were hoping you could help us regarding the incident at Dr. Majer's home last weekend. Is there somewhere that we could talk, a table perhaps where I could lay some photos down for you to look at?"

"Of course," the prince said, "there is an office area here." They followed him into the suite, but Sarah let her eyes linger on the men as they walked through. She didn't like going into an interior room with this many people between them and the door. The room they entered was equipped with computer monitors, a fax machine, and several phones amid papers scattered about. They sat at a round table as Don put his briefcase on the floor.

"Would you like a drink?" the prince asked as they took a seat. In the afternoon sun, away from the dim lights at the Majer household, Sarah saw he was much younger than she had originally thought. The sounds of the soccer game drifted in, and she heard the men laugh. Face and posture relaxed, Sarah's mind was on full alert as the prince left the room. Don leaned down to his briefcase and put his hand inside his suit coat, nudging his gun back a bit. Sarah, seeing the gun, sat a bit straighter, checking her own weapon against her body.

Don laid about twenty photographs out on the table, preparing his questions and conversation. Someone turned up the TV, and Sarah could no longer hear voices in the other room. As the prince came in and placed the coffee and cups in front of them, he nodded at her. She realized she was expected to pour. She took Don's cup as he began to hold the photos up to the prince, handing them to him, one by one, as

Sarah kept an eye on the doorway. The prince took each picture, taking his time, sipping a light yellow liquid from a clear bottle. Putting his feet up on a chair, he selected a photo and leaned back, relaxed, holding it up and looking at Don.

"This is my cousin," he said. "We grew up together, went to college together."

Don appeared to be surprised. "We're misinformed, sir. I probably just have it mislabeled. Will you give me that name again?" He took a pen from his pocket and scribbled a name on the back of the photo. "How about this one?" he asked, shoving it across the table.

"Ah, that's my oldest brother, now in the military." He gave the photo back to Don. Don moved a photo from under another one and handed it to the prince. He smiled. "Yes, that's the family picture, my parents, brothers, and sisters."

He stopped, looked at Don, then back at the photo. The older woman in the photo was not the woman from the Majer party, and Sarah could see that he realized what he had just said. Don merely smiled and handed him the next photo. Frowning now, Prince Abdel put his feet back on the floor and laid the picture on the table, bending closer to look. He was looking at it too long, too thoroughly, and true to form, she watched his breathing change, become shallower. "This man is familiar, but I can't say who he is," he said. He handed the picture back to Don. "Is this connected to the incident with Ms. Booker?" he asked. Don nodded. "Are these people, or my family, suspected in any way?"

"We are just trying to make any connection we can," Don said sincerely, reaching for another photo.

Abdel stood, looking down at both of them. "We had nothing to do with her abduction or injury. How could my family be involved with that woman? For that matter, how could I?" He walked several steps away and then turned, looking at Don.

Sarah was motionless, watching Abdel's eyes and body posture as Don turned in his seat to answer him. "I don't think you had any part in this. Since you're in town, we hoped you might be able to identify anyone that we have questions about. We don't have the opportunity to talk with someone of your stature, or from your country, very often. Do you come here frequently?"

The prince looked through the doorway toward the television, crossed his arms, and then walked back to the table. "This is my first time in this city. I came to see how Dr. Majer's sister and her family were doing. They were in need of help, and I do what I can." He shrugged.

"How long do you plan to stay?" Don asked with an easy smile.

A door slammed, and Sarah heard a man's voice, speaking in a Middle Eastern dialect. A tall man wearing an odd-colored baseball cap came into the room, took off his coat, and smiled at the young prince. Sarah felt a jolt of recognition as he walked toward them, the male version of Prince Abdel's "mother." Sarah recognized him from the store with Annie, and she saw him remember her. He introduced himself as a cousin and scooped up some of the photos lying on the table, talking to Don about the pictures. Don seemed relaxed, nodding at the man, explaining that they were here seeking help with the case that involved Ms. Booker.

Sarah smiled, trying to melt into the background. She slid her gaze to the prince. Was he the man who had hurt Annie? Or had it been this new man? Or any of the men here? She felt very much the only woman in the suite.

The man nodded, looking quickly through the photos, and Sarah noticed the picture of Abdel's family was gone. He identified the prince's brother and cousin. Don thanked him, leaning down to put the photos back into his briefcase.

"Let's go. This is all we needed. Thank you, gentlemen. Frankly, we are at a loss." Don held out his hands, palms up, in the classic submissive posture. "Who would do this, particularly here?" Sarah stood, following Don, and looked at the man's coat that he'd tossed over a chair. It was the same one he had worn at Sam's, the small store by Annie's house. She smiled as they left the room, thanking the prince, and moved to the door.

They walked silently toward the elevators. "I'll be damned," Don said as the elevator doors closed. "This is as weird as the hidden door in the bathroom. We definitely have a brother and sister." He instructed everyone to hold their position.

They walked into the coffee shop in the hotel lobby, taking a booth that looked out on the street. "That was intense," he said. "Man, I hate situations where we get stuck in an interior area without a clear view of the surrounding rooms, don't you?"

"The prince certainly lied," Sarah said. "At least twice. And that man that came in was definitely the man Annie and I saw near her house. He recognized me, Don."

Don ordered a piece of pie and coffee while Sarah asked for water. There were only two other people in the restaurant, both at the counter, and Sarah relaxed into the booth.

"Did you know that I speak most of their languages?" Don said.

"No, how on earth?"

"My dad was in the oil business, and I practically grew up over there."

"What did the man say when he came into the suite?"

"Essentially, what the hell is going on?" Don laughed. "They think we are so unprepared for them, but we're catching up, Sarah."

"I liked your line about never having the opportunity to speak with someone of his stature. Who were the other photos of?"

"Guys I went to school with over there, about a thousand years ago," he said with a laugh. "Now we've got the mystery man's fingerprints, and I'm headed for the lab. Bet you anything they match the ones we found in the basement. I'm sure he never would have touched them if he'd known we were going to be there."

Sarah glanced out the window. A movement caught her eye, and she saw the man, the same one they'd just talked with, moving with a limp down the sidewalk. He was wearing the strange-colored baseball cap and got into a small tan compact car. She sat up, remembering that car with the red sticker and the man with the baseball cap. She'd seen it the day she'd gone to Annie's mother's clinic.

"There goes that man, the brother, or whatever. Don, I've seen him in that car before. Damn. The day I went to the Milwaukee Women's Clinic with Ms. Booker."

"All right, here's what we're going to do," Don said. "First of all, pray that we were good enough not to alarm them, and keep surveillance in place in case we weren't. Secondly, I'll get this stuff through the lab in record speed. Maybe we'll have a face to go with those prints. If that's him, Sarah, it's the man that you shot at."

"The man who shot me," she said, adrenaline and a little anger crawling across her.

"You know what has me worried? Even if this all comes out clearly, even if the prints match, how in hell are we going to do anything about it? The State Department is sending someone up here tonight or tomorrow morning. They'll guide us through what we can do about the prince. If the man is not connected to the prince's group, he's ours." He gestured at the waitress and looked at Sarah. "Get Ms. Booker home and then call me, all right? By the way, how are you feeling?"

"I'm sore, but I'm fine," she said with a little shrug. It was the truth.

He was looking out into the street. "Can I admit something to you?"

Sarah nodded.

"The other night scared the hell out of me. How about you? It's been a long time since I've had to pull my gun."

"I didn't have time to be scared. But yes, somewhere in there my knees were shaking. I've never been in so many parts of this investigation before. Is there anything else I should know?"

"No. The psychiatrist wants to see you at least once more, and it'll take I.A. a couple more days to clear the paperwork on the shooting. You're officially on limited duty. I want you to stay close to Ms. Booker and get her up north. I checked, Sarah. You haven't had time off in over a year. You have to stop that, or you won't be worth anything to me, or worse, yourself."

They left the coffee shop, and Don drove silently for a while, then cleared his throat. "I'm going to give you carte blanche with the Booker woman, Sarah," he said. "If this gets to be something else, I want you to come to me. Talk to me about it. Deal?" Sarah nodded, knowing they were having more than one conversation.

Sarah spent some time in her office, glad to find Dr. Hatawabe's information already on her computer, and she integrated it into Annie's case file. She shut her computer down and looked out at the winter sun, now just about gone. Standing in the doorway, she wondered if she should have talked to Don about her feelings. Still, if Annie took another assignment in Iraq, it wouldn't matter.

❖

Kilie Williams and Hannah Booker were there when Sarah walked into Annie's hospital room. Hannah looked worn out and gave Sarah a gentle hug.

"Are we ready?" she asked. Annie looked like she had gotten

some rest. Sarah turned to the other women. "Tomorrow, we'll be out of town. You both have my card with my numbers, and of course, you have Annie's phone numbers. Is there anything I should know or that I should do?"

Both Kilie and Hannah shook their heads. "She'll be fine. She has her instructions from both of us, and no alcohol with those pills. Wait, you're hurt too," Hannah said, moving toward Sarah. "Okay, lift that shirt."

Sarah backed away. "Can't a girl have any privacy? Come on, Hannah."

"Nope, let me look at my art work."

Sarah dropped the bag, pulling her shirt up.

"Let me see," Annie said, walking over to them.

Hannah peeled away a portion of the tape, causing Sarah to jump. "Looks good. Remember, keep a tight rein on Annie."

"No, that doesn't look good," Annie said. "It looks like she's been shot, and that's enough, Mom. You're talking as if I'm not here. Let's go, I want out of here."

They moved down the hallway, walking to the nurses' station. Hannah and the doctor stopped to fill out the paperwork as Annie and Sarah waited for the elevator. Annie grabbed Sarah's arm. "Sarah, look."

Sarah wheeled and saw a tall, dark-haired nurse dressed in blue hospital scrubs going behind the desk. She was walking right in front of Kilie and Hannah, almost a twin to the man Sarah had sat across from that afternoon. Sarah ran, bumping a nurse, but the woman went through a door before she could get there. She yelled at Hannah, "Who was that?"

"Who?" Hannah asked.

"That nurse, the one in blue, the one that just went through this door." Sarah opened the door cautiously, putting her hand on her gun inside her jacket. She stepped into the exit stairway and could hear footsteps below her, running. "Do any of you know that woman?" she asked, turning to face everyone.

Surprised faces looked back at her. No one had noticed her. Hannah looked at Sarah. "Isn't that something? In all my years and work, I've always wondered how the human mind and eyes cannot seem to work together at specific moments." Sarah pulled out her phone and called

Scott. They would need to talk to everyone who had been standing there.

Sarah alerted hospital security, but the search proved to be futile. She seemed to have just disappeared. Sarah questioned those in the area, but no one got a good look at the woman.

Moments later, Scott walked out of the elevator with Don.

"What is this about?" Hannah said. "Is she the woman who hurt Annie and Sarah? I thought it was a man."

"It was a man, Hannah, but this woman is tied to him somehow, and that's why I want Annie out of here," Sarah said. She introduced Don to the two women.

"Don, it was the same woman from Majer's party. Almost a twin to the man we saw this afternoon. Damned doppelganger. No wonder this is confusing. Wait, Annie, could you give us a sketch of the woman?"

Annie sat down at the desk with a pad of paper and a pencil. She had the woman on the paper in just a matter of minutes. "I still can't draw that man, but this isn't a problem, and I've seen her twice," she said, handing the paper to Don.

"That's her," Don said and sent Scott to the personnel office. "Sarah, there's a car waiting outside the emergency room entrance. Get Ms. Booker's car, pull it up beside the other car, and I'll follow you. I want at least two cars at her house tonight and perimeter walks every half hour."

CHAPTER TWENTY-TWO

Annie rummaged around in her kitchen cupboards looking for a vase for her flowers and noticed the missing pans, pots, and bowls. Sarah said the kitchen was a mess the night she'd pulled the gun on the girls. *Well, at least Mary remembered my penchant for a neat kitchen and left it organized*, she thought. *She should have taken them all, and then I could have shopped*, she thought. I *love to shop for a kitchen almost as much as Ellen Kennedy loves to shop for clothes.*

Flowers arranged, she flipped on the deck lights and looked toward the lake. Light snow fell steadily. Don and Sarah laughed, and Annie looked toward the den with a smile. How long had it been since she'd heard *that* kind of laughter in this house? *Sounds wonderful*, she thought, taking food out of the freezer and turning the oven on.

She turned back to the accumulating snow, and a random thought slid across her mind. She stopped, staring at nothing. She would never go back to Iraq. Ever. The psychiatrist at the clinic had said she was living in anger, not interest, in her job. Was that true? Anger wasn't feeling alive. She had loved this job so much, once. In the last three years it had been the only part of her that had felt real.

Annie wrapped her arms around herself. What else would she do? At the very least the network would have a place for her. Or she could teach. Rebecca would love that. She loved art, but she didn't think it would sustain her. She rubbed her forehead, aware that her head was hurting. She went for her pain pills just as Sarah laughed again, and Annie thought of her walking toward her bed in the hospital. Every part of her body moved just right. She'd been watching Sarah's body since the night she met her.

❖

Sarah was in the den, laughing at Don as he tried to start a fire. Finally, the flames caught and Don flopped down on the couch with a contented sigh. "This is nice," he said. "Look at the space. I'd kill for a house like this."

Sarah realized that she'd liked this house from the moment she first walked into it. Had it been Annie or Mary who had done the colors and the furniture? The room and its built-in bookcases glowed warmly in the soft lights. The carpeting that usually looked off-white now appeared the color of honey, and the colorful accents seemed to vibrate softly in the mellow lights. She could hear Annie clattering dishes in the kitchen. She exhaled. They were home, and it felt good.

Annie came into the room. "Did someone go home with Mom? I don't like it that she's involved with this."

Don nodded. "I had Frazier follow her home, just in case."

Annie looked relieved and sat in her rocking chair by the fire. "Nice fire, Don. Would you like to stay for dinner?"

"Thanks, but I can't. Here's where we are, Ms. Booker."

"The name's Annie." She smiled at him.

Sarah watched his reaction to Annie's smile with an inward laugh. *You're had, mister.* He cleared his throat, glancing at Sarah as if he knew what she was thinking, and explained the prince's diplomatic immunity as the FBI had to deal with it. Then he talked about the fingerprints and the DNA. He omitted Dr. Majer's sister since the final results weren't back. Annie listened, and when he was done, she looked at Sarah with a humorous expression.

"He knows what he's talking about."

"That's why he's the boss," Sarah said, "and he speaks most of their languages."

"Wish I did," Annie said. "It would have been very helpful when I was over there. How did you manage that?"

"I was practically raised there. My dad was an oil executive around the world but mostly in the MidEast. I have followed your reports with a lot of interest."

Annie grimaced and leaned back in her chair. "Remember them

well because I'm not sure what I'm going to do next, and believe me, I've had the time to think about this over the last few weeks." She stared into the fire and was quiet for a few moments. "When were you there?"

Sarah had left her boots by the back door in the kitchen and got up to find warmer socks. *It's always cold in this state*, she grumbled to herself and leaned back into the room. "I'm going to change clothes," she said to Annie.

Annie nodded. "Look on my desk before you come back."

Sarah took some sweatpants and a sweatshirt out of the dresser she had been using, looking through her clothes for heavy socks. Not finding the warm ones she thought she'd brought, she went into Annie's bedroom. Knowing Annie wouldn't care if she borrowed some of hers, she opened a drawer. She stopped and stared. There lay a gun, a standard police-issue 9mm, holstered properly, but a gun. Sarah took it out to make sure it was empty. It was. She put it back carefully, curious why Annie had a gun and wondering where the clip was. Annie had been adamant about not liking them or having them around her.

The next drawer had the socks she was looking for, and she sat on the bed, putting them on, thinking about the trip to Green Bay. Not tonight, it was too late and they both needed rest.

Switching on the lights in Annie's office, she grinned when she saw the country music CDs on the desktop. She carried them into the den and Annie looked up with a playful expression.

Don looked at his watch. "We have two people at the hospital personnel office, trying to identify your sketch. Scott will let you know if they find her. And now, ladies, I have to go. When this is all over, and it will be, will you stop by my office? I'd like to talk with you, Annie."

Outside, he stopped, outlining the two cars posted at the house and reminding them that there would be perimeter checks every half hour or so. He had Sarah check the alarm system and the computer.

Settling back into the den, Sarah lay on the couch and Annie sat down in her rocking chair. The fire popped a few times, and Sarah stretched, trying to find energy but found none. She closed her eyes.

"I want a beer," Annie said.

"No, not with that medication," Sarah said without opening her eyes. She could hear Annie going through the CDs, then quiet. She opened her eyes to find Annie's face, frowning, about five inches away from hers.

"My God, Annie." Sarah jumped and sat up.

"Beer," Annie said softly but firmly.

"No. That was the only thing Dr. Williams said you couldn't have. Alcohol."

"This is dumb," Annie said, going back to her chair. She held out a Dixie Chicks CD with a questioning look on her face.

"Love 'em," Sarah said. Annie put some discs into the stereo. "I borrowed a pair of your socks and noticed the gun. When did you pick that up?"

"The day you came to Mom's clinic. My brother Will got it for me. How about helping me learn to handle it?"

Sarah sat up and braced her legs on the coffee table. "Come here," she said, patting her legs.

Annie turned the music on and was in her lap almost immediately, snuggling into her, sighing. Sarah brushed the hair back from Annie's face. "I like your haircut. I kept meaning to tell you but forgot."

"I got it the day I got the gun. I thought I might as well make a clean sweep. Haircut and gun, kind of goes together, don't you think?" She smiled up at Sarah, who just shook her head. "The network keeps me in the trendiest styles so I can go on air at any given moment."

"I just wanted you to know that I noticed," Sarah said, running her fingers through the layered hair.

"Oh, girl, those brown eyes of yours are always on the move. I don't think you miss much." Annie gave her a crooked smile that made Sarah want to kiss her.

"How's your head?" Sarah asked, gently lifting the hair, looking at the stitches.

"I've been taking the mother of all pain pills. How about you?"

"Living on ibuprofen," Sarah said. "We're a pair, aren't we?" She picked up Annie's hand. "Where shall we start?"

Annie traced Sarah's mouth with her fingers. "I suppose not where I'd like?"

"Rules, damned pesky things," Sarah said. "I could get fired, Annie. I'm out to the agency. It's in my file, but clients are absolutely forbidden and I've never—" Annie quieted her with a finger on Sarah's lips.

"Okay, I'll play nice. I know you're from Arizona. Are you a cowboy...a cowgirl...a cowperson? What the hell do you call those people these days?" She laughed.

"I wouldn't know, but I do love horses. You know, the motorcycle jacket thing. Do you ride?"

Sarah took a sudden deep breath as Annie snuggled deeper. "I ride. My grandparents had a stable next to their cabin, so I grew up on them, and I've ridden a lot at Kilie and Nicki's too. Wouldn't be any good in a rodeo, but I like them. I learned to hunt and fish at my grandparents' cabin too."

Sarah raised her eyebrows. "You hunt? I thought you didn't like guns."

"I did until I started seeing how people use them against each other. I'll tell you about Grandpa, but that's why I need your help with this gun." She pressed Sarah's hand against her mouth. "Thanks for the beautiful crow carving. See it up there, on the mantel? Rainbow's End, right, where the horses are?"

"How did you know the name of the ranch?"

"The card was taped to the inside of the box."

"Nina and Sherry, always advertising." Sarah chuckled. "By the way, where do you keep the clips for that gun?"

Annie laughed.

"What?" Sarah said, wondering what so funny about ammunition for a gun. Annie sat up.

"The clips are in the bottom drawer, the sex toy drawer." She grinned at Sarah.

Sarah burst out laughing. "The sex toys?"

"When I started going overseas I'd look around and pick up new ideas, fun things." She sat up with an impish look and held her hand out. "Come on. I'm starving. Let's eat," Annie said. "The night you had dinner with my family, Dad gave me some of his stew and I froze it. It's been in the oven since we got home tonight, so it should be ready."

Sarah's stomach started to grumble as she followed Annie to the kitchen. "I just remembered. Do I still get to see your painting?"

Wheeling around from the stove, Annie looked at Sarah for a moment, then turned back. "I hadn't even thought of it. Let me get this on the table." She placed large stoneware bowls on the table with utensils and napkins. "What do you know about the brother and sister, the ones that you think have been following me?"

"Do you have any idea who they are? You've seen them both now, at Sam's and Majer's party, the hospital."

"They're familiar. That's all I know. I have thought about him until my brain hurts, but I can't connect, and that's strange for me. And her? I can't figure out if she's familiar because they look alike, or if I've actually run into her. It was a shock to see her at the hospital."

"We have their information out overseas. We'll find them. Both Don and I feel they're connected with Majer's group. Getting you out of town will give us time to work on it without worrying about them hurting you again." Sarah tackled the food but felt adrenaline start to edge into her one more time.

Annie was quiet, her eyebrows knit.

"What?" Sarah asked.

"Just instinct, experience. I always have it, like an internal warning. Something's off here. Don't you feel it?" She stared at space for a moment. "I don't think these people are part of the terrorist group. I think they're involved with the prince. We're not ready."

"We're ready, and if they are involved with the prince, we'll know. We'll find out." Sarah fought the increasing edginess, wanting to just sit in the warm kitchen with Annie and enjoy the food. "Tell me about learning to hunt."

Annie's face relaxed. "About my granddad?" Sarah nodded. "He was quite a man, my father's father. He was determined that his granddaughters, all of us, would learn to hunt just like the men. He even taught Mom, and you know what? She's a pretty good shot. He took Molly and me out in the woods behind the cabin with two guns, a small shotgun, and a twenty-two rifle. He handed each one of us a gun and said we were going to learn to shoot. Molly was sixteen and I was twelve, so I got the twenty-two. We shot tin cans, bottles, whatever he could find to put in front of us."

Annie's eyes twinkled. "We progressed to rabbits and squirrels. Will had teased both of us unmercifully all year about being girls and not being able to shoot. Grandpa evened it all up, and after a whole summer of shooting in the woods behind the cabin, he took us on a 'special' pheasant hunt with Will. I didn't hit anything, nor did Will, but Molly shot two of them. Grandpa was so proud of her, and Will never teased us again. That night we had to clean them, behind the cabin, and it was awful. To this day, when I smell burnt hair or feathers, I think of pheasant."

"So you know how to shoot a rifle or a shotgun, but not a pistol?"

"I target shoot with Will now and then, but nothing like I've got in there in the drawer. Will said it's much faster than anything I've shot before."

Sarah nodded. "Will is right, and we'll practice. I promise. We'll take some time up in Green Bay. Did you eat what you shot?"

"I love squirrel and rabbit." Annie grinned. "You just ate some."

"What?" Sarah stopped and Annie started to laugh.

"There was rabbit in that stew. Dad, Molly, and Will did some hunting last month. In the winter we get together and hunt."

"Where? I didn't know you could hunt in town."

"Right here, out in the woods beside my house. I'm in the county, not the city, and this land is grandfathered for hunting."

They took coffee back to the den, and Annie talked about hunting with her family. Sarah leaned her head back on the sofa and closed her eyes.

"Can I lie in your lap again?" Annie asked and curled into Sarah when she nodded. "This is much better than the hospital." She reached up into Sarah's dark hair, playing with the curls.

Sarah pulled her closer. "I love touching you, even when I'm not supposed to."

"Want to hear something funny?"

"How funny?"

"I told Rebecca, when I first got home, that I was fairly certain you and I didn't bat on the same team."

"How could you not know?"

"I'm pretty sure I've lost my gaydar."

"Good, you don't need to be looking anywhere else," Sarah said. "I hope you have."

"That's not nice, FBI Agent Moore. Tell me about the person who got you into the FBI and then left you."

"You want to hear about Patricia? I don't know if there are enough mean words in the dictionary to describe our relationship."

"Were you the same age?"

"Thereabouts. It's been over eight years since that disaster. We hooked up briefly in college, then lost sight of one another and found each other again. Crazy."

"What was she like? Did she like sports, books, or just bodies?"

"No, well, yes, all of the above. She's a drummer in a band."

"What? You're putting me on."

"Nope. She's a drummer for the Last Girls, an all-girl band in California, or that's where they were when I last heard from her, just after I moved here. She called me, drunk or high, whatever. She was trashed. She was a smart, pretty girl, Annie. Just couldn't get it together. I never met anyone as well read as she was. It's just a shame. And she did want me out of town. Patricia could always find someone more interesting. She had met a musician, some dark-haired guy that looked like he was going to stick a gun in your ribs any moment."

"A guy? That's always an option, isn't it? I don't know what I'd do in that situation."

"There's not much you can do, believe me. I came home, unexpectedly, and when I walked in on them in my bed, she didn't even bother to cover herself. That stays with me."

"I'm sorry," Annie said. "That's an ugly story. Anyone else?"

"Sure, but nothing that stuck. I'm always so busy and sleeping when I'm not." She looked down into Annie's face, realizing she hadn't really cared until now. "Where do you go with Mary now?"

Annie scrubbed her hands over her face. "I'd just like to salvage a friendship out of this. When she was in Switzerland, she yelled a lot. I was kind of crazy myself and told her to go home, but she wouldn't leave. I'd never seen her that angry. In my opinion, we officially split right there." She was quiet for a moment. "Do you really want to hear this?"

Sarah nodded, staring down at the green eyes. She had never seen so many shades of green as Annie's eyes.

"I don't think we said more than twenty personal words to each other on the trip home. We had both just shut down, and I didn't even want to be here. I stayed with Rebecca for a couple of weeks. Mary came back here and moved into the guest bedroom. We never slept together again, and should have just stopped right there, but Mary wouldn't. She said to keep trying, but it was over. She never mentioned the word 'love' again."

Annie slipped a warm hand under Sarah's sweatshirt, letting it lie lightly on her stomach. "I think she was already seeing Meg but wasn't sure enough to make a move. She finally did tell me just before this last trip."

The logs in the fireplace shifted and Annie got up, poking them around. "I'm ready to move on, Sarah. She already has, and frankly, I'm glad she has Meg. I can see how happy she is. I have to forgive myself for not listening all those years, or worse, not paying attention."

"Why didn't you? Pay attention, I mean?"

Annie sat down in the rocking chair and was quiet, thinking. "When Jack first took me over there, I fell in love with our troops and the cause. Those boys and girls, the men and women are so…American. And the Iraqis. It's such a different culture. I was fascinated. Then everyone began to die, and it began to be people I knew. I'd come home and send their parents or wives and husbands notes, especially if I had photos. Then there were just too many. I couldn't keep up." She stopped and took a drink of coffee. "The thing in Saudi Arabia happened and I changed. Mary would list all the ways I was becoming someone else, and I didn't know how to fix it. Everything I did just made it worse, made me restless. I couldn't find one single place to connect with her any longer. I used to leave here, go back, and practically drive myself crazy trying to think of ways to make us work. I never could find the answer."

"Was there been anyone else besides Mary?"

"As a matter of fact, the answer is almost. It was Kerry, the English photojournalist, the woman who took those pictures I gave you. At the last minute, it just wasn't enough, but she came the closest." Her voice trailed off and she looked away. "I haven't wanted anyone to touch me. When I was younger, I always took all of this for granted, but the

attack in Saudi Arabia really messed with my head, and hell, my body."
Annie yawned, and Sarah noticed the smudges were back under her
eyes again.

"Annie, I have to check the computer, and then I think we both
need some rest. How about it? Bedtime?"

Annie nodded. "Whew, I'm beat. It's that stupid pill. You're right.
Time for bed."

❖

Hamel stood in the woods, watching the FBI around the reporter's
house. He had timed the walks. About every twenty to thirty minutes.
The car was there, and he was certain the two women were inside.
This time he couldn't miss. He turned to start the long walk back to
his own car, cursing at his hurting leg. If he didn't get Jack Keegan's
photographs, Amer's contact here was going to kill him. This time he
wouldn't miss, and the reporter would give him the evidence. Then
she'd pay the price for coming back to Iraq. Arrogant Western women.
Even his sister knew enough to fear him.

Chapter Twenty-three

Annie's voice in the darkness woke her, and Sarah grabbed her gun off the nightstand as she ran to the hallway, all senses trying to wake up. Holding the gun in front of her, Sarah poked her head into Annie's bedroom, inching inside. She turned in a slow circle looking at the entire room. Moonlight lay across the floor and part of the bed.

Annie was sitting up with her arms around her knees. Sarah let the gun drop and sat on the bed.

"Annie," Sarah said. "Wake up. You're dreaming." Annie dropped her head onto her knees, crying. Sarah crawled across the bed, pulled her down, and held her.

"It's okay. It's a nightmare. I've got you now." She tucked Annie's head under her chin and pulled her body into her own, rubbing her back and shoulders until she quieted. Annie whispered something, threw her arm around Sarah's waist, and then was still.

Except for Annie's breathing, the room was quiet again, but Sarah's noisy mind, fully on guard, kept her awake. She thought about the prince and his little group, then the Majers. She was angry, almost too furious to lie still. She pulled Annie closer, breathing in her warm scent.

❖

Bright sunlight and the smell of coffee woke Sarah next. She rolled over, wondering how she'd gotten into Annie's bed, than she remembered the nightmare. Sitting, she could hear the shower in

Annie's bathroom, and she went across the hallway to her own room, anticipating the trip to Green Bay today. She dressed in navy cargo pants and a white button-down shirt with heavy socks and boots. Tucking her shirt in, she pulled a heavy blue sweater over it and began to brush her damp hair. She thought about holding Annie last night, her soft body against her own, and she knew the next time, if there was a next time, she would want more. The last woman she'd actually fallen asleep with had been Patricia in another city and another time. She tossed her bags on the bed.

Turning her phone on, Sarah walked down the hallway but stopped at the office, staring. Annie had headphones on and was barefoot, in a dark green long-sleeved T-shirt and jeans with a book in front of her face, dancing to whatever she was listening to. Sarah grinned, enjoying the body moving to the rhythm. Annie turned and caught sight of her, ripping the headphones off.

"Morning," she said, "want to dance?"

"What's this?" Sarah asked, touching the glasses Annie was wearing.

"Vanity, thy name is Annie." She laughed, setting the glasses on the desk. "Ready for coffee...or dancing?" She ran her hands through Sarah's hair and snuggled close with her arms around her neck.

Sarah breathed Annie's rainy scent and closed her eyes. "We'd better stick with coffee," she said and took Annie's hand, leading her to the kitchen on shaky legs.

Annie chattered as she bustled around the kitchen, making thin pancakes with peaches on top. Sarah watched, heart beating rapidly, replaying last night in Annie's bed. *How did it get to this? She has the sexiest voice I've ever heard, and all she has to do is speak or look at me and I almost have heart failure. Intentions*, she thought, looking down at the table.

"Why did I wake up with you in my bed this morning?" Annie asked, cutting up her pancake.

"You had a nightmare last night. It got me out of bed in a hurry, and I just never went back."

"The pain pills make me a little stupid. That's too bad. Or maybe Rebecca's right. I'm slowing down." She poured more syrup on the pancake. "By the way, are you going home to your apartment for clothes or anything before we leave today?"

"I need clean clothes?" Sarah said, reaching for another pancake and more peaches.

"No, I'm asking if I can go along, see your place where you live." Annie's smile didn't quite reach her eyes.

"Absolutely, but what's up, Booker?"

"It was so wonderful this morning, waking up with you. Like crawling out of a deep fog. I'd like to keep that feeling for just a bit longer."

Sarah got caught in Annie's eyes, feeling her entire body shift toward her, but her phone rang and she reached for it.

"Well," she said finally, "thanks for the call. I appreciate it, Don." She hung up and looked at Annie. "Now I can tell you what I wouldn't say last night. Our DNA just confirmed that the man and woman are your friend's oldest kids. That would be Majer's niece and nephew."

Annie's eyes swung up. "Nyalia's kids?"

"I wanted to make sure before I told you, Annie."

"No, Nyalia wouldn't do that to me."

"Annie," Sarah said, putting the phone down and reaching for her hand. "She may not know."

Annie jumped up from the table. "Wrong, you're wrong! Damned straight she knows. She knows it all." Annie started out of the room, then turned, coming back, angry energy crackling around her. Sarah sat very still, engulfed in the sight, watching the green eyes turn electric.

"Sarah, I've been talking with her for well over two years. Been in her home, helped her with her two youngest daughters." Annie slammed into the chair next to her. "Damn and damn again! That's where I've seen them, now I remember him. She had pictures of them in her house, in Baghdad. They were younger, of course,, but still, it's them." She laid her head on the table. "I can't believe this."

"Don is going out there right now to pick up Dr. Majer and his sister. I need to sign this trip off at the office. Let me get Scott in here, and he'll stay with you while I'm gone. You finish packing and I'll just swing back for you. Remember, we've got the walk-by every half hour, so don't be alarmed when you see someone outside."

"Okay, gumshoe. I'll be here."

❖

The office was busy as Sarah walked toward Don's office. He was sitting at his desk, suit coat thrown over a chair. He looked up when she came in.

"How was last night?" he asked.

"It was quiet, had a nice meal, went to bed early. We're getting out of town, at last. Did you pick up the Majers?"

"They're downstairs, talking to their lawyer. As I told you on the phone, the man and woman that have been around Annie are Majer's niece and nephew. Her sister's oldest children."

"Do you think she knew what they were going to do at the party?"

"She wouldn't talk because her brother, Dr. Majer, wouldn't let her. From what little conversation that did occur, I have the feeling that she was aware of some of this, but certainly didn't have all the facts. And, Sarah, as you said, she went into that bathroom just before Ms. Booker."

Sarah asked about the prince and the information from Dr. Hatawabe that she'd given the lab yesterday.

"Still nothing on your new information. Good notes, by the way. We'll have something today, I'm sure. Surveillance says the prince's little group is packing up, getting ready to leave. They've checked out at the desk. I've got Customs ready at the airport, just in case Majer's nephew Hamel is with them. We'll detain him if he is. The men from the Chicago State Department are on their way up, so we'll be able to talk with them legally, but not for long. Whenever he wants to leave, the prince can go."

"I told Annie about Majer's sister and she exploded. She considered the woman a friend."

"It's going to be a long day. We'll formally arrest Dr. Majer today. I've already informed his lawyer. As a matter of fact, I have some photos we picked up at the Majers', and Annie might be able to give us some information. What I'm trying to connect is the female, Majer's niece. Why would she be working with her brother to harm Annie? Unless they're a team, working together for the prince."

"That's what Annie said last night. Maybe she's right. Well, we'll be gone today, and that'll give you time to work on this without worrying about her." Sarah reached for her coat, anxious to get going. "All right, I'm gone."

"Sarah, just a minute. Remember, we may have their mother, but we don't know where these two people are, especially the woman. We got an ID from the hospital. I've got people on their way out there now, to her apartment. Be careful."

Sarah nodded as she put her coat back on. She left and checked the clock in the hall. It was almost noon. As the elevator doors opened, Scott Frazier walked out, taking his gloves off.

"Scott." Sarah reached for his arm. "Who's at the house?"

"What?" He stopped. "I thought we had them here."

"Who?"

"I was monitoring Don on the computer as he picked up the Majers. He said they picked up the man, the woman, and their mother." He looked unsure. "I told Ms. Booker we were leaving and why. She asked why you hadn't called."

"Oh, Scott, no." Sarah ran the few steps back to Don's office, leaning into his door. "Scott misunderstood and pulled the surveillance from Annie's house. He's here, with the other car as well. Call the locals and see if they can get someone out there. I'll take Scott with me." Don stood immediately, grabbing his phone.

Scott apologized all the way up to the parking ramp in the elevator, but Sarah barely heard him. She ran toward the car, listening to Annie's message on her phone. Sarah dialed but could only get Annie's voicemail. It'd been well over an hour since she'd left. As she tried to get the car keys out of her pocket, her phone rang and she hoped it was Annie, but it was Don. He'd called the state police for an escort out to the Booker house.

Sarah had a moment of pure panic and her hand shook so badly that she couldn't get the key in the ignition. Exhaling, she got a firm hold on her mind, got the key in, and drove down the parking ramp, praying the local police were on their way.

CHAPTER TWENTY-FOUR

Annie cleaned up in the kitchen after Sarah left for her office. She thought about waking up with Sarah that morning. Sarah's warm skin and breath on her face had surprised her, then flooded her with hunger. God, had she ever been this empty? In the last three years her body had betrayed her constantly. "Damn," she said and stood. Desire had to count for something. Sarah quieted her, gave her room to think. It was something she'd never found with Mary.

She went to the office, thinking of the trip today, and opened the loft door for her heavy boots. She put her phone in her pocket, added the charger to the bag, and slid her laptop into its case. She put her glasses into a metal case and tossed them into the other bag. A book on the desk caught her eye, and she slid it and another into the bag, wondering if Sarah was going to stay in Green Bay with her. She had forgotten to ask. Maybe Scott would know. She walked to the living room, and he looked up, smiling.

"Guess what? They've got them all downtown." He stood, shutting down the laptop. "That means we can all go home. It's over, Ms. Booker."

"I haven't heard from Sarah," she said. "Wouldn't she have called?"

"She may not know, but I was listening to the transmission between Don and the office when he picked up the Majers and the whole group." He disconnected the wires, wrapping them into the case.

"Majer's niece and nephew too? His sister's kids?"

"Yes, and I'm heading back to the office. It's over." He pulled his suit coat on, smiling at her.

Annie stood at the front windows and watched the cars leave. It didn't feel right. Sarah would have called. She dialed Sarah's phone but got her voicemail again and left a message, asking about the information Scott had given her. She checked the alarm system and walked back to her bedroom. Perhaps Sarah was on her way home.

Taking dark green slacks out of the closet, she selected a sweater to match and hung them in the bathroom. Looking back at her bedroom, she felt like she was leaving on assignment, everything strewn between here and her office. Annie reached over for a towel. Her life was changing, again.

A soft but distinct thud sounded above her, and Annie looked up at the bathroom ceiling. She thought it was snow falling off the roof, but then knew she was wrong. There was a straight pane of glass right above her head, a studio window. The floor creaked softly, and Annie realized there was someone in the studio, in the house. She moved quickly to the drawer with the gun and then the two clips. Annie knew every creak in that floor and remembered she had left the loft door unlocked.

Instincts honed by years in hollowed-out buildings, ditches, and unknown terrain kicked in, and Annie stepped into the hallway. The air was very still.

The most secluded place would be the back bedroom, but Sarah's room had the best view of the hallway. Annie moved quickly to the closet that faced the doorway. Ducking under hanging clothing, she pushed herself against the back wall, then looked down at herself, at her dark jeans and long-sleeved T-shirt. She straightened her head behind the clothing, face covered in the shadows. Her hands shook as she put the clip into the gun, and she forced herself to think of everything she could remember from the day Will had given her the gun. Clip in first, check safety, hold still, and pull firmly but lightly. It would be fast. Annie put the gun between her legs, holding it with both her knees and her hands, checking the safety again, waiting. Annie had a perfect memory of her grandfather, standing in the woods with her and Molly. "Don't shut your eyes. Look where you're shooting."

There was a sudden noise in the office, and Annie strained her ears. The telephone rang like a warning, and she could feel sweat trickling down her back as she tightened her knees and her hands.

A click sounded in the kitchen as the French doors opened and closed, then soft voices, male and female. Annie remembered Sarah had her car. They probably didn't know she was here. A woman passed in front of the room. Annie recognized her. Nyalia's daughter. Within seconds Annie could hear her in the room next to her and then in her own bedroom across the hall. *What irony*, she thought, *take fire in the Middle East, and get shot in my own home, by a woman.*

The telephone began to ring again in the quiet house, and she reached into her pocket, turning her phone off. Annie waited, barely breathing. She could hear someone in her office, drawers opening, things falling on the floor. The woman appeared in her doorway, gun in front of her, turning slowly, eyes passing the closet where Annie was hiding. As she started into the room, sirens sounded from outside, and she stopped, stepping back out into the hallway, saying something to the other person. They were quiet for a moment and then a male spoke. The woman stepped back into the room in front of Annie. She pressed her back against the wall. Her head was turned toward the doorway, looking away from Annie's hiding spot. For a moment even the air felt sharp, as the garage door opener started to grind and the sirens screamed loudly. *Thank God*, Annie thought, *Sarah's here. I won't have to shoot.* The woman pushed straighter against the wall with her head still turned toward the hallway, listening.

Everything happened at once. Sarah called out her name, and the woman stepped out into the hallway, gun pointed at Sarah's voice. Annie yelled "No!" and pulled the trigger, watching as the woman slammed into the opposite wall under the force of the bullet, blood spraying across the light colors. The noise was enormous, and Annie saw the woman's head turn, a surprised expression on her face, as she struggled back to her feet, fully facing Annie now, gun pointing at her. Someone else shot and the woman fell. She stayed down. Annie heard more gunshots outside the house.

Several moments of dead silence followed, and Annie scrambled out of the closet on her hands and knees, peeking over the bed at the body lying in the hallway. The woman was breathing.

Sarah was calling her name, and she tried to answer, but nothing came out of her mouth. Annie cleared her throat and tried again. "Here," she called.

She could hear a man saying, "Shots fired," but she didn't move, wouldn't move, until she saw Sarah. Sarah looked in the door at Annie kneeling on the other side of the bed. "Are you all right?" she said, holstering her gun and moving quickly to Annie.

Annie stood, handing Sarah the gun, and then fell into her. "She was going to shoot you," she said, wrapping her arms tightly around her. Annie's ears rang from the noise of the gun, and the smell still sizzled around them.

Don walked in the door. "What happened, Sarah? Annie?"

"I shot Nyalia's daughter," Annie said into Sarah's coat. "She was going to shoot Sarah." She stiffened. "Dammit, I shot someone."

Don turned and walked to the woman in the hall, pulling on latex gloves. Sarah took Annie to the kitchen and then went back to Don, squatting down beside him. "She's alive, and I have her gun," he said. "Scott shot the brother, Hamel, on the deck, but he didn't survive. It's the man from the DuMont Hotel, Majer's nephew." He placed his fingers on the woman's neck. "Strong pulse."

"I came inside and the deck doors were open, so I called for Annie," Sarah said, handing Annie's gun to Don. "It all happened so fast. Just as I was starting to see the woman, Annie yelled something and shot. The woman fell against the wall and then straightened up and pointed the gun into the bedroom, so I shot too. Looks like Annie hit the right shoulder area and I got her here." Sarah pointed at the blood on the right side of the woman's chest.

Don just shook his head. "The man abandoned his sister and went out through the patio doors." Don leaned over the unconscious woman. "There's an ambulance on the way. Locals and crime scene people will be here soon too." He looked up at Sarah. "Do you have any idea how fast you and that state trooper were going on the interstate?"

❖

After speaking to Scott for a few minutes, Sarah poured a cup of coffee, keeping an eye on Annie sitting at the table. Annie was watching the local police and the FBI go in and out of her house and someone was stretching crime scene tape around the deck. She had given her statement to the police in a clear, coherent voice, but she was quiet, sitting straight, and Sarah saw the professional mask cover her face.

Don followed the medical technicians with the wounded woman

down the hallway and held the kitchen door as they moved to the ambulance. He watched Annie's eyes follow the gurney and raised his eyebrows at Sarah.

Annie spoke to Don. "Where is Prince Abdel? Has he left yet?"

Don shook his head. "They're about to leave the hotel. I just spoke with surveillance. We need to talk with Abdel, but I don't know how we're going to hold him for very long. Customs will hold him for a while, and State is meeting me there, but—"

"Why do we need the prince now?" Sarah interrupted. "Hamel's dead and we have his sister."

"Because Abdel collaborated with the Majers, Sarah. That puts it back into my case."

"I have an idea," Annie said. "Let me get my local TV affiliate down there, at the airport. They can be there before him, and I'll interview him."

"No!" Don and Sarah said together.

"Why not? This is a perfect setup. He'll see it as an opportunity for publicity. The prince has the perfect mindset for this, and you know he won't give you or the State Department anything. Plus, he seems to want to talk with me."

"Booker," Sarah groaned.

"Listen to me. He's not only got the ego, but there isn't a man of the prince's position who would want to be embarrassed in a public place, especially by a woman." Annie was calm and confident. "I guarantee you that he'll talk to me. It's my job. Just brief me on what you want, the information you need. Actually, I can probably get him to stay for a while, and you can ask him what you need. How long do you need him? I'll just front him with the interview."

Sarah and Don were quiet, thinking about what she had just said. It went against everything Sarah wanted. They'd just be putting Annie out there again. "I don't think I can let you walk in front of him again, Annie. You've done enough," she said, lacing her fingers with Annie's.

"Sarah, remember what I said? What's left? Death? Fear is worse. This is the only chance we'll have to face him. Otherwise, he's back in his cave." Her eyes begged, but her face was the one from television, composed and unafraid.

Annie turned to Don. "The local producer was in Kosovo with me.

He'll give me a hand, and this is a perfect moment for him to get in on the action."

"That might work," Don said, just as Sarah had known he would.

CHAPTER TWENTY-FIVE

Sarah and Annie made the familiar drive to the airport in silence. The afternoon sun outlined Annie's profile. Sarah's heart clenched as it had at the airport when Annie had left for New York City. She exhaled slowly and reached across the seat, taking Annie's hand into hers and rubbing it with her thumb. Annie seemed focused on a faraway place, but she squeezed Sarah's hand and finally spoke as they pulled into the parking ramp at the airport.

"Can you find out if my local guys have arrived?"

Sarah called Don. "We're in the parking enclosure. Where is everyone?" She looked across at Annie. "They're all in place. Are you ready?"

"Yes." Annie looked down, searching through her coat and pulling out a notebook and a pen. She held them up for Sarah to see. "Told you. I always have them on me, somewhere." She put her hand on the door, than turned back to Sarah. "Is today Thursday?"

Sarah nodded and raised her eyebrows in a question.

"It was a little over three weeks ago when you picked me up here at the airport." She laid her hand on Sarah's cheek, tracing it with her fingers. They lingered on her lips, and then she turned, opening the car door. In the elevator, Sarah wordlessly pulled her into her arms for a moment and Annie leaned in with a sigh. The doors to the international terminal opened, and they walked toward the local TV producer and cameramen waiting beside their equipment. Annie flipped her notebook open, writing as she and the producer talked. Don, Mike Easton, and two men were sitting in the waiting area. They got up when they saw Sarah and Annie.

The prince had his back to her. He turned to look at Annie, frowned for a moment, and then smiled when he saw the TV cameras. Annie had been right.

Sarah walked past the group while Don and Mike stayed behind Annie and the television equipment. Annie said something to the prince that made him turn and look at Sarah with a smile. Annie gestured at the cameras and tossed her coat over a seat, composed and confident. Sarah looked at the other men, sitting in the concourse chairs. They seemed relaxed but were watching the prince and the cameras closely. Annie's eyes raked over them and then came back to Sarah's.

Why does this feel so dangerous, Sarah wondered, checking the area. The terminal was quiet with only a few people in the comfortable seats. Annie had said this was just an interview, and she'd done thousands of them. Sarah looked back at her, at her apparent ease and comfort.

The prince had his head slightly cocked, listening closely to Annie as she fixed a microphone on his clothing and then one on hers. She nodded at him, then turned to face the camera and began to speak, her back to the prince's men. Sarah was riveted onto the group as Don and Mike walked casually to stand closer to Annie as she spoke. Sarah slid her hand inside her coat, touching her gun.

The prince answered Annie's questions, smiling easily, and she said something to him. He stopped smiling and said, "No," very loudly, dropping his hands into fists at his side. Annie, still smiling, tucked her hair behind her ear. She spoke again, and Sarah wished she were close enough to hear. The young prince was clearly angry. Annie said something to the cameraman and the prince, gesturing at the seats. Sarah walked toward them as Annie folded down into a seat with Prince Abdel next to her.

Abdel let his head drop, staring at the floor. Finally, he looked at Annie. "I wanted to tell you that night at Majer's. This truly was not my doing, but I had no choice."

Annie frowned at him just as Don leaned over, saying something to him in his own language. He turned to the men from the State Department and Prince Abdel agreed to talk with them.

❖

Pinks and reds from the setting sun shimmered around Annie and Sarah as they walked from Sarah's office. Annie took Sarah's hand for a moment. "Your hands are cold again."

"I'm just tired, and yours are always so warm." Sarah opened the door to the conference room where Don and the State Department officials were talking with Prince Abdel.

Don looked at Sarah. "Abdel has a problem. Hamel had his sisters."

"Sarah, you were right," Annie said softly. She sat down, smiling at the prince. "Abdel, talk with us. I just want to know that I'm safe now. That's all. If you can help me in any way, I'll be satisfied for my part. Perhaps these men can help you find your sisters."

The prince looked at her for several moments and then sat across from her. "I really didn't come here to hurt you, Ms. Booker. I didn't even know you would be here until Dr. Majer told us you were back. Hamel and his sister followed you."

"Your sisters?" Annie asked. "Were you perhaps related to Hamel in some way?" She never took her eyes from him.

"My sister married him in Paris," he said, leaning on his elbows on the table. "My family, of course, has never accepted the marriage, but my sister was rebellious, refused to come home. Then she lured my youngest sister to stay with her. My family has forbidden any contact, but my brothers and I have never given up."

Sarah asked what would happen to his sisters now.

"I don't even know how to find them. Hamel's sister coordinated the communications. They ran the business together, and you say she is dead."

"No," Don said, "she's not dead. She's at the hospital, but I'm afraid Hamel didn't make it."

The prince asked Don for a drink before he continued. He looked at Annie. "Hamel has been working with Amer al-Sadr, operating a trade with women from several countries since his father was killed, and you just happened to be there." He stopped. "You argued with them at the party at my home, and then you came back into Iraq, as if nothing had happened. He was furious. Your friend, Jack Keegan, had photos of Hamel with Amer and some of his men. They killed your associate, but your soldiers were too quick. They didn't want you, Ms. Booker.

They wanted the photos. Jack Keegan was going to give them to the new Iraqi government to shut Hamel out of the country and prove that Amer was profiting off the war."

Annie became very still, looking at him as silence gathered around them. She finally dropped her head. "That's why I couldn't draw his face. Something in my mind remembered."

"The hospital says the sister's going to survive? Do you think we could negotiate?" Don said to the men from the State Department. "Or will you want to hold the sister on other charges? They both collaborated with known terrorists at the very least, not to mention the sex trade with the women here." He looked at Abdel. "As did you, sir."

One of the men from the State Department said, "Perhaps we can negotiate the whereabouts of your sisters, Abdel, in return for deportation, including her mother and sisters. I'm certain our counterparts over there would welcome the information. Don, let's go to the hospital and see if Majer's niece is awake. The prince can go with us. He's not under arrest."

Don nodded, and everyone stood. "Sarah, you and Annie go on home. It's been a hell of a day. I'm not sure you'll want to go to your house, Annie."

She was silent for a moment, "No, I don't think so."

Sarah got up. "We'll stay at my place. Let's go home, Annie."

❖

They picked up Thai food on the way to Sarah's apartment, and Annie called her parents, then left Rebecca a message. As they got out of the car, Annie pointed up into one of the trees.

"Will you look at that? A crow."

"At this time of night? That's unusual. They're usually nested by now."

"They waited for us, Sarah." The crow called out just as she spoke. It lifted its huge wings to fly.

Annie laughed as she turned in Sarah's living room. "This is wonderful. Look at the colors and the artwork. My heavens, where did you get all this?" She picked up a large wood carving of a bird sitting in the corner. "What is this?"

"It's a roadrunner, a bird common to the Southwest. Kind of a quirky bird. You'd like it. Especially the male with its colors." Sarah put the food out on her kitchen table, then closed the blinds on the windows. "Come on. Food's out, and I even have a beer or two." She set two bottles on the table and then looked at Annie. "Wait, did you take any of those pills today?"

"Oh God, are we going to go through that again?"

"Yes."

"Well then, the answer is no," Annie said, smiling sweetly and grabbing the bottle before Sarah could get a hand on it. "I'm hungry, as usual. Let's eat."

"By the way, what did you ask the prince at the airport? Whatever it was, you got his attention."

"I asked him why he attacked me. His apology at Majer's party just wouldn't leave my mind, and my thick head finally realized he was trying to tell me something."

Sarah frowned. "Why?"

"Abdel is young but not stupid, and it looks like he cares about his sisters. Or maybe it's gotten to be a matter of pride. I'd bet anything it was Hamel who was doing the assaulting in France, wouldn't you?"

"Wasn't he a piece of work? What did you say to Abdel that made him smile at me before the interview?"

"I said you were the most attractive woman I'd ever known."

Sarah blushed, totally at a loss for words.

Annie grinned at Sarah's red face and changed the subject. "Where did you get the Indian rugs on the walls? Your grandmother?"

"Some of the blankets are from Grandmother, but I've just picked up what I liked through the years. We share a love of colors, don't we?"

"It's our eyes, Sarah. We probably see colors much the same."

Sarah watched Annie look at her living room, hoping they saw more than colors the same way. After they ate, Sarah led Annie through the apartment and stopped in her bedroom. "My bed's kind of small. I'll sleep on the couch."

Annie looked at her. "You must be kidding." She walked out of the room, her voice trailing behind her. "Have anything I could wear to sleep in?"

Sarah nodded, but Annie was gone. She shook her head and yelled after her, "I'm going to shower. Make yourself at home." She grabbed some flannel boxers, a T-shirt, and warm socks, heading for the bathroom. "Damn," she said softly, "I'm tired."

❖

After the shower Sarah walked into her office just as Annie picked up a photo off her desk.

"Who's this?" Annie asked and turned to see Sarah in the boxers, T-shirt, and socks. The sight silenced her, and she missed Sarah's response. "I'm sorry, what did you say?"

"I said, my family." Sarah looked over Annie's shoulder, putting her hands on Annie's hips and leaned into her. "That's Mom, Dad, my sister, her husband, two kids, and our dog." Annie smelled the lavender soap, felt Sarah's body against her, and quickly set the frame on the desk before she dropped it.

Sarah leaned into her again and picked up another photograph. "Look at Dad." It was her father, holding up the biggest large-mouthed bass Annie had ever seen.

"That's huge. You fish in Arizona?"

Sarah nodded. "We fish a lot."

"Good," Annie said, "I've got a boat and we'll go out on Lake Michigan. Have you been out there yet?"

"No one's ever asked me." Sarah covered her mouth, yawning again. "But if you're asking, I'd love to go. See any books you want?"

"You'd give your books away?"

"To you, of course."

Annie gave a little laugh. "Well spoken." She pointed at the family photo. "Does your mother work, or is she retired like your dad? She looks younger than him."

"She'd love to hear you say that. She's five years younger than he is and is a working archeologist. She works for a national museum, actually. My mom is something else. Well, you talked with her."

"That explains your degree in archeology."

"Enter Patricia. Did I have a brain?"

"Your mother sounds very energetic. I enjoyed the conversation, and you're one of her favorite topics." Annie turned to the other wall. "Sarah, what's this?" She was looking at the photos of crows and the carvings.

"You're the first person I've met that likes crows like I do," Sarah said, picking up a small statue. It was carved from black onyx and sitting on a piece of pyrite. "Do you know much about them?"

"Some. They're highly organized and mate for life."

"They're all black. There's no difference in color between the male and female, and they're probably the smartest bird on the planet. Survivors." Sarah set the statue down. "Annie, let's go sit on the couch. I can't believe I'm this tired. I'll sleep out there tonight."

"Didn't like sleeping with me last night?"

"Don't say that. I'm just trying to make you comfortable, and you've had a rough day."

"Good, then we'll sleep together. I don't take up much room." Annie patted her legs, and Sarah collapsed into her lap.

"Oh," she groaned, "this feels wonderful."

Annie looked down at Sarah lying in her lap and knew it would just take minutes. She bent, kissing her, tasting the tang of beer on her mouth. "Go to sleep. I'm going to sit here and shake the dust out of the rafters." She ran her fingers through Sarah's dark wavy hair.

"You've had quite a day." Sarah touched her mouth where Annie's had just been.

"I want to go see that woman in the hospital tomorrow."

Sarah reached up to touch Annie's face. "How are you? I think we should talk. I mean about the shooting and Hamel."

"I need to think about it for a while, actually." Annie's breath hitched. "You shot someone too, for the second time. The thing at the airport, that's just my job, and Hamel? At least I know and it's over."

Annie was quiet and Sarah looked up at her. "Tell me where you've been, Annie," Sarah said.

Annie started to talk about her first winter in Kosovo, watching Sarah's long eyelashes droop and come to rest against her cheeks. Sarah was soon asleep. Annie sat quietly, finishing her beer, studying the sleeping woman. She reached down, pulling Sarah's T-shirt up just enough to look at the stitches across the taut muscles.

"Dammit, Booker," she whispered, angry tears in her eyes. "You got someone hurt, someone you care about. Sarah, I just found you."

She stared out into the space in Sarah's living room, replaying the woman in the house today. She never thought she'd have to fire a gun in her own home. Then she thought about the woman's eyes just before the car bomb. It had been an appraising look, as if she knew she was only a drawing on a piece of paper, another woman from another country. Annie laid her head on the back of the couch and groaned softly. *Christ, stop it, Booker. You've got to let it go. You can't solve it. You can't change it. All you can do is leave it and never go back.*

She got up carefully, wiping her eyes with her hands, and covered Sarah with a blanket. Finding a long T-shirt, she took a long shower and wandered back to Sarah's office. She looked at the family photo again, studying it for several minutes. Sarah was a beautiful combination of both of her parents. She had her mother's wonderfully sculpted mouth and her dad's long, lean body lines. But where did she get those beautiful eyes? The photo wasn't clear enough. She reached for a book and saw another photo in a silver frame, a much younger Sarah. She put it back carefully, walked back to the living room, and sat on the other end of the couch, putting Sarah's feet in her lap. She stared out into space, then rubbed her tired eyes, looking back at Sarah. Was it her imagination, or did this woman always smell like the outdoors? Like fresh air and lavender? She grinned and whispered, "Damn straight we'll sleep together, Moore. I think you're officially off duty."

CHAPTER TWENTY-SIX

S arah woke up on the couch, one low light still on in the room. Annie was asleep, her head on Sarah's stomach and arms wrapped around her waist. Sarah lifted her head, looking down her own body at the sleeping woman. *I've got to move*, she thought and ran her fingers through the brown-blond hair lying across her ribs.

"Annie," she said softly.

Annie raised her head, disoriented, and Sarah held her arms out. She crawled up Sarah's body, reaching between the two of them, and pulled both of their T-shirts up as she moved. She mumbled "better" in a sleepy voice. Warm skin touched warm skin.

"Fall asleep?" Sarah said. She heard her voice shake. Every single cell in her body was moving toward Annie.

"Mmm, still asleep. Want to feel your skin."

Sarah kissed her ear, her cheek, and then her lips. Annie groaned. Sarah pulled her closer, soft skin skimming soft skin.

"Annie," she whispered just as Annie struggled to her knees, straddling Sarah's hips, and pulled her shirt off. Sarah stopped breathing as the naked woman hovered above her, slender as smoke. Annie cupped Sarah's face with her hands, hair falling forward onto Sarah. She kissed her mouth. Once, twice, and then she stretched lightly and fully on top of her once again. The only sound was their own labored breathing. Sarah, helpless in front of her own desire, turned Annie over, fingers running roughly over shoulders and breasts, harshly across ribs to hips. She felt Annie flinch beneath her relentless hands.

"Christ," Sarah's voice hitched with an uneven breath. She scooped Annie up, going for the bed. She couldn't believe how little she weighed.

Sarah couldn't have said where her clothes went except that they were gone, and she was kissing the hollow of Annie's throat, a shoulder, and a perfect erect nipple. Annie shivered. Sarah looked down into shadowy unfocused eyes and kissed her, hard, her restless hands stopping inside Annie's thighs.

Afterward, Annie curled into her, talking and kissing her softly. Her hands and voice lulled Sarah's body. Sleepy with satisfaction, Sarah closed her eyes. Annie had the sexiest voice she'd ever heard. Annie's soft mouth nibbled on Sarah's skin in between words and hands caressed her hips, across her stomach. Her heart jumped as Annie's soft voice, sweet mouth, and gently aggressive hands charmed her body back into slow, unhurried sex. Finally exhausted, they fell asleep in each other's arms.

❖

A shaft of moonlight lay across the foot of the bed as Sarah woke, stretching into Annie's warm body, breathing sex mixed with her rainy scent. Annie had quietly, almost shyly, seduced her. Sarah stared at the dark. No one had ever done that before. Emotion shook through her. Now that she had touched and tasted her, she would always want her, even when she left.

Annie's body trembled against Sarah, caught in a dream. "Sarah, be careful," she mumbled.

"Baby," Sarah whispered, smoothing her hair, trying to wake her.

"A dream," Annie said as she woke. She pulled Sarah on top of her. "A dream about you."

❖

At 10:05 in the morning, Sarah's cell phone woke them. Arms and legs disentangled and everything moved at once. Sarah grabbed the phone. "Damn," she said. It was Don.

Annie laughed and asked about a toothbrush. Don was talking, but Sarah wasn't listening. Her eyes were glued to Annie's naked body. She had to ask him to repeat himself. Twice. She hung up as Annie came back in, a borrowed toothbrush in her mouth.

"Here, let me help," she said around the toothbrush, picking up Sarah's clothes from the floor.

"Damned meetings," Sarah said as Annie tossed clothing at her.

Annie maneuvered the toothbrush around in her mouth, grabbing Sarah's feet, pulling her socks on and finally, tugging her off the bed, ending up in her lap.

"Do we have to go?" Annie looked longingly at the bed.

"Freaking meetings," Sarah grumbled again and then looked at Annie. "Is that my toothbrush?"

Annie took it out of her mouth and kissed her.

Sarah talked about her ranch as they drove to Annie's house in bright winter sunlight. She glanced across the car at Annie. Everything made them smile and lean toward one another. Annie inched slowly toward Sarah. By the time they drove into the driveway, Annie was almost in her lap with her hands under her shirt. Sarah almost drove into the wall.

Walking inside silenced both of them. Yellow tape was stretched across the deck, drawn drapes darkened the rooms, and the kitchen was still cluttered with yesterday's mess. Sarah put her arm around Annie's waist and walked with her to the bedroom. Annie sighed and went to change clothes. Sarah walked out on the deck, ducking under the yellow crime tape and around the side through the snow. The small bottom pane in the loft was still open and Sarah frowned at it. It should have been closed yesterday. She looked at the prints in the snow. The man had gone in first just as he had before, then opened the patio doors for the woman. Sarah followed the trail out to the woods to an old panel truck. She pulled out her phone and called Don.

"We knew the truck was there but haven't had the time, Sarah. The lab team will be back there in less than two hours. We'll finish up and close this out." She could hear him organizing out loud as his voice rambled on. "Can you make the meeting? We'll wrap this up and get you some down time."

They hung up and Sarah looked at her watch as she walked back to the house. Clouds had captured the sun. She stood on the deck, looking down at the lake. The falling snow looked like fog creeping up the slope. Bending over the railing, she noticed coyote tracks trailing across the snow. She gripped the rail. *Annie will leave again*, she thought. *She's too good not to, and that's what she's supposed to do.* She shivered as light snow blew around her.

The doors opened and Annie came out onto the deck, shrugging into her coat. She wore a yellow sweatshirt with jeans and boots.

"Where have you been?" Annie asked. The bright sweatshirt reflected the tan still on her face, like a small sun in the now gray winter surrounding them.

"Trying to see how they got into the house," she said. "The vehicle they used yesterday is out there."

"How did they do it?" Annie walked past her, looking out into the woods.

"The same as before, the garage to the loft. I was driving your car, and they didn't think anyone was here. The crime scene folks will be out soon and they'll take the vehicle. Also, we'll have to close that shutter in your loft." She pointed up at the open window.

Annie nodded, looking down at the lake as the cold wind bit at them. "Look, Sarah, lake effect snow. The wind's shifted, and the lake's snowing on us." She wrapped her arms around her and put her mouth close to Sarah's ear. "We managed just fine in your bed last night. I really don't take up much room."

"You're the first woman I've had in my apartment or that bed."

"I want to be there again."

Sarah put her arms on Annie's shoulders. "We'll finish all of this at the meeting this morning. Annie, where do we go from here?"

"I'm cooking dinner for you tonight." Annie reached for her hand. "Come with me. I have something for you."

Annie took Sarah inside to the kitchen and said, "Wait here."

Several minutes later she was back, and she told Sarah to turn around as she carefully propped the painting on the chair. "Now, stand over there by the doors, and, yes, I closed the window in the loft." Sarah started to grin. "Take a few steps forward until you're almost against the doors," Annie said. "Okay, now turn around."

Sarah glanced first at Annie's face, now shy, a look that Sarah had never seen before. Then she looked at the painting. She pulled in a breath, stunned.

"It's not done, but—" Annie said, but Sarah interrupted.

"When was this, Annie? I mean, I can see it's the couch in the den." The painting of Sarah was like a touch, explicit in its desire.

"The first night you stayed here, after your workout."

Sarah put her arms tightly around Annie, not trusting her voice.

"Okay, now that's a first for both of us." Annie's voice was soft against her ear. "I've never let anyone see a painting before it was finished, and I was the first woman in your own bed. We're even."

Sarah stared at the painting over Annie's shoulder. *My God*, she thought, *where do feelings begin?* "Thank you, baby. It's beautiful." She cleared her throat. "Annie, you were just so unexpected." She leaned in to kiss her. "What time tonight?"

"Just come home," Annie said.

❖

Annie watched Sarah drive out of the driveway into the blowing snow. The ruined hallway made her edgy, and she refused to look at it as she walked back to the kitchen. Her dad had said he'd come out today and look at the damage. She thought he had his work cut out for him. The phone shrilled in the quiet house, making her jump.

"What are you?" Annie asked Rebecca. "Psychic?"

"Just dial 1-888—"

"Shut up, moron."

"I'm off today, but my kids are in school. Yes! I have about one hour before I have to take my mom shopping. What are you up to? Your message last night was kind of cryptic. I thought maybe someone died."

"That's not funny, Rebecca." Annie's voice shook as she sat down in a chair, surprised to find tears in her eyes.

"Wait a minute, are you crying? I'll be right there." Rebecca hung up.

Annie sat for a moment and then went for the coffeepot, wiping her eyes. "What's going on with me?" she muttered, then thought of yesterday and last night. Stress and hormones came to mind.

"Come here." Annie didn't even say hello when Rebecca walked in her back door. She just grabbed her hand and pulled her down the hallway in front of the guest bedroom.

"Holy shit," Rebecca said, looking at the shattered wall and hallway. "Is that blood?"

Annie tightened her jaw. "I shot someone here yesterday. Sarah did too, and the FBI killed a man on the deck."

Rebecca stared. "What? Damn. Who?"

"The people who were following me were the people who hurt me in Saudi Arabia, and I think it's finally over."

Rebecca put her arms around her, tugging her away from the ruined area. "Come on, let's get out of here. I need coffee."

She poured them both coffee, getting Annie settled in the kitchen. "Start from the beginning, I want to hear it all." Twenty minutes later, Rebecca sighed, going for more coffee. "Like I said, your life scares me to death."

Someone knocked on her kitchen door, and Annie's dad poked his head inside. Annie walked over and hugged him. He pushed her back a bit and then hugged her again.

"You have to quit this, you know," he said. "You're scaring your mother and me to death."

Annie swallowed hard. "I know, and I'm going to stop." She took his hand and led him down the hall. He whistled softly. "Annie, damn," he said, staring at the damage. "All right, let me get the boys in here. We'll take care of this."

Annie covered the painting as her dad's crew came inside. She looked up at Rebecca. "You know what, Slider? It's my life and I can change it." She picked up the phone, calling Bill Simpson in New York City. Rebecca smiled for the first time.

"All right, first step taken. Now let's talk about that gorgeous FBI agent you're hanging out with." Rebecca had a smug grin on her face. "By the way, I couldn't help but notice that painting. My God, Annie. Whew!"

"Isn't she yummy?"

Rebecca gave a quick laugh. "She looks like a model. My God, that silver suit at the party. But you noticed that, I'm sure."

"Of course. My head just got beat up. My eyes haven't died. Anyway, I'm—"

"Engaged?" Rebecca finished her sentence.

"Idiot." Annie actually giggled.

"Finish what you were saying, what are you?"

"Smitten."

Rebecca pumped her fist in the air. "Yes! I knew it when I saw you two at the party. Wait until I talk with your mom."

"Too late. She's already caught me leering, more than once." Annie felt her face heat up. "Isn't she delicious?"

"Ha!" Rebecca said with a laugh. "I don't believe it, Annie. I wish I had a camera. You're blushing. All right, let's have all the details, and do you realize you're describing her as food?"

"Remember the problem I mentioned at your house? Intimacy?"

Rebecca's eyebrows shot up.

"Finally," Annie said, "but it's different. It's like I'm starting from the beginning." She couldn't put a word to it. "I think my life's just a little too public and too fast for her."

"Listen to yourself. You're on national TV, and you spend most of your time in some godforsaken land. I mean, why on earth would that unnerve the average person, even an FBI agent?"

"I know, but I'm not sure what to do. I'm not going back to Iraq. I know that, but I'm not sure what I want to do."

"How about becoming a stay-at-home college professor?"

Annie felt around in her mind for the right words. "Sarah is a first for me, in so many ways. I actually get butterflies when she puts her arms around me, and I can't remember that happening to me before."

Rebecca grinned. "It's about time."

CHAPTER TWENTY-SEVEN

The lake had taken the snow back, and the sun was fighting to shine by the time Sarah reached her office. Sarah booted her computer and went to her case site, working on Annie's information until it was complete. "Case done," she said. "Debrief. Pack up my clothes and things at Annie's house." Damn, that was a lonely thought.

She decided what she was going to do, at least about work, and began straightening her office. Sarah looked at the photos of Annie taped above her desk. A memory of last night and Annie hovering above her, slender and naked, swept through her mind. "Hot," she said and sat down suddenly. "That second time was just plain hot." She had loved that sexy slow seduction. She jammed papers into her briefcase. *I may have to* pack up *tonight, but I'm not going to* give up.

Thirty minutes later she opened the door of the conference room after a meeting with the HR office. Eleven people were at Don's table, and Sarah took the chair next to him. "Let's get this side of the case done with first," Don said and started the recap of two years' progress regarding illegal Iraqis.

"I think this is about it," Don said finally. "It's going to take them a long time to reorganize and become this efficient again. They've taken to the back roads on us, hand-delivering messages and information via bicycles or cars, resorting to computers and airplanes only when they have to. That means they're slower. We've arrested over two hundred people in the city alone. A special unit is on its way from Virginia now. They finished in Detroit last month and found enough evidence with our group to come here. Sarah, you and Sam will be debriefed by them when they arrive." Sam Coates, Sarah's counterpart on the immigration side of the case, nodded at Don, but Sarah shook her head. Don raised his eyebrows but continued talking. "Have we gotten through all the boxes that we found at the Majers'?" He looked at Sam.

"No. It's enormous in its scope, and some of it will go out to other cities that are involved. It was much bigger than we first thought, and, Sarah, you might tell Ms. Booker that she wasn't the only journalist that they caught in their little scheme. It was a good one." Sam slid a piece of paper across the table to Sarah. "Give that to her and tell her there are more. I've notified their local offices, and they'll follow up with them, just as we have with Ms. Booker."

"I think Majer was in charge, unless there's new information?" Don said.

"Yes, in the Midwest, in this four-state area. But the Atlanta task force reported a similar situation last month. I think we've just got the tip of the iceberg. They must have thought, because Milwaukee is a relatively small city, that we would give up and concentrate on the Chicago group. Actually, we were about to when Ms. Booker's case came up."

"All right, now let's get the Booker thing sorted out," Don said. "Hell, I remember when the worst thing we had to deal with was the mob or the guys in Florida." He shook his head. "The Jaish al-Basca Web site from Baghdad got us involved in the beginning, but the two cases came together when Sarah and I looked into some names that Ms. Booker gave us. One of them was Dr. Atoli Majer, a respected professor of Islamic religions here at the university."

"Anything new?" Sarah asked.

"Only that, much to my shock, Prince Abdel didn't lie to us. For those of you that weren't involved, let me tell you about Dr. Majer's family." Don placed a huge file box on the table. "This file may become the primer on these families as they struggle to survive over there.

"Majer came here, got himself established at the university after nine-eleven, and began to filter Iraqis into the country. He had a sister still in Baghdad, a professor who taught English, among other things. Her husband, an engineer, fled Iraq with their two adult children when things began to get rough. She stayed in Baghdad with their two young girls and steered Iraqis to her brother here in Milwaukee. Her husband was killed, but the two adult children, a man and a woman, stayed and were trained in Afghanistan. The son, Hamel, began a human trafficking trade. Majer wanted them here, to help him smuggle illegals into our country, but Hamel refused. Worse, he picked up a silent partner in Iraq, the anti-American cleric Amer al-Sadr, a powerful man that the new Iraqi government wants to shut down."

Don pointed out each person on the plasma screen on the conference room wall. "The Iraqi government is going to love our information. This may be enough to prosecute Amer, something they've been trying very hard to do for quite a while."

He walked back to the table. "At the beginning, Hamel grabbed one of Prince Abdel's sisters, married her in Paris, and then attempted to extort her family as well. He also managed to get another of her sisters into his little den and got away with it for a while, but it didn't take Abdel's family long to sever those ties. But they didn't count on their younger sons, Abdel and his brothers, trying to save their sisters. Hamel's older sister, Sheikha, ran his operations over here, and after we went through her apartment this morning, we may be able to help the prince find his sisters. Also, Sarah, you might want to know that Hamel was tracking Annie's car through her GPS system on his laptop."

"How did you get all this information?" someone asked.

"From the prince, the Majers, and Ms. Booker," Don answered, taking a drink of coffee. "Dr. Majer's niece, Sheikha, came in illegally, and he got her into one of the hospitals here as a nurse. According to the people who hired her at the hospital, she was good. The State Department will take it from here."

He walked down the table. "Ms. Booker got us into a party at the Majers', Hamel and his sister attempted to abduct Ms. Booker, and you all know what happened there. That was also the first time we met the prince. The next day, Sarah and I talked with the prince at his hotel, and while we were there, Hamel came in. We were able to match the fingerprints from the hotel with those in Majer's basement."

Don shuffled some paper on the table. "To cut to the chase on all of this, Majer's nephew and niece, Hamel and his sister, broke into Ms. Booker's house yesterday, and both Ms. Booker and Sarah had to shoot her. Scott Frazier killed Hamel outside of the house as he abandoned his sister and tried to get away. Sarah had gone inside and Scott had taken the perimeter. At this point, we couldn't legally keep the prince in the country, and it was Ms. Booker's suggestion that she interview him at the airport. She maintained it was something the prince would never turn down, and she was right."

Sarah spoke up. "We were getting ready to take her up north yesterday when the shooting occurred. Just for the record, Ms. Booker predicted they'd move faster than we anticipated. Her years of experience were right on the money."

Don nodded. "There is no doubt in my mind that Majer's niece would have killed both Sarah and Ms. Booker, as would her brother. She is recovering in the hospital, and it appears she's going to be a valuable source of information. She's already told us that Hamel was after the photos that Ms. Booker found and gave to us. State will take Majer's sister's case, along with her injured daughter, but we'll run with the charges against Dr. Majer."

Don cleared his throat. "Ms. Booker isn't the first citizen to help us, but remember they have many skills and know their specific fields very well. Hell, we take people in the National Guard every day, away from their jobs in the private sector, train them, and sometimes kill them in Iraq. They do a wonderful job, just as Ms. Booker did hers, something not one of us in this room could have done the way she did. Because of her, Abdel willingly cooperated with us."

He stopped and looked out at the group. "Any questions?"

"Sarah, what about Jaish al-Basca?" Sam asked.

"It's in the hands of New York City and Josh Palmer now, but honestly, Sam, I don't think it's connected. The group is fundamentalist in nature, and it appears they don't get out of Iraq. However, when she goes back there, it'll be something she'll have to watch. As Don said, if they hadn't threatened Ms. Booker in the first place, we wouldn't have been with her and been able to follow through."

Sam smiled. "We're learning as we go."

Don ended the meeting and asked Sarah to wait a minute.

"What now?" he asked, sitting beside her as the room cleared.

"What do you mean?"

"I mean, nice job on the case. As Sam said, we're learning. The postmortem showed that it was Hamel that traded shots with you in Majer's basement, and speaking of learning, Dr. Majer lied to us about that door. He lied about a lot of things, didn't he? He showed the prince and Hamel the door. You and I were wrong about that." He took a floor plan from the display on the wall. "Didn't you wonder where Hamel went after you shot him? We already had the house sealed. Think about it." He laid the floor plan in front of her. It showed a diagram of the Majers' basement. "Look at this, another hidden room. Well, not so much hidden, just a pocket." He stabbed the paper with his finger. "According to Majer, it was designed just for moments like we were involved in, and all the time we were looking for him, he was just on the other side of this wall."

"Hamel tried to kill Annie because she survived his attack three years ago and then threw it in his face by going back to Iraq," Sarah said. "He needed the photos Jack Keegan gave to Annie, but those men don't like women who can't take a hint, do they? His sister tried to help him, and she was almost killed doing it." She shook her head. "People never change. We're still dying over ego. What makes me mad is that they hide it in religion or culture."

Don nodded. "Don't forget that both of you have to give a formal statement. Set it up and come in tomorrow. The locals are satisfied with the statements you gave yesterday. What's next?"

"Are you talking about my job or Annie?"

"Both."

"I am going to take some of the mountain of vacation I have piled up. I already got it approved, and that's why I won't be here when the special unit comes in. And Annie? I don't know." She took a deep breath. "I'm going to have dinner at her house tonight and we'll see what happens." She sat up straighter and fiddled with the pen he had laid down.

He looked at his watch. "And for another four hours, I am still technically your direct superior, so what's stopping you?" He grabbed the pen from her hand. "You're going to stab me. I can see it coming."

Sarah laughed. "Do I look that nervous? That's why I'm taking some time off. I want to go home, see my family, play some golf, and maybe fish a bit. I'll do that, no matter what happens."

"Is she going to continue on the job? The network will fight to keep her and you know it."

"They should, she's excellent."

"There's only one way you'll know, Sarah. Ask her. That way you'll have a clear head, and even if it's bad news, and it may be, you'll know which way the flag's blowing."

"The flag's blowing? Just ask? My brain freezes up every time I even think of talking to her. I suppose you're right. I'll never know if I don't ask."

CHAPTER TWENTY-EIGHT

A cold wind blew snow across Sarah's headlights as she pulled into Annie's driveway just as it had the first night she had driven Annie home from the airport. It felt like a thousand days ago. She turned the car off, leaning back for a moment. *If Annie refuses to live in fear, what's wrong with me? All I have to do is ask.*

Stepping into the kitchen, she saw Annie bending over the oven, her cute little bottom up in the air. "Honey, I'm home," Sarah said.

"What did you say?"

"I said, honey, I'm home," Sarah repeated, hanging her coat on the hook beside the door. A spicy aroma tickled her nose. "Is that enchiladas I smell?" Sarah asked, starting for the stove, but Annie stepped in front of her, oven mitts on both hands and dish towel over her shoulder.

"Did you forget something?"

"Just following my nose," Sarah said, taking another breath, but Annie stood fast.

"Pay the cook first, and then you get fed."

Sarah dropped her hands to Annie's hips and backed her into the wall, planting every bit of herself onto each piece of Annie that she could touch. She kissed her mouth hard and put her hands up under the bright yellow sweatshirt, groaning softly at the feel of skin. Annie kissed her back and put her gloved hands on Sarah's shoulders. Sarah finally pulled back.

"I can't move." Annie let her head fall back. "Guess I asked for that, but give me a moment here."

"I've been thinking of this since the moment I left," Sarah whispered into her ear.

Annie moved, taking one of Sarah's hands in her oven mitt, pulling her past the table and to the carpeting. Oven mitts fell to the floor as hands jerked her shirt out of her pants and fingers undid her bra.

"Annie, just a minute…" Sarah said and then groaned as warm hands covered her breasts, teasing the nipples. Then Annie began to tickle her. Both of them laughing, they slowly slid to the floor, Annie on top, and finally, when there were no more buttons, zippers, snaps, or clothes, Annie kissed her, hands everywhere.

"I want you, now," Annie muttered, biting Sarah's ear, moving down her shoulder with tiny nips. She began to tickle her again. Sarah's mind blurred, somewhere between laughter and raw desire. She somehow got Annie's sweatshirt off, then started working on the jeans with shaking hands just as Annie's fingers slid inside her. She almost went over the edge and grabbed Annie's hand.

"Wait, wait…just a minute, let's do this together," Sarah said, getting Annie's jeans off and pulling the warm body onto her.

Annie was almost panting. "Hurry, I'm ready," she said as Sarah's fingers slipped inside, and somehow they managed to come together.

"Sweet mother, Annie." Sarah was Jell-O. "Sex and tickling. On the floor?"

Annie rolled over, pulling Sarah on top and looked up into her face, eyes wet, almost gray. "Don't move."

Sarah's head fell onto Annie's shoulder. "I couldn't move if I wanted to. Where did that come from?"

"I'm just waking up," Annie said, wrapping her legs around Sarah.

"I'm cold," Sarah said.

"Then I'll just have to warm you up again."

"Here," Sarah said, bracing her back against the wall and pulling Annie into her lap. "You keep surprising me, sneaking up on me. You know I won't stop." She ruffled the brown-gold hair.

"Please don't stop." Annie's breath was warm on Sarah's skin.

"We'll starve to death together. They'll find our bones."

"I don't care. They can have my bones. Besides, we're not going to starve. We're only a few feet from a huge meal. I have to feed you, keep your strength up."

Sarah's stomach rumbled at the mention of food, and they started to sort through the clothing strewn around.

"See what I've cooked for you. Although it might be a little cold now." Annie pulled Sarah up, gesturing at the table. Tex-Mex chicken enchiladas, refried beans with Annie's dad's hot sauce, and more.

"This is beyond astonishing," Sarah said, popping the cap off a beer. She watched Annie pull her sweatshirt over bare breasts and drew a shaky breath.

Annie propped her elbows on the table and put her chin in her hands, trying for a smile but ending up with a kind of dreamy look on her face.

Sarah took a bite and closed her eyes. "Wonderful."

Annie beamed as she put food on her plate, avoiding her dad's hot sauce. They talked between bites of food, hunger trumping polite eating.

"Did you finish up at work?" Annie asked. "And what does that mean in your world?"

"It means we tie up all the loose ends, and that probably will take a while. It's so complicated. Don coordinates the two cases."

"What about the Web site?" Annie asked.

"From now on that will be handled by the New York office as they continue to coordinate with other foreign agencies. They'll keep Don in the loop, but you are officially off the radar as of this afternoon, thank God. We both have to give formal statements tomorrow, but that's all."

"Am I allowed to say that you catch bullets with your teeth?"

"Only if I can say you leapt buildings in a single bound." They looked at one another across the table. Sarah gathered her courage. "Annie, are you going back there?"

"Why?"

"No fair answering a question with a question."

"I thought we could talk about that tonight," Annie said tentatively. Sarah's heart hammered in her chest, watching Annie's face.

Annie moved to Sarah's lap again, snuggling into her, kissing her face, her eyes, and her mouth. "You've made me feel. That hasn't happened in a long time, but I've never felt like this." She kissed Sarah again, slowly and thoroughly. "You said that I was unexpected. Believe me, Sarah, I didn't expect you either. Or to care. Not like this." She took a deep breath. "So, to answer your question, the answer is no. I don't know what I'm going to do, but I know what I'm not going to do. I spoke with Bill Simpson after you left today and asked for an extended leave. I have so much vacation that I could be off a year and still get paid."

Sarah put her mouth by Annie's ear. "Want to run away with me?"

"Do you mean that?" Weeks of emotion seemed to slam into Annie, and she leaned back, tears in her eyes. "Where?"

"I mean it, and anywhere you want to go. Like you, I have a mountain of time available, and I got approval today, before I came home. I'm officially off duty for quite a while."

"I don't care where we go, as long as we're together."

"Okay, I know you're probably all traveled out, but I've never seen the Pacific Northwest. Have you been there?"

"Just on business, never for pleasure. What are the chances of that, as much as I've traveled in the last ten years?"

They talked about going to Sarah's home in Arizona. Sarah suggested driving Annie's car, as long as she could drive, of course, making Annie laugh.

"Let's turn the hot tub on and have another beer in there."

"Hot tub?"

"The one in my bathroom."

"Ah, the secret door?" Annie nodded. "Go start the tub, Annie, I'll take care of the dishes."

❖

Annie hummed all the way into the bathroom. She touched the panel and the walls receded, opening to two large panes of glass that revealed the backyard, down to the lake. Lights twinkled in the clear cold winter night, and she gave a small sigh of happiness. She turned the tub on and then music. Sarah walked in with the beer just as Annie took the last of her clothes off.

The candles cast soft lights and a faint fragrance around the room as Sarah sank into the water with a sigh. Looking out the window, Sarah could see the whole yard, the lake, and a tiny trace of moon.

Sarah cleared her throat. "All right, I just have one more question. Rebecca. Why do you call her Slider?"

Annie started to laugh and told her about her high school softball team that made it to the state tournament. "It was the bottom of the ninth, I'm on second and Rebecca's on first, two out." Annie imitated an announcer's voice. "We're down a run and Rebecca's the one with wheels. The coach gave her the sign to steal. Rebecca looks down the baseline at me, fear all over her face. She had never stolen a base in her life." Annie laughed harder, shaking her head. "I'm trying to be encouraging, but laughing, nodding at her, something like, 'c'mon, you can do it.' Rebecca's shaking her head at me like, 'no, I can't.' So the pitch goes and we go. I made it to third and looked back. Rebecca's lying in the dirt, a good two feet away from the base." Annie was laughing so hard there were tears in her eyes.

"Did she fall down?"

"No, but she wished she had, oh Lord," Annie said. "She tried to slide, but she just stopped in the dirt, two feet off the bag. Their second baseman caught the ball and just walked over, tagging her out. Needless to say, we lost." Annie ducked her head in the water, washing the tears off her face. "Poor Rebecca, there are people out there today, myself included, that still call her Slider, and honestly, she's a good sport about it. Well, sometimes."

"Great story, and I promise never to tease her about it." Sarah tipped her beer back for a drink. "I meant to tell you, they talked to your friend, the English journalist."

"Really? I haven't heard a thing from her. She was very good to me. Thanks for following up."

Sarah looked at the clock just as Annie yawned. "Ready for bed?"

❖

Annie gave her a look and crawled out, snuffing candles and turning off dials. She left wearing only her smile, and Sarah's eyes gobbled her up. *I'm going to drool*, she thought, and let her head fall forward. She lifted her head just in time to be hit in the face by a towel, laughter trailing from the bedroom.

"I'll shut the house down." Annie's voice floated in, along with a scent that made Sarah close her eyes. Annie's perfume.

Sarah walked into the bedroom toweling off as Annie came in wearing absolutely nothing but the painting she was carrying. Annie held it, diagonally, across herself. Upside down. She saw Annie's right breast and left leg.

"You look like a Picasso nude," Sarah said.

Annie was staring into space, not listening. She put the painting down, still upside down.

"Hey, I'm upside down."

"What?" Annie said.

Sarah pointed at the painting. "I'm upside down."

"Oh." Annie giggled and righted it. "I just had the best idea. I don't have to go to the MidEast to report on the war. I can do a series right here, in America. Look what's happened to me, to us. The split in our country, the changes, the possibility of another attack. You could be my inside source and—"

"Oh no," Sarah said, holding out her hand. "Come here."

Laughing, she leapt on Sarah, knocking her back on the bed. "When I finish that painting, where would you like me to hang it?"

"Right in here so every night when you go to bed, you have to look at it and think of me."

Annie propped herself on an elbow, looking down at Sarah. "Don't you mean, when *we* go to bed, *we* have to look at it?"

Sarah looked at the soft skin covering firm muscles, and put her hand on a hip, rubbing softly. "Yes. That's exactly what I mean."

About the Author

Born and raised in the Midwest, C.P. Rowlands attended college in Iowa and lived in the Southwest and on the West Coast before returning to Wisconsin. She is an artist in addition to having worked in radio, sales, and various other jobs. She has two children, two grandchildren, a cat, and an incredible partner of nineteen years. It's a very good life.

Books Available From Bold Strokes Books

truelesbianlove.com by Carsen Taite. Mackenzie Lewis and Dr. Jordan Wagner have very different ideas about love, but discover truelesbianlove is closer than a click away. (978-1-60282-071-5)

Justice at Risk by John Morgan Wilson. Benjamin Justice's blind date leads to a rare opportunity for legitimate work, but a reckless risk changes his life forever. (978-1-60282-059-3)

Run to Me by Lisa Girolami. Burned by the four-letter word called love, the only thing Beth Standish wants to do is run for—or maybe from—her life. (978-1-60282-034-0)

Split the Aces by Jove Belle. In the neon glare of Sin City, two women ride a wave of passion that threatens to consume them in a world of fast money and fast times. (978-1-60282-033-3)

Uncharted Passage by Julie Cannon. Two women on a vacation that turns deadly face down one of nature's most ruthless killers—and find themselves falling in love. (978-1-60282-032-6)

Night Call by Radclyffe. All medevac helicopter pilot Jett McNally wants to do is fly and forget about the horror and heartbreak she left behind in the Middle East, but anesthesiologist Tristan Holmes has other plans. (978-1-60282-031-9)

Lake Effect Snow by C.P. Rowlands. News correspondent Annie T. Booker and FBI Agent Sarah Moore struggle to stay one step ahead of disaster as Annie's life becomes the war zone she once reported on. Eclipse EBook (978-1-60282-068-5)

Revision of Justice by John Morgan Wilson. Murder shifts into high gear, propelling Benjamin Justice into a raging fire that consumes the Hollywood Hills, burning steadily toward the famous Hollywood Sign—and the identity of a cold-blooded killer. Gay Mystery. (978-1-60282-058-6)

I Dare You by Larkin Rose. Stripper by night, corporate raider by day, Kelsey's only looking for sex and power, until she meets a woman who stirs her heart and her body. (978-1-60282-030-2)

Truth Behind the Mask by Lesley Davis. Erith Baylor is drawn to Sentinel Pagan Osborne's quiet strength, but the secrets between them strain duty and family ties. (978-1-60282-029-6)

Cooper's Deale by KI Thompson. Two would-be lovers and a decidedly inopportune murder spell trouble for Addy Cooper, no matter which way the cards fall. (978-1-60282-028-9)

Romantic Interludes 1: Discovery ed. by Radclyffe and Stacia Seaman. An anthology of sensual, erotic contemporary love stories from the best-selling Bold Strokes authors. (978-1-60282-027-2)

A Guarded Heart by Jennifer Fulton. The last place FBI Special Agent Pat Roussel expects to find herself is assigned to an illicit private security gig baby-sitting a celebrity. (Ebook) (978-1-60282-067-8)

Saving Grace by Jennifer Fulton. Champion swimmer Dawn Beaumont, injured in a car crash she caused, flees to Moon Island, where scientist Grace Ramsay welcomes her. (Ebook) (978-1-60282-066-1)

The Sacred Shore by Jennifer Fulton. Successful tech industry survivor Merris Randall does not believe in love at first sight until she meets Olivia Pearce. (Ebook) (978-1-60282-065-4)

Passion Bay by Jennifer Fulton. Two women from different ends of the earth meet in paradise. Author's expanded edition. (Ebook) (978-1-60282-064-7)

Never Wake by Gabrielle Goldsby. After a brutal attack, Emma Webster becomes a self-sentenced prisoner inside her condo—until the world outside her window goes silent. (Ebook) (978-1-60282-063-0)

The Caretaker's Daughter by Gabrielle Goldsby. Against the backdrop of a nineteenth-century English country estate, two women struggle to find love. (Ebook) (978-1-60282-062-3)

Simple Justice by John Morgan Wilson. When a pretty-boy cokehead is murdered, former LA reporter Benjamin Justice and his reluctant new partner, Alexandra Templeton, must unveil the real killer. (978-1-60282-057-9)

Remember Tomorrow by Gabrielle Goldsby. Cees Bannigan and Arieanna Simon find that a successful relationship rests in remembering the mistakes of the past. (978-1-60282-026-5)

Put Away Wet by Susan Smith. Jocelyn "Joey" Fellows has just been savagely dumped—when she posts an online personal ad, she discovers more than just the great sex she expected. (978-1-60282-025-8)

Homecoming by Nell Stark. Sarah Storm loses everything that matters—family, future dreams, and love—will her new "straight" roommate cause Sarah to take a chance at happiness? (978-1-60282-024-1)

The Three by Meghan O'Brien. A daring, provocative exploration of love and sexuality. Two lovers, Elin and Kael, struggle to survive in a postapocalyptic world. (Ebook) (978-1-60282-056-2)

Falling Star by Gill McKnight. Solley Rayner hopes a few weeks with her family will help heal her shattered dreams, but she hasn't counted on meeting a woman who stirs her heart. (978-1-60282-023-4)

Lethal Affairs by Kim Baldwin and Xenia Alexiou. Elite operative Domino is no stranger to peril, but her investigation of journalist Hayley Ward will test more than her skills. (978-1-60282-022-7)

A Place to Rest by Erin Dutton. Sawyer Drake doesn't know what she wants from life until she meets Jori Diamantina—only trouble is, Jori doesn't seem to share her desire. (978-1-60282-021-0)

Warrior's Valor by Gun Brooke. Dwyn Izsontro and Emeron D'Artansis must put aside personal animosity and unwelcome attraction to defeat an enemy of the Protector of the Realm. (978-1-60282-020-3)

Finding Home by Georgia Beers. Take two polar-opposite women with an attraction for one another they're trying desperately to ignore, throw in a far-too-observant dog, and then sit back and enjoy the romance. (978-1-60282-019-7)

Word of Honor by Radclyffe. All Secret Service Agent Cameron Roberts and First Daughter Blair Powell want is a small intimate wedding, but the paparazzi and a domestic terrorist have other plans. (978-1-60282-018-0)

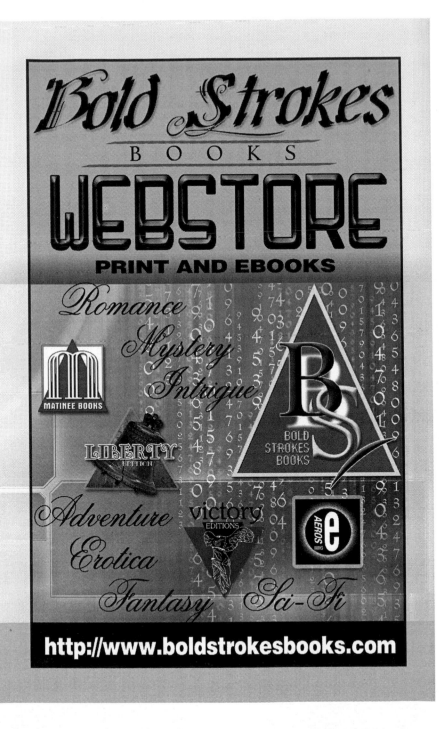